MY WOLF'S BANE
SHAPES OF AUTUMN, BOOK ONE

VERONICA BLADE

I0630377

PUBLISHING

Gardnerville, Nevada

MY WOLF'S BANE, SHAPES OF AUTUMN BOOK ONE

Crush Publishing, Inc
Gardnerville, NV 89460

ISBN 978-0-9853434-6-0

Cover design and layout by Rose Nomura

Printed in the United States of America

MY WOLF'S BANE
SHAPES OF AUTUMN, BOOK ONE

EXCERPT

THE SMELL OF *unwashed wolf closed in on me, fur tickling my skin and fetid breath in my face. I trembled, hot tears burning my eyes. The wolf snarled and I scrambled back as he leapt toward me.*

"Autumn. Autumn, wake up." Zack pulled me off the pillow by my shoulders.

I lifted my head and rubbed my eyes, trying to wipe away the mental fuzz. But I was aware enough to notice my comforter wasn't anywhere near us, certainly not separating me from him. I must have kicked it off during my nightmare.

"Are you okay?" Zack was sitting directly in front of me, his thighs straddling mine, heat from his bare skin radiating through me.

I nodded.

He exhaled in relief and leaned back to sit on his heels. "Heard you scream and I ran up here. Been calling your name over and over, but you wouldn't wake up. Scared me for a minute there."

I'd been having that same dream where I was being chased. "I was running from wolves."

He brushed a finger down my cheek. "It was just a dream."

"More like a nightmare," I whispered, my gaze locking onto his. He wore nothing but a pair of boxers. As my ragged breath slowed, I realized the only other thing between us was my threadbare tank top and skimpy panties.

"Autumn." His breathing quickened and he growled so low it sounded like a purr. Then he tilted my face to meet his and drew closer until I felt his breath on my skin. "You're too beautiful."

My Wolf's Bane
VERONICA BLADE

FREE E-BOOK OFFER

For a limited time, *Thrown To The Wolves: The Legend of Hannah & Eli (Shapes of Autumn Prequel)* is available for free from my website.

Find out more at VeronicaBlade.com

FOR ALLIE

To give you life after Twilight

CHAPTER ONE

SCOOPING UP MY backpack, I abandoned my geriatric car and forged through the double doors of the school. The patter of my sandals echoed through the hallway as I smiled at a group of classmates passing by.

My nose detected the bathroom before my eyes did, filling with the smell of disinfectant and... paint? Whatever. I'd take the toxic fumes over my former home school days, where my parents had kept me trapped without a social life.

Inside the empty restroom, I rummaged through my backpack for my makeup bag. I set it on the edge of the sink, then surveyed the damage. At least I'd had time to do my hair before I'd stormed out of the house. Long, dark brown hair cascaded over my shoulders in thick waves. My face was a different story though. Evidence of sleep deprivation circled my eyes and my normally olive skin was pale.

As I stared at my reflection, I wondered how to handle my very dead car without involving my mom or dad. After the bomb they'd dropped last night—that we'd be moving *again* in just a few weeks—I didn't want to speak to either of them. I mean, what kind of parents uproot their kid two to three times a year? There had to be a way to convince them to stay until I graduated, maybe get me started in college. Then I could make my own choices.

The restroom door swung open behind me, letting in the dull roar of voices and banging lockers, and a younger girl disappeared into a stall. Was it time for my first class already? I checked the time on my cell and realized I'd been holding the mascara brush for several minutes, yet my lashes were still naked. Crap.

I tossed the makeup bag into my backpack, slung it over my shoulder and whipped open the door. Barreling out of the bathroom, I slammed into what felt like a walking boulder. I ricocheted off the human rock and my backpack hit the wall behind me, throwing me off balance and pitching me forward into the hard, linoleum tile.

My palms cushioned my fall, but I winced as pain spiked up my wrists. On all fours, I lifted my chin and peeked through my curtain of dark hair.

He wore a black tee that molded to his wide, muscular shoulders and jeans that fit over powerful legs. Wow. I'd thought my soon-to-be-ex-boyfriend was cute, but this guy...

"You okay?" the hottie asked in a sexy, gravelly voice, stretching a hand toward me. His hand wrapped around mine and effortlessly pulled me up, as if I weighed no more than my calculus book. Maybe it was the throbbing in my limbs or the warmth of his hands on my elbows. Or maybe it was his earthy scent invading my senses, but a wave of dizziness hit me and I tipped forward.

His hands shot to my hips to steady me. "Easy there."

I stared into his deep, green eyes as my palms rested on his hard biceps for support. Lord, he smelled good, like the forest after rain.

My breath hitched.

The scuffling of feet and rustling clothes seemed quieter than it should've been. I glanced over my shoulder to see what was up. Nearly everyone in the hallway had their eyes fixed on me. No doubt, most of them had witnessed me doing the Humpty-Dumpty and, by the end of the day, the incident would be all over school. Probably even caught on video and uploaded to You-Tube, me with no makeup and totally un-cute. Ugh.

Hot Guy may have been standing right in front of the bathroom in my way, but I shouldn't have been speeding. I opened my mouth to apologize when I recognized Daniel's voice.

"That's *my* girl you're touching, freak." Daniel sneered, flicked his long, dirty-blond hair over his shoulder and clamped onto my wrist. "Hands off."

Hot Guy nudged me aside and stepped forward until he almost butted chests with Daniel. "You need to learn some manners."

"Oh, yeah? You gonna try to teach me, girly boy?"

Though I knew Daniel was acting like an idiot, the school gossip mill didn't need any more material on me today. I was more than finished with Daniel, but

I didn't necessarily want him to get a public smack-down—even though he probably deserved it. Wedging myself between them, I twisted to meet Daniel's gaze. "Let's just go."

"Good idea." Daniel gave Hot Guy another scalding look before grabbing my hand and jerking me away. I breathed a sigh of relief that I wouldn't have to referee a brawl.

"Ass hat," Hot Guy muttered.

Daniel kept walking, practically dragging me along. He couldn't have heard the insult or he would've stopped and turned on Hot Guy. But I had heard it so clearly. Weird.

"Hang on and I'll walk you to class." Daniel paused at his locker and spun the combination lock.

"Sure," I said absently. I glanced over my shoulder to Hot Guy, who was leaning against a locker fiddling with his cell phone. The least I could do was give him an apologetic smile and mime, "Sorry."

I didn't get a chance. His gaze met mine, his mouth twisting as he raised one brow. Okay, so this wasn't going to be an easy fix. Hot Guy seemed too old to be in high school anyway. Probably a college student dropping off his younger sibling, which meant I'd never see him again.

I wanted to keep staring at his perfectly sculpted nose, angular cheekbones and deep brown hair that fell haphazardly over his forehead, but he spun and strolled off in the opposite direction. A tug of my hand drew my focus back to my future ex-boyfriend.

"Hold up," I said. The warning bell sounded, but I barely heard it as I yanked my hand from his. "Why'd you have to act like such a psycho?"

Daniel shrugged, as though the answer was obvious. "He was touching you."

I laughed. "Seriously?"

"You're mine, Autumn. No other guy can ever touch you again." He said it like he couldn't believe I'd even question him.

"I'm *no one's* property," I hissed. "Besides, I tripped and he was just helping me up."

"Why are you defending that loser?" His voice rose and his face flushed.

My hands balled into fists. "Because I don't like how you treat people."

"What are you talking about?" He gave me a look that said it all—I was insane. I opened my mouth to start in on him, but his eyes swept the corridor before he said, "We're gonna be late for class."

Daniel was right. The hall was deserted. A stream of mild curses spewed from my mouth as I sprinted to homeroom with only seconds to spare.

† † †

Just before lunch, I scribbled notes in my textbook and tried to concentrate on the current assignment, but my mind drifted to Hot Guy. Why had I heard his insult when Daniel obviously hadn't?

The bell rang and I gathered my books and headed to the cafeteria. As soon as I entered the corridor, I caught a whiff of cinnamon and orange. John's signature scent, since he always chewed this weird gum. I glanced around, expecting him to be right next to me.

A moment later, John stood beside me and that same cinnamon-orange scent heightened. But why had I smelled it before he even got there?

"Hey." I flashed him a smile.

Daniel and my friend Gina didn't talk to super-geeks like John. I did though, ever since a few weeks ago when I'd watched him get between little Benny Frampton and two big jocks.

To avoid witnessing carnage, I'd rushed over and flirted with the bullies. John took his cue and got the kid out of their way. Ever since then, I never treated John like a nerd, no matter how much Daniel and Gina protested my friendship with him. To me, he was Brave John, my friend.

"Heard what happened this morning," John said as he fell into step with me, "but I see you're still in one piece."

Ah, the gossip mill running fast, as usual. "Yeah. Good as new," I said, marveling at how my hands and knees weren't sore at all. First the amazing hearing, then the super-human sense of smell and now the lack of bruises. Weird. Was I sick or something?

"So you want to see a movie tomorrow?" he asked. "I bet Maya would come."

My jeans vibrated. I stopped to juggle books to my other arm and reached into my pocket to read the text. It was from my mom. *Coming home directly after school, sweetheart?*

I groaned, answered the text and shoved the phone back in my pocket. "Unfortunately, I can't go *anywhere* this weekend."

"Oh." He nodded slowly, frowning. "Grounded again?"

"Yep."

"How much do you owe this time?"

As we passed other students along the hallway, I flicked the lapel of my new leather jacket and wagged a finger toward my jeans. "These weren't cheap. I think my latest shopping euphoria gave me amnesia that I *still* owed my parents."

When they gave me an advance, it had to be paid back before leaving the house the following weekend. That was the rule. Paying my debts and keeping my agreements was supposed to teach me discipline. Why couldn't they just hand over an allowance, with no strings attached, like other parents?

"Wait." John took hold of my arm, stopping me in my tracks. "Have you told Daniel yet? He won't be too thrilled about his girlfriend ditching his party."

Daniel had exercised astounding patience over my parents' rigid rules and nine pm curfews, but missing his party? He'd probably dump me... which would save me the trouble of breaking up with him.

"True." I landed a playful punch on John's bicep as an arm wrapped around my waist, spinning me around and pulling me against a firm chest.

"Hi, babe," Daniel said. Always on the alert with him now, I flattened my palms against his stomach, ready to shove him away.

When we'd first started dating a couple of months ago, Daniel did the sweetest things, like bring me daisies stolen from his mom's garden. He'd won me over all the way the day he'd changed my flat tire. But in the last few days, Daniel had gone from loving and considerate to demanding and offensive. Worse, he'd become hard of hearing when it came to the word "no," and I wasn't in the mood to fend off his pawing. I was so over him, no matter how uber-popular he was.

"Hey, Daniel," John said.

Daniel ignored him. John rolled his eyes, then ambled away.

"You could try being nice," I said, moving out of Daniel's grasp. I wanted to end it with him right then, but a hallway swarming with people wasn't the best place. "What'd John ever do to you?"

Daniel snorted. "He annoys me. I don't know why you give that dork the time of day. C'mon, let's eat."

Dork or not, eating with John and my other best friend, Maya, sounded like much more fun. But Gina still needed to know I couldn't go with her to Daniel's party. An A-lister like her wouldn't have a problem finding someone else, but she'd probably blow the whole thing out of proportion anyway. Maybe she'd even dump me.

Gina had been my first friend at Verdugo Hills Academy and introduced me to the cool people. She always had my back. At first, hanging with school royalty had been exciting, but being popular wasn't all it was cracked up to be. It took me three months with *Gina* to realize I preferred Maya and John, people who were easy to be around.

Daniel led me to the lunchroom and, after collecting some food, we settled next to each other at our usual table. Gina had beaten us there, stunning in a pink sleeveless blouse with ruffles for straps. Her short, auburn hair had been blown straight, bringing out the natural red highlights. As always, her makeup was flawless, just like her heart-shaped face.

Which reminded me that I still wasn't wearing any makeup.

Her friend Natalie, who'd never warmed up to me, huddled with her. Natalie had potential beauty, but her ever-present scowl and matching mood always overpowered those piercing hazel eyes and short cap of black, curly hair.

Gina stopped talking mid-sentence and turned to us with a grin. "Hey, guys."

"I'll see you later," Natalie told her, rising from the bench. She wrinkled her nose at me, then left. I knew Natalie was just jealous that Gina hung out with me more, but knowing Natalie's reasons didn't make her any less irritating. Thankfully, once I showed up, she didn't usually stick around long.

I returned Gina's smile, but it faltered in anticipation of her reaction to my house arrest. "How's it going?"

"Babe, I'll be back." Daniel's beefy hand darted out for the sandwich on his tray, then he left without waiting for a reply. Relieved to have him gone, I watched him join a couple of his friends.

"God, who died?" Gina asked.

"What do you mean?" Oh, crap, was my reluctance to confess that obvious?

"Look at you." She quirked a brow. "You're so junior high without makeup."

"Oh, yeah." I lifted one shoulder. "Ran short on time this morning."

Maya appeared at our table, looking amazing even holding a plastic food tray. She was a guy's embodiment of perfection with her long, wavy blond hair and voluptuous body. She occasionally complained how hard it was to find a bra that fit around her narrow ribcage, but could still hold all she had to offer. Like all that cleavage was such a burden. Poor thing.

"Hey, Autumn." Maya turned to Gina, her tone going flat. "Hi."

"Nice shirt." Gina smiled sweetly. "How generous of your brother to go through his clothes for you."

My mouth dropped open. Gina had never been nice to Maya, but she usually limited their interaction to giving her the cold shoulder. "Gina, what the hell?" I demanded.

"Holy Underwear Model." Gina's gaze riveted to her right. "Who's the hottie sitting with Trevor?"

Following the path of her gaze, I froze. The din of voices, the distant clanging of trays and the smell of grease faded away when I recognized the guy with the dark hair and green eyes I'd gotten lost in.

My stomach dipped.

CHAPTER TWO

MAYA GLANCED BEHIND her. "That's Zack De Luca."

"And?" Gina prompted.

"Trevor's cousin." Maya laid her tray on the table, but remained standing.

As if he could feel me staring at him, Zack turned his gaze on me. I gave him a welcoming smile, hoping he'd forget I'd bulldozed into him earlier and how my dickhead boyfriend had behaved. No such luck. He narrowed his eyes and shook his head.

I instantly deflated. "What's his deal?"

"Zack just enrolled. He's been visiting weekends and summers for years, but now he's here for good."

Maya had crushed on Trevor since grade school and knew everything about him and, it seemed, his relatives. I couldn't understand why she and Trevor hadn't already hooked up.

"Did he fail a couple grades? He looks old enough to be in college." I surreptitiously checked out the boys again, while I broke off a piece of my grilled cheese sandwich. Trevor's hair was a little lighter and his features less angular, but both guys excelled in the cute department. Zack more so.

"Almost the same age as Trevor. He's a senior like us," Maya said, glancing back at them. "Though he's grown about a foot and bulked up since I saw him last."

"Steroids?" I asked.

Maya laughed. "He's always looked older than Trevor."

"He could have that aging disease," I offered.

Gina still hadn't taken her eyes off him. "Who cares? He's smokin' hot. You can practically see his six-pack through his T-shirt."

Maya rolled her eyes as if Gina were insane to prefer Zack over Trevor. "I could find out more about him, if you want me to."

Gina turned to Maya with a sneer. "You're such a stalker."

"Whatever, Gina. It's called being nice," Maya said through gritted teeth. "Something you don't have a lot of experience with."

Gina made a face at Maya, then focused on me. "You've been hogging the cutest guy in school for weeks. If Zack fell madly in love with me, the hottest guy would be *mine*. Compared to him, Daniel looks like he's got chromosome issues."

Even if I still liked Daniel, I couldn't be offended at the absolute truth. Everything about Zack was exactly right. As if feeling my gaze, he turned sharply in my direction again. My dad once wore the same expression when he discovered the decaying remains of a cat under our house.

My cheeks heated and I dropped my gaze to pluck a potato chip from my plate.

Maya moved next to me for a better view of the guys. "Must be awkward starting a new school when the year is almost over."

Before I could stop myself, my eyes found their way back to Zack.

"Not when you're that hot. He'll be just fine." Gina's fork banged onto the plastic tray when she tossed it and stood. "Time to introduce myself."

As I watched Zack, the hair on the back of my neck stood at attention. There was something different about him... almost feral. I wanted to caution Gina, but she'd probably call me paranoid.

Gina sashayed over to Zack, coyly twisting her hair around a finger. Trevor got up, leaving them alone. I eyed them under my lashes as Gina said something. Zack chuckled and she laughed.

At that moment, I hated them both—him for making me feel like week-old garbage and Gina for making him smile when all I got was a scowl. To distract myself, I picked up my sandwich and concentrated on Maya.

"Gina's in rare form today." The soda can hissed as Maya popped the top, her gaze straying back to Trevor. He looked away when their eyes met.

"Yeah, sorry about that. I don't know what's up with her." I let my hair fall forward to hide my face as I snuck a peek at Trevor, who was staring at Maya again. "You should talk to Trevor. I really think he likes you."

Her eyes cut to mine. "How could a guy be interested in anyone else when you're around?"

"What?" My mouth dropped open.

"C'mon, Autumn," she said, but there wasn't any bitterness in her voice. More like she'd accepted her fate. "You have perfect olive skin that never gets a zit and never needs a tan, you're tall and thin and I'd kill for all that glorious, black hair."

I eyed the locks cascading over my shoulder. "Dark brown, actually. Boring. And besides, Trevor keeps staring at *you*, not me. I bet he'd go for it if you asked."

She rolled her eyes and flicked a thumb at Zack. "He seems nice."

Obviously, Maya hadn't noticed him scowling at me. "I wouldn't know." I focused on my tray, tracing little circles with my index finger. Hopefully, she'd drop the subject.

"On the way here, I saw him talking to some of the math geeks in the hallway. It's like he's not too full of himself to be seen with the unpopular kids. Can't say that about Gina or Daniel." Maya slid her sandwich out of the baggie. "John told me you're grounded."

My gaze shot to Gina's hand resting on Zack's forearm. She certainly moved quickly. "Yeah, but I haven't told Gina yet, so don't say anything, okay?"

"You want me to come over Saturday night and keep you company?"

"You're not going to Daniel's party?"

"Are you kidding?" She grimaced and waved a hand. "His last party was a drunken hook-up fest. I'd rather have a girl's night with you. Do our toes, rent a movie."

"Sounds awesome." The ick factor that had slowly built all morning fell away. What would I do without Maya? Oh, God, if my parents followed through with their plans, I'd find out soon enough. As if on cue, my phone vibrated.

"Wow, your parents just don't let up."

"I know," I said, answering my mom's text with what I wanted for dinner. She couldn't have asked me this morning? I theorized that them making me reply throughout the day was just another way of keeping tabs on me. I pressed the send button and focused on Maya again. "Uhm..."

She eyed me with a frown. "What's wrong?"

I took a deep breath and pushed away the threatening anxiety. "We're moving again."

Her face fell. "When?"

"Not sure. Before graduation, most likely." I pressed my lips together at the thought of leaving our pretty little home in the foothills north of Los Angeles. But it wasn't just that I liked the house and the city. I'd live in a hut if it meant I could grow roots. I hadn't known Maya long, but I'd become closer to her and John than any friends before. "I can't bear the thought of moving again and leaving you guys."

"Then stay with me. My mom and dad would love that. They're *so* not over my brother going away to college."

Live with Maya? For a second, I fantasized about taking a class or two at the local college. But even if her parents said yes, I couldn't mooch off them forever. Eventually, I'd have to get a job to pay for food and somewhere to live. I had a lot to do before striking out on my own, starting with earning money for a new car before the old one choked out its last sputter. The way it died in the parking lot this morning, that last sputter could be sooner than I expected.

Butterflies did a march in my stomach, but I forced a smile. "That's something to think about. Thanks."

Gina sauntered back to our table and reclaimed her seat. "He has a girlfriend." She didn't seem too broken up about it though.

"Bummer for you." I bit into my sandwich, trying not to imagine Zack with a girlfriend, his deep green eyes gazing into hers, his full lips... My attraction to him was ridiculous considering how he scowled at me.

"Maybe, maybe not." Gina snuck another peek at him.

I hurriedly swallowed to talk. "You can't go after someone else's boyfriend."

"I won't need to." She gave a half laugh. "People break up all the time. And I doubt she's prettier than me."

"There's always someone prettier, Gina." Maya rolled her eyes. "Besides, some people care more about substance than appearance."

"Only the *average* girls say things like that." Gina's cold stare would have come in handy during last summer's heat wave.

"What's the matter with you?" I asked. Her bitchiness had reached new heights.

Maya picked up her tray. "I'll catch you later, Autumn."

I gave Maya an apologetic look, then turned and glared. "Gina!"

"What?" She gave me her innocent face.

"You make no effort with her."

Her face scrunched up as if I'd suggested she spend the night locked in a room full of roaches. "Why would I want to do that?"

"Because she's my friend? Same reason I try to be nice to Natalie." I lifted my brows expectantly.

"Oh, my God!" She giggled. "You should see the dress she bought for Daniel's party. Wicked. But mine is sexier. You and I will be the hottest girls there, easy."

Knowing it was a losing battle, I sighed. "Uh, speaking of Daniel's party, remember our last couple shopping sprees?"

"Sure." Gina scanned the room, probably hunting for Zack, but I steeled myself to stay tuned to Gina. If Zack caught me staring again, I'd look stalker-ish. Or, even worse, desperate.

I hesitated, my teeth holding my bottom lip hostage. "That money I spent with you? I borrowed it from my parents, planning to work it off during the week."

"Yeah, so?" She brushed her auburn hair off her shoulder, then stiffened, her eyes fixing on me and narrowing. "Don't even tell me you're grounded."

"I'm sorry, Gina. I—"

"We've been planning this for two months." Her nostrils flared, lips tightening. "I can't believe you did this to me."

I sighed. "You act like you have no one else to go with. What about Natalie?" Yes, I'd broken my word, but her attitude was over the top. "And at least you get to go to the party. I'll be stuck at home with my parents. I'm not any happier about this than you."

"Whatever." She crumpled her napkin, tossed it on the table, then stomped off.

Now I was free to spend the rest of lunch with Maya. But beyond Gina's retreating back, John and Maya stood with Zack, who seemed engrossed in something she'd said. Just great. Seemed like I was the only one at school he didn't like.

As if knowing I was watching, he turned. I silently cursed for getting caught staring, yet couldn't take my eyes off him. After a long moment, he returned his attention to *my* friends.

Was it extra noisy in the cafeteria today or just my imagination? Whatever. I took my tray to the trash bin, knowing the warning bell would ring soon.

Daniel waved at me from across the cafeteria and mouthed, "See you later."

I hoped not. Except I still needed to break up with him.

Gina approached Daniel and his posse. Zack still chatted with John and Maya—which made both groups off limits. Damn.

If I had superhuman powers, I'd turn invisible right then. And no one would've noticed.

I headed to English Lit. Alone.

My phone vibrated and I sighed, reaching into my pocket. It was my mom again, reminding me I was grounded and offering to let Maya stay over. Knowing she'd keep texting me if I didn't answer her right away, I stopped to type in my thanks, then I continued down the corridor. Thankfully, my mom knew I wasn't allowed to text during class, which gave me a reprieve.

Seeing the restroom, I darted inside to finally put on some makeup, since I had a little time to spare. A few minutes later, feeling cute for the first time all day, I rushed into the crowded classroom and claimed my usual spot.

Oh, goody, Zack was in that class and he'd taken a seat two rows over to my left. He was facing the front of the class as though I didn't exist. I inwardly groaned, then flipped my hair over to form a wall between us. Peering between the dark strands, I eyed him on the sly. I only got his profile, but that and his muscular shoulders were plenty satisfying.

Once class began, I tried to forget Zack was a few seats away, but I couldn't. His presence added an awkward tension I could live without. And we had a pop quiz to brighten my day—which I hadn't prepared for.

On the upside, my day probably wouldn't get any worse.

† † †

When the final bell rang at the end of last class, I gathered my books and bailed.

Seeing Gina in the corridor ahead of me, I hoped she'd ignore me. Luckily, she kept a brisk pace and didn't look back. Closer to the exit, she slowed until she stood in front of Zack. He smiled at her and listened attentively. After scribbling on a piece of paper, she handed it to him, then walked backward grinning. He mouthed, "I'll call you."

Flirting when he had a girlfriend. Yuck.

I continued on toward the parking lot, passing them. A moment later, I sensed Zack behind me, but didn't turn around to confirm it, since he might think I was keeping tabs on him. Just before the curb on the way to my car, Ashley waved me over.

Gina didn't approve of being friendly to juniors, but I liked Ashley. She was one of those people who didn't make you wonder where you stood.

"Hey, Autumn." She gave me a shy smile. "I'm having some people over on Saturday night and thought you might like to come."

I couldn't go to *any* party, much less blow off Gina for someone else. Wait... throwing a party on the same night as Daniel? I couldn't imagine her competing with the most popular guy at school *on purpose*. She wanted a good turnout, right? I frowned. "Uhm, this Saturday is Daniel's party."

"Oh," she said in a small voice. "I thought it was *next* weekend." Ashley's gaze dropped to her feet, her bottom lip jutting into a pout before wandering off. Poor Ashley.

I turned in a circle to scan the crowd, searching for Daniel, who usually met me at my car. I couldn't wait to say my piece and finally be free of him. Instead, I saw Zack sitting on a wall about three feet away. Except for his narrowed eyes, his face was a mask as he stared at me.

Over the sound of skateboard wheels banging

against the sidewalk, honks signaling rides to potential passengers and car doors slamming, I heard Zack scoff.

"What a piece of work," he whispered to himself, his eyes still glued to me.

I shouldn't have been able to hear him over the noise, right? But his words had been so clear. Wait... had he heard me too? I paused a moment to replay my conversation with Ashley and cringed. I'd sounded kind of snobby. Yeah, as if that was going to make Zack think any better of me.

Whatever. He wasn't going to give me a chance anyway and why should I care what he thought? I just hoped Ashley hadn't taken it the wrong way, too. I scanned the parking lot, just in time to see her drive away with her mom. I'd have to fix it with her later.

I spun around, headed to my car and shoved my backpack through the window. I didn't know where Daniel was or how long he'd be, but if I didn't text my mom soon, she'd probably show up. I hated it when she did that. I hit the buttons of my cell saying I was hanging out with Daniel for a few minutes, but would be on my way soon.

Leaning against the door, I waved at John and Maya as they cruised by.

Daniel's dirty-blond head and beefy body suddenly blocked my view. "Hey, babe."

"Hi." I gave him a weak smile, not looking forward to a confrontation. After what he'd said earlier about no one ever touching me again, he probably wouldn't let me go easily. I could totally pass on the inevitable drama.

"I'm grounded," I blurted out. "I can't go to your party."

His face fell. "Oh. I had plans for us."

I didn't even want to know what those plans were. "Yeah, about that. Uh, we need to talk."

"Daniel!" a guy shouted from across the lot.

"Gotta go." He gave me a quick kiss without giving me a chance to evade it, then took off.

Damn. I was still officially stuck to him. Resigned, I nudged my backpack over and settled in the driver's seat of my ancient sedan. I turned the key in the ignition, then cursed under my breath. Today had sucked so much, I'd forgotten all about my car needing resuscitation.

John and Maya had already left. I could call one of them back to get me, but John depended on rides from someone else and Maya wouldn't have time to come back, drop me off and still make it home in time to babysit her little brother.

Unless I could get my car to start, my only choice would be to call my mom or dad for a ride. Taking a deep breath and crossing my fingers, I waited a moment, then turned the key again.

Silence.

A head appeared in my window and I jumped. Realizing it was Zack and not a serial killer, my muscles relaxed a little. I gazed at him, mesmerized by his deep, green eyes.

The corners of his mouth twitched. "Car trouble?"

CHAPTER THREE

APPARENTLY, ZACK SHARED his smiles with everyone *except* me.

"Yeah." I teeter-tottered between being embarrassed for being seen by him in my dilapidated car, and fear that he couldn't or wouldn't save me. "Car won't start."

Zack blew out a breath, then motioned to the hood of the car. When I didn't move, he stared at the sky for a moment before saying, "Release the hood, so I can check it out."

He'd spoken slowly, like I had a learning disability. Heat rushed into my cheeks. I reached around my knees where the lever should've been, but my hand came up empty. Where was it? I'd found it before. If I just had another minute...

"Move and I'll do it."

I scrambled out, bumping shoulders with him as I squeezed past. Wow, the guy was all muscle. I cursed the butterflies fluttering like crazy in my stomach, vowing not to get a crush on a guy who had such a low opinion of me.

Zack immediately found the release, then propped up the hood. I darted around to the front to see what he'd do. The engine looked like grease-covered metal. It could've been a time machine and I wouldn't have known the difference.

"So what do you think?" I asked.

"If I knew..." he paused to eye me from under his brows, "I'd already be fixing it and one step closer to being gone."

I gritted my teeth. "If you're going to be a jerk about it, why bother helping me at all?"

"Because my mom raised me right." His gaze fell on my mouth and, for an instant, his eyes darkened. Just when I thought we were having a moment, his lips thinned as he met my eyes. "If you prefer, I could leave."

"That would make you even more of a douche," I said, sticking a hand on my hip and praying he'd stay.

The corner of his mouth quirked and he resumed scrutinizing the engine.

I breathed a sigh of relief, but I didn't want to press my luck. To keep myself occupied, I counted the flattened gum spots in the asphalt while listening to his occasional mutters. What I really wanted to do was get a closer look at the seat of his pants, but I didn't want to get caught ogling him. Again.

"Rear passenger side tire is a little low," he said, almost like he was talking to my car. "You should stop and get some air soon."

"Okay, thanks." Sure, he'd been rude before, but he didn't have to stop to help me and he could've let my tire go completely flat. Maybe he was finally warming up to me. My insides turned to jelly at the thought. I sidled up next to him and leaned over to peer at the engine. "So... you know a lot about cars?"

Except for his eyes that studied the engine as if mentally taking it apart, Zack didn't move a muscle or even glance my way. "I know enough."

That didn't curb my curiosity. "Where'd you learn? Your dad teach you?"

"No."

Several seconds passed and he didn't say anything more. So much for making conversation. Considering how little he apparently thought of me, what had I expected? Maybe he'd lighten up if I apologized for bumping into him and told him I was dumping Daniel. I opened my mouth to speak, but Zack beat me to it.

"See the way the clamp isn't connecting to the battery?" He pointed at a big, rectangular thing.

Grateful for the break in his silence, I studied the box. "The vibrations wiggled it free?"

"That would be my guess." He flashed me a grin and nudged me with his elbow. My insides warmed. "Maybe under all that hair and spiffy clothes is a car geek just itching to bust free," he said.

That was probably as close to a compliment as I was going to get from Zack. I returned his smile.

His grin disappeared in a flash and his eyes grew cold as he jiggled the cables. "Okay, try it again," he ordered, averting his gaze.

Climbing back into the car, I turned the key and it sparked to life. Oh, thank God! I got out again to thank him, but left the motor running, just in case. "So it was just the connection?"

He mumbled, then let the hood drop shut and strode off without saying another word.

Just because he had atrocious manners—when he wasn't saving my ass—didn't mean I had to stoop to his level. Besides, people were always nicer when you were friendly. "Thank you!"

He didn't even turn around. Sometimes, taking the high road sucked.

Oh, what the hell. "Maybe you should fix that personality next!" I shouted, but he was already driving away in an old, faded red Jeep. As Zack cleared the gate, a yellow Corvette eased away from the curb and into the lane behind him.

† † †

I whooshed through the front door of my house, dropping my backpack in the entryway. This house was newer than the others we'd lived in, with high ceilings and plenty of wide-open spaces. Mom managed to make it homey despite the lack of furniture and knick-knacks, always keeping fresh flowers on the fireplace mantle, a soft rug over the hardwood floors and warm hues covering the walls.

"Mom? Dad?" I called out.

Faint voices from their bedroom wafted down to the ground floor, reminding me how much I'd be working over the weekend in my dad's office upstairs.

But I'd have to embrace slavedom in order to win back my freedom. Maybe if I started working tonight and only stopped to eat and sleep... A thrill rippled through me at the thought of salvaging my Sunday. One thing at a time though. Right now, the only thing on my mind was talking my parents out of uprooting me again.

Bolting to the bottom of the stairs, I sprang, intending to take them two at a time. Instead, I soared over four steps, my feet landing with a thud on the fifth.

Sure, five-feet-eight was tall for a girl, but even my dad couldn't hop that many steps as effortlessly as I just had. Unless, I'd already taken one step before doing the three. Had I?

My heart pounded, not with exertion, but sudden fear. Was my body freaking out or was I going crazy?

Eyeing the first landing, I braced myself, then leapt again. My foot slipped on the third step and my knee smacked into the hard corner. I teetered backward and caught the railing before tumbling to level ground. Pain sliced through my leg.

My knee throbbed as I hobbled the rest of the stairs one step at a time, then limped down the hallway toward my parents' bedroom. Testing myself for suddenly developed superpowers had been a lame idea.

By the time I stood over the threshold to their room, any discomfort had completely vanished. Like I hadn't already had enough weirdness for one day with my freaky sense of smell and heightened hearing.

Speaking of smell, the nicotine stench in the house was particularly pungent today. Before I could give it more thought, I noticed my mom smiling up at me from her cross-legged position on the floor. A thin mist of smoke from the lit cigarette between her fingers swirled up toward the ceiling. I glanced at the window that was cracked open only a smidgen and wondered why my parents hadn't already flung themselves through the window to get some oxygen.

"Autumn." Dad's blond head popped up from behind his laptop. He grinned at me as he set the computer aside to reveal all six feet two inches of him. "How was your day?"

"Hi, sweetheart." My mom's nearly black hair swished over her arm as she reached over to cram a T-shirt into one of several very full plastic bags. Donations to the thrift store, no doubt. Mom liked to travel light, so she always purged just before we moved.

My stomach twisted at the thought of starting all over somewhere else. Worse, with school almost over, why bother enrolling me wherever we ended up? I'd be back to homeschooling.

"Something wrong?" Mom asked, exhaling as she flicked ashes into the ashtray.

Yes, something was definitely wrong, but my urge to rehash it with them died as soon as I'd seen the loaded bags. What was the point when they already knew how I felt? "I'm fine," I lied, giving them a tight smile. "I have a lot of homework though. See you for dinner."

I slogged down the hall to my room. After kicking off my shoes, I wiggled my toes in the silky fuzz of the white faux fur rug at the foot of my bed and drew in a lungful of air. Mom or Dad must have been smoking in my room recently. Gross. I glanced at my dresser to see a stack of folded clothes that had been dropped off. With another breath came the scent of laundry detergent. From across the room.

I didn't know how I was able to smell it from that far away, but at that moment, I didn't care. Fatigue nagged me. Maybe after a nap, I could forget my rotten day.

Sprawling over my purple comforter, I closed my eyes. Noises surrounded me—the patter of my mom's feet as she went downstairs, a dish clattering against the counter, the refrigerator door opening and closing, water rushing through the pipes. How could I possibly hear all that?

From my prone position, I brought my knee to my chest and rolled up my jeans. My knee appeared perfectly normal. No swelling, no scratch. But as much as it had hurt bashing into the step, there should've been something to show for the pain.

My new super-hearing, crazy sense of smell and fast healing couldn't be my imagination.

But it had to be.

I was just a normal girl who'd been reading too many vampire romances and werewolf tales.

† † †

Wolves howled in the distance.

I crouched perfectly still, huddled against a moss-covered tree trunk, surrounded by the scent of damp earth and pine.

The snarls grew louder and leaves rustled. The wolves were getting closer. Sweat trickled down my temple and my breath froze in my lungs as I braced myself for the inevitable.

I sucked in air and bolted upright, my heart thudding against my ribcage. I rubbed my eyes, then scanned the walls around me. *My* room. No wolves. I released my breath and flopped back onto my pillow.

It had been years since I'd dreamed of them. Why now?

The sun had lowered, casting shadows on the walls. It had to be almost dinner time. My stomach growled in confirmation. Shrugging off my nightmare, I headed downstairs.

When I settled at the table to eat with my parents, I was too disturbed over the day's events to concentrate on food. Wayward boyfriends, bitchy friends, my inevitable return to home schooling... And then there were my heightened senses and accelerated healing—which were my imagination, of course.

"How are your classes going?" My mom eyed me over her plate of rice, sautéed vegetables and stuffed tomatoes.

She didn't fool me. Their love for me was the one constant in my life, but they took it to extremes. One more thing to add to the list of oddities about my parents: they asked a lot of questions about my teachers, my friends and anyone else I mentioned. But if someone else asked questions about us, they got twitchy.

Like in Reno, Nevada, when I was fourteen-years-old, the waiter at a restaurant was curious why we were vegetarians and asked what school I went to. We'd moved a week later. Or a couple years ago when our neighbors in St. George, Utah had asked, in what seemed like polite conversation, where we were from—I'd told them. That time, I'd only had a few days before being whisked away.

Way to make me earn my adulthood by loving me to death. I adored them, but their backseat-driving and paranoia drove me crazy. And drove me away.

They weren't exactly over-sharers either, so my info deprivation only fueled my imagination. I used to wonder if I'd been kidnapped, but blew it off since I looked too much like my mom. Had something bad happened to make them so overcautious? I'd asked, but never got any straight answers. Ironically, I'd hated their aversion to sharing information, yet I'd developed the same affliction with them.

Until I knew the reason for their paranoia, omitting details and giving my parents a more pleasant version of reality would keep them from worrying as much—and from ruining my life.

"Aced my history test." Which was odd since I hadn't studied at all. Like I'd suddenly gotten way smarter. "But I'm not sure why any of that matters since I won't be graduating with everyone else." I set my glass on the table with a bang.

Dad cleared his throat. "We're doing what's best for this family."

"Whatever," I mumbled.

Mom took a sip from her glass of juice, her gaze still steady on mine. "You should know, your father accepted that job today."

So it was official. My eyes stung. "When does it start?"

Dad reached over to squeeze my hand. "We're still working that out."

My parents shelled out money for my private

school, so we couldn't be poor. But if we stayed here and they turned down work, could they still afford the tuition? Whether we stayed or left, I was screwed.

I blinked away the burn in my eyes as I withdrew my hand from his and got up. "Thanks for dinner." After loading my plate into the dishwasher, I headed to my room to mope in private.

Just as I settled on the bed and turned on the TV, a rap sounded on my door. Apparently, going five minutes without laying eyes on me was too long. "Come in."

Mom and Dad appeared in the doorway, each holding a glowing cigarette between their fingers. I wondered if it was a conspiracy to stink up my room.

With only the dim light from my TV barely reaching their faces, they could almost pass for teenagers. They insisted that their vegetarian diet and jogging every night kept them young. Except they smoked. Go figure.

"Did you want to talk about it?" Dad asked.

I muted the TV. "Is it going to change anything?" I fired back.

He shook his head. "We've made our decision."

Exactly. They'd still haul me from city to city and they weren't going to give me a pardon on the debt or unground me.

"Then I have nothing to say." I switched the sound back on and turned to the TV.

Mom peeked past Dad's shoulder, her amber eyes narrowing just before closing the door.

Damn them.

Restless, I jumped off the bed and opened the window for some fresh air. I looked past the neighbor's parted curtains to their ghastly, paisley-patterned wallpaper, which I hadn't been able to see yesterday.

Yep, even my vision was better.

Maybe my improved senses were stress-related. Like the way moms were capable of great strength to save their child. If I did away with the stress, maybe my body would start metabolizing normally again. Maybe that's all there was to it.

After my shower, I threw on some pajamas, then went in search of dessert. Maybe after getting some chocolate in my system, I'd feel normal.

A *lot* of chocolate.

"We're leaving for our run, sweetheart," my dad said as I descended the stairs. "We'll be gone an hour or so. You'll be okay while we're out?"

I blew out a breath, slipping in a groan for their benefit. "I think I can handle being home alone for an hour. Maybe one day, when I'm thirty or forty, you can leave me alone *all day.*"

Dad laughed, my irritation soaring over his head. Mom gave me a scolding look before following him out the front door.

On the way to the fridge, I shook out my arms to relax. An unfamiliar energy, like a power surge, centered in my chest and spread out. My pulse hammered. What the hell was that? Panic crept up on me. Maybe I had a brain aneurysm or something.

As my breathing calmed and the tingles faded, I

could almost believe I was okay and that most likely it was just my crappy day that had taken its toll. Yeah, that's all there was to it.

Grabbing a juice bottle from the fridge, I held it in one hand and twisted off the cap with the other. The bottle burst and liquid sprayed. I winced as shards of glass sliced through my palm and blood flowed down to my fingertips, blending with the spilled juice.

My heart pounded. I sucked in a few long breaths which seemed to dull the pain. With trembling hands, I threw the glass shards in the garbage, then ran water over my palm to survey the damage. The cool stream soothed my frayed nerves and washed the blood down the drain.

How had I shattered the bottle with my bare hands? Defective bottle? It had to be. I couldn't imagine the amount of strength it would take to crush a glass bottle.

Strangely, all the pain had faded, even though it had only been a matter of seconds since I'd broken the bottle. Flipping my hands over and back again, I couldn't find the source of the blood. How was that possible? Blood would've required an opening to pass through. And yet, no such opening existed.

No avoiding it now. Something was definitely up.

A logical explanation had to exist somewhere, but I had no idea where to start. The last place I'd go for information was my parents. The way they worried about me, I'd probably find myself in the hospital. Next thing you know, I'd be the subject of some weird experiment.

CHAPTER FOUR

I'D FALLEN ASLEEP at my laptop last night, surfing the Internet for anything on powers or accelerated healing. The Marvel comic sites told me about superheroes with special abilities. But I already knew I wasn't a superhero. I needed to know *why* it was happening. I had some other ideas for research, but had to hold off until later, after I worked off my debt to my parents.

Dad had plenty for me to do—filing, data entry, billing. I even started a website for him. He did graphic design, but his true love was computer forensics. He'd examine the hard drive for evidence of hacking or whatever he was hired to investigate. And that required traveling. But why did we have to move for every single job when he could leave us behind and return when he finished?

By the time Maya texted me Saturday afternoon to let me know she'd be there soon, I'd whittled my debt to almost nothing.

"Anything else you need done?" I waited for my dad's reply while he typed in code for a website.

"Always. There's another stack of filing." Dad smiled, blue eyes twinkling, and pointed to the top of the file cabinet. "How's it going with Daniel? Haven't seen much of him lately."

My love life was the last thing I wanted to discuss with my dad. "Fine. He has some friends over tonight. I was supposed to go, but I'm grounded." I shrugged. "I'll see him Monday."

He nodded slowly, eyes narrowed. "Did he do something?"

Damn, my dad had good instincts. "No. I promise."

"And how are *you* doing?" Dad's eyes bored into mine, as though he could hypnotize me into coughing up whatever might be bothering me. But I'd never tell my parents about my school problems or I could lose what few days there I had left. I wasn't going to spill that I was crazy enough to think I might have superpowers either. Best-case scenario, they'd think I was losing my mind and keep even closer tabs on me. They hovered enough as it was.

"You mean other than being forced to move again?" I asked, struggling to keep the attitude out of my voice.

He sighed.

There, that would throw him off the subject of Daniel and school. If anyone could make me talk, it was my dad. "I didn't realize it was so late," I said, checking my cell. "Maya will be here soon. Okay if I do this tomorrow?"

Maya usually spent Sundays with her family. With me avoiding Daniel, and Gina avoiding me, I'd have tons of time to earn money.

"Sure." He smiled and returned his attention to the computer monitor just as the doorbell chimed.

I hurried downstairs and relieved Maya of her overnight bag. Still holding her pink, vinyl makeup box and a small, paper sack, she followed me to my room. I locked the door and turned up the music, so we could speak freely without anyone eavesdropping.

"Gina still mad?" Setting the pink box on a chair, she flopped on the bed, small bottles clinking against each other inside the sack.

"Yep." I waved her into the connecting bathroom. "Pedicures first."

A few minutes later, the jet tub's motor kicked on and bubbles rose up from the steamy water. We leaned against the tile wall and let the water beat against the bottoms of our heels.

I was dying to tell her about my super-powers, but if they went away and I couldn't prove it, I'd look crazy. Maybe sitting on it for a while would be better than blurting it out and paying for it later.

"What's new with Trevor?" I asked.

"Nothing." She stared into the bubbly liquid.

"Maybe it's time to make a move. How long have you been crushing on him?"

Maya groaned. "Too long. But a guy has to give me *some* kind of sign before I'm that brave. How are you and Daniel getting along?"

I still planned to dump him, but didn't want the added pressure of Maya rushing me, since I clearly sucked at the whole breakup thing. "We're fine."

When we finished our pedicures and had given each other cucumber and avocado facials, I whipped out the makeup. It was almost a waste to do full makeup if we weren't going anywhere, but we loved trying new things, whether anyone saw us or not.

"I'll do yours first," I said. Setting the box in the sink, I put the toilet seat lid down for her to sit. I dipped the giant brush in the bronzer, then swished it over her cheekbones, nose and forehead. After rummaging through the box, I found the right shadow. "Close your eyes."

Maya obeyed. "What do you think of Zack?"

"He seems like a bit of a jerk." Which was why I loathed the way my stomach fluttered at the mere mention of his name. I concentrated on getting the mascara on thick enough without clumping.

"Then he's just your type." Maya chuckled. A few seconds went by before she noticed me staring at her. "What?"

"You think Daniel's a jerk?"

"Me and everyone else." She held out her hand. "Give me the mirror, so I can see what you've done."

I passed it to her. "If that's true, how can he be the most popular guy in school?"

"It's an illusion. When you're king of Verdugo Hills Academy, everyone's afraid to cross you."

"He used to be so sweet," I mumbled, peeking over the mirror.

"They're all nice in the beginning," Maya said as she examined her eyeliner.

"Sometimes they stay that way," I said, thinking how much my parents adored each other, even after nearly twenty years together. "But you'll never have that if you don't put yourself out there." I waited a beat, but she didn't comment. "So, what do you think?"

"Interesting." She turned her face side-to-side, examining my work from every angle. "The eyeliner's thicker than I usually do, but you balanced it with the clear lip gloss. I look nice."

"You look *phenomenal*." I mentally patted myself on the back for impressing Maya, my makeup guru. "Hey, what if you flirted with Trevor? You know, be receptive?"

She blinked. "I'm not receptive?"

"You're the queen of casual. We hung out for weeks before I stopped wondering if you liked me. He probably has no clue."

"Really?"

"Yeah." I chuckled. "Just flash him a smile. You don't even have to use words."

Maya frowned as she processed that. I almost grinned at my matchmaking attempt, then remembered my own disastrous love life.

CHAPTER FIVE

WHILE MY PARENTS went out for their run Sunday evening, I cleaned and organized my room. With arms full of dirty clothes, I shot out of the hallway and nearly crashed into the wall. I leaned an elbow against the doorjamb for balance as the world shifted around me, blurred for an instant, then sharpened.

What the hell?

I proceeded with caution, moving slower to keep track of the hallway in relation to myself. Taking the stairs went smoothly enough, but as I took a step through the doorway of the laundry room, tingles of energy snaked through my stomach, chest and limbs. When the heel of my foot landed on a nearly invisible puddle of water, I overcompensated by pulling back. My other foot skidded across the floor and I hydroplaned. My free hand shot out to break the fall and the fleshy part of my thumb caught on a loose screw in the threshold. Blood pooled in my palm.

I stared at my hand, feeling queasy. Then, right before my eyes, the opening slowly closed. Within moments, there was no sign of even a scratch.

Whoa.

As if to demonstrate my power, another swell of energy moved through my hands.

Okay, I would not freak. I would calmly and systematically figure out what the hell was happening to me. Had I been exposed to a chemical or radiation? My new intermittent abilities couldn't be hereditary. Aside from their hovering, my parents were totally normal. And if they knew anything, they would've told me.

I couldn't confide in them or they'd probably worry that an aneurysm was bringing on freakish abilities and would lead to death or something. Sorting out what was going on was enough without adding their neuroses into the mix.

Maybe I should see a doctor. Except the only way to keep it from my parents would be to see someone I didn't know and pay cash from my car savings. That was a last resort. Besides, they'd have to document the case and what if someone evil found out about me who wanted to use my powers to rule the world? Yeah, my imagination was running wild. Still, I didn't want to become someone's experiment.

Sneakers pattered outside and I realized I'd sat there scrutinizing my hand for several minutes. I jumped up, rinsed off my hand and straightened my clothing.

Breathe... Breathe.

I strolled into the living room just as the front door swung open. "How was your run?"

"Great," my mom answered, hanging her keys on a hook by the door. "We're going to watch a movie.

Would you like to join us?" She pulled a cigarette from her pack and fished in her pocket for a lighter.

"Not tonight, thanks. I have some research to do for a class." I couldn't possibly concentrate on anything other than figuring out what was going on with me.

† † †

As I drove to school Monday morning, to prevent getting into a car crash or something and miraculously healing in front of someone, I kept the radio off and ignored anything else that might distract me. I'd have to remember to be careful of my movements at school too, so I wouldn't accidentally leap a tall building in a single bound, or some such crap, and draw attention to my newly developed weirdness.

I'd researched again last night, using all the words and phrases I could think of. I'd even checked diseases, but nothing about superpowers and accelerated healing popped up. There were all sorts of websites on herbs and acupuncture to *promote* healing. Not helpful.

Seeing a roadwork sign and cars bottle-necked up ahead, I slowed. By the time I passed the orange cones, I'd lost five minutes.

When I parked in the school lot and rounded the hood of my car, the passenger-side rear tire caught my eye. Damn, it was almost totally flat. Zack had mentioned it Friday, but I'd forgotten all about it. I needed to remember to stop for air after school.

On the way to the school entrance, I saw Daniel in

my peripheral vision leaning against his car. I wasn't in danger of being late, but I no longer had time to dive into a long and probably heated conversation with Daniel. I pretended not to see him, but he darted out from between cars and captured my hand.

Oblivious to my cringing, he lowered his head to try to kiss me, his long, blond hair whipping around and tickling my nose. I stiffened and prepared myself for a confrontation.

"Hey guys. What's up?" Gina's eyes narrowed a moment at his arm around my waist.

"Oh, hi." I gave her a small smile, not sure if she was still mad at me.

Gina grinned, like she was totally over it. I didn't want to be her bestie anymore, but I didn't want us unfriendly either. She'd get another chance to make up for being such a hag on Friday.

"I'll see you at lunch." Daniel freed my waist and left without kissing me goodbye. Whew.

Gina walked with me through the school entrance and stopped at her locker. "The party was crazy. I had such a blast."

She definitely seemed back to her less-bitchy self. "You look awfully cheery. Did you hook up with someone at the party?"

"Yes, and he's gorgeous." Gina beamed as she dragged a book from her locker.

"And?" The juicy details would take my mind off my epic fail with Daniel, among other things.

She turned to face me. "The thing is... I might really like this guy. Maybe I should see him a couple more times before I say much. Don't want to jinx it."

So much for distraction.

† † †

I nearly choked on the thick smell of grease that hung in the corridor as I headed to the cafeteria. My super sense of smell didn't do much for my appetite.

Daniel and Gina beat me to our table. They sat next to each other, shoulders brushing like they were deep in conversation. For a second, I considered going straight to Maya and pretending Daniel and Gina didn't exist. But that would be too rude.

After getting my food, I closed in on them. Gina noticed me, then returned to a normal sitting position as Daniel glanced over his shoulder. I shot them a weird look and was about to ask them about their big secret when Maya stopped by our table. She'd let her hair go natural and golden waves fell around her face. Her makeup was almost the same as I'd done it Saturday, but somehow improved upon.

She glanced to her right. "There they are, looking mighty fine."

Following her gaze, I spotted Trevor. Next to him sat Zack, appearing every bit as delectable as ever. His straight dark hair spiked up and he'd dressed in faded jeans and a solid black T-shirt. It was basic, yet looked anything but plain on him.

"Ooh-la-la." Gina clicked her tongue.

Daniel snorted. "Those guys are total losers."

Like a bullet, Zack's eyes shot to mine. I hung with the two most beautiful girls in school and he was looking at *me*? I thought he didn't like me. He grimaced before looking away, reminding me nothing had changed.

"I'll see you later, Autumn." Maya twirled and walked toward John's table.

I stared after Maya, longing to go with her. Normally, I would've sat down by now. To stall, I whipped out my cell and texted my mom just to say hello. There, I'd beaten her to it. Still standing, I contemplated how to spend the rest of lunch at John and Maya's table without Daniel or Gina making a scene.

"I haven't seen Jeff today. Is he okay?" Gina asked Daniel.

"Yeah. He's still hung over from Saturday."

Gina tucked an auburn lock of hair behind her ear. "That's some hangover."

"Moderation isn't one of Jeff's strong points," Daniel said.

I yawned, my gaze wandering to John's table. "I need to talk to Maya for a minute."

Gina beamed. "We'll hold your spot for you."

"Yeah, I'll walk you to class in a bit." Daniel shot me a quick look and returned his focus to Gina as though I were an afterthought. No giving me crap about hanging with my less popular friends? Something had to be up, but I wasn't going to question my good fortune. I snapped up my tray and high-tailed it.

Two other girls and a guy sat with John and Maya. The only free spot next to John allowed a full view of

Zack. Taking the seat, I smiled, which was easy since I was so glad to be away from Daniel and Gina. "Hey."

John's brows rose. "Gina and your boyfriend let you go?"

I shrugged, barely containing my joy.

Maya glanced over at them, then gave me a grin. "They seem just fine without you."

A moment later, proving once again I was powerless against Zack's pull, my line of vision adjusted a fraction to include him. And suddenly he was watching me. Damn. Caught ogling again.

Twisting around, I let my hair form a barrier between us. But I could feel the energy emanating from him, like a beam coming straight for me. Just as I snuck another peek at him from under my lashes, he rose, emptied his tray and left. I wondered where he was going when he still had most of lunch period left. Well, good. With him gone, I could enjoy my meal with my real friends.

After lunch, Daniel walked me to English Lit. Near the entrance of my class, he leaned in. He didn't smell like his usual self. There was something extra. Perfume? It was all over him and reminded me of Gina.

"We've barely seen each other for days." He moved closer. I automatically backed against the wall and he caged me in with his arms. "After school, want to go for coffee or something?"

No, I didn't want to go anywhere with him. But I needed him to stick around so I could dump him.

"I'll see you after school." I ducked under his arm, making my getaway. Thankfully, Daniel and I didn't have any classes together. We probably wouldn't cross paths again until school was over.

Several desks away from Zack, I took my seat and swiveled toward the door, so Zack could only see my back. The bell rang.

"Everyone face the board, please. Autumn," Mr. Farajian boomed.

Zack chuckled softly and my cheeks heated. Lifting my chin, I aimed it at the teacher and managed to get through the entire period without glancing at Zack. Keeping my mind on my studies was a different matter entirely.

There had to be someone I could talk to about my strange new abilities. Maya's mom maybe? Except super-human powers were kind of a big deal and what if she talked to my parents?

When the bell rang again, I rose and moved around my desk. With my eyes anywhere but on Zack, I darted into the aisle. When he bumped into me, my step faltered and I lost my balance. His hands shot to my shoulders to steady me and I spun around.

His hands moved to my hips. "Falling for me again? It's either that or I give you vertigo," he said softly, a smile playing on his lips.

My gaze dropped to his mouth, then lower. Zack had a dimple in his chin. A very sexy dimple.

"I..." I what? The pressure of his thumb at my hip bone turned my brain into soup and I couldn't squeak out even one syllable.

"Are you okay?" A frown marred his forehead.

"Yeah, sure."

The lines over his brows disappeared and he shook his head as if wiping away cobwebs. "You should get going, don't you think? Daniel's probably waiting for you." He smirked, then dropped his hands. "That one's a keeper, huh?"

My brain engaged and I returned his smirk. "And you're so much cooler?" I turned and headed to my next class.

Once I rounded the corner, I exhaled, sure I didn't sense Zack close by. I couldn't think about how I knew when he was near. Couldn't think about a lot of things right now. I just needed to watch where I went and how fast I moved, especially where Zack was concerned.

After my last class, I stopped at my locker. As I rooted around for the books to take home, I felt thick arms wrap around my waist, lips nuzzling the back of my neck.

"You ready to go to Bill's Bean and Brew? We're due for some quality time together," Daniel whispered in my ear.

No, I wasn't ready for that at all. But it would give me the perfect opportunity to end things. That is, if we actually made it to the coffee shop and not some deserted road for *quality time.* But since I really wanted to have that talk with him, I'd take what I could get and fend him off.

"I'll meet you outside." I shoved my books back in the locker and faced him, fully expecting to dodge him when he swooped. Instead, he flashed me that same sweet smile he used to give me before we started dating. Too bad the sweetness wouldn't last.

Daniel took off. I turned to follow when I noticed Zack sauntering toward me. Why couldn't his locker be at the other end of the hallway?

Zack gave me a thumbs up, mouthing, "He's a winner," as he passed me.

I hated that Daniel was such a creep and Zack had judged me by that.

I needed to get this breakup on.

Sighing, I resumed the book search, loaded up my backpack and headed to Daniel's car. Right outside the double doors, I saw Gina twisting her hair around her finger as she talked to Zack.

Could he be the mystery guy she'd hooked up with at the party over the weekend? Except that Gina had said Zack had a girlfriend. Maybe he'd recently become available.

Zack seemed to like Gina just fine, but he couldn't stand me. A feeling deep inside me fought its way up. Jealousy. Which I needed to get over, because Zack didn't like me at all. He and Gina were probably perfect for each other. They could sit together at lunch and judge everyone.

As I approached my car, I noticed the rear tire all plump and healthy. I searched the lot, expecting to see someone walking away with a car-jack. No such luck.

Who'd filled it up? If my dad had noticed—which was unlikely since I'd parked across the street yesterday where he couldn't see that side of my car—he would've insisted on driving me to school or at least mentioned it to me and warned me to be careful. Zack maybe?

I dumped my backpack in the Taurus and scanned the parking lot for Zack. Instead, I spotted Daniel's black Audi gleaming just several cars away. Daniel casually leaned against the passenger side, glaring in another direction and oblivious to my presence. I followed the path of his gaze to Zack and Gina, wondering what Zack had done to annoy him—besides being way hotter than him.

"Hey," I said, as I approached.

"Hi, babe. You should park your car on the street, so we don't have to rush back before the gates get locked."

I backtracked to my car, but halted two steps later and spun around. Knowing Daniel, he'd invite Jeff and Natalie. We wouldn't be alone at all. "I can't go for coffee."

"Okay, but you said you wanted to talk. Get in and we'll drive around the block or something."

Which was what I'd wanted. But did I really want to be trapped in his car with him?

"Actually, I really need your help with something," Daniel said, his blue eyes pleading. "I'd rather not talk about it here."

I sighed and climbed into the Audi. I was about to put on my seatbelt when he gripped my arm.

"Not so fast." He leaned over, cupping my face. "You look really pretty today."

I leaned back, so Daniel's mouth couldn't reach me. Instead of noticing my retreat, he gazed past me and frowned. Glancing over my shoulder, I saw Gina and Zack talking at his car. My tummy fluttered. So not the reaction I wanted when seeing Zack. He gave Gina a wave, then went back into the school.

"What's with you and Zack?" I asked.

Daniel pivoted in his seat and started the engine. "For starters, he's a total tool."

Whatever. I probably wasn't going to get anything else out of Daniel, so didn't try.

As he barreled through the gate and swerved into the lane, which was how he always drove, I pondered what I'd say. How did you go about telling someone you don't like them anymore?

My palms moistened and I racked my brain for the right words. Then I stared out the window and noticed we were a few hundred yards from Angeles National Forest—with plenty of secluded spots hidden by trees. Why was I not surprised that he'd driven me to a very private place to park?

Daniel killed the engine under a covering of trees and unhooked his seatbelt.

I scooted toward the door. "We're not *parking* this time, Daniel. We need to talk."

"We can do that later." Daniel lunged, his mouth devouring mine. As he squished against me, my elbow wedged against the door and his weight on my chest pressed into my air passages. I couldn't breathe.

CHAPTER SIX

"DANIEL!" I SHOUTED. "I wanted to talk, not make out."

He lifted his head, brows drawn. "You mean you were serious?"

"Yes." I shoved, but his full weight made him hard to budge. Disgusting. "Get off."

"I don't mind getting off. Just put your hand right here—"

"You know what?" I gritted my teeth. "Just take me to my car. Now." He didn't even deserve the speech, whatever it may have been. After today, I'd never speak to his stupid ass again. He'd get the idea soon enough.

"What? We just got here." He aimed for my mouth, his tongue poking past my lips.

I shoved harder, blasting his back into the dashboard.

"Ow!"

"I said *no*." I adjusted my shirt.

"Damn it, Autumn. You've kept me waiting for weeks. I swear, I'm not waiting until prom night."

"Prom night?" My face skewed. He assumed I'd sleep with him then? Oh, he had some nerve.

"Come on, baby. I promise you'll love it." Daniel reached over and hit the button to make my seat recline, then he pounced. In a flash, he was climbing over to my side, trying to kiss me again.

I turned my head. "If you don't get off me right now, I'm going to scream." My arms thrashed until my palm connected with his chin. He yelped. "I'm not kidding. Let me go."

"Fine." He clambered over to his own seat and rubbed his jaw. "But I'm done waiting, Autumn. You'd better start getting your priorities straight."

"Screw you, Daniel." I shifted in the seat so my back faced him. The creep didn't speak another word after he started up the Audi. A few blocks from the school, I couldn't take it anymore. I didn't want to be in the same city with him, much less the confined space of a car. "Pull over and let me out."

"What?" He glanced at me briefly.

"I said stop. I can walk the rest of the way."

"Whatever." Daniel swerved dangerously and bumped the curb.

"Don't you dare come near me ever again," I hissed. Without looking at him, I swung the door open, leaped out and slammed the door shut. His tires screeched behind me.

Still trembling from rage, I texted my mom to tell her I'd been delayed, then sprinted to the school. The run felt good, liberating. Barely winded from the exertion, I climbed into my car and leaned back in the driver's seat.

What an ass. I shouldn't have waited so long to dump him.

A knock on my window made me jump and my stomach clenched, thinking it was Daniel. Not out of fear, but revulsion.

Zack motioned for me to roll the window down and I did. A whiff of his woodsy, earthy scent invaded my nose and I stared into piercing green eyes.

"Car not starting again?" He pulled his cell out and looked at the screen.

To check the time, I assumed. Apparently, subtlety wasn't a quality Zack possessed. If he was short on time, why did he bother stopping at all? "What are you still doing here?" I asked.

"Detention."

"On your second day at a new school?" I scrunched my nose.

He exhaled and aimed his eyes at the sky. "Tried to break up a fight, then your boyfriend said I started it."

Daniel rated high on the douche meter, for sure, but *that* high? "What about the guys who were fighting? They pin it on you too?"

"Yep." He straightened and folded his arms over his chest.

I made a conscious effort to keep my jaw from dropping. Zack didn't seem the type of guy to let someone walk all over him that way. Daniel and his creepy friends would fully deserve anything Zack dished out.

He rolled his eyes. "Are you stranded or not?"

I blinked, still stuck on Daniel and his evil deed.

"I haven't tried."

"Why don't you try it *now*?" He lifted one brow.

"Geez, no one's forcing you to stay. I'm sure you have more interesting things to do."

"Yeah, like get to work, which I'll be even later for if you don't speed things up." He gave me the hurry up motion with his hand. "Start it."

I turned the key and the car fired to life right away. My gaze returned to the open window, but Zack was already yards away.

"Zack. Wait." Leaving the motor running, I scrambled out of my car and chased after him.

He pivoted on his heel and faced me. "What?"

"Did you fix my flat?"

His eyes darted to my tire. "Somebody did."

"So it wasn't you?"

"You think *I* fixed it for you?" Zack gave me a really good are-you-crazy-look.

I lifted my chin. "You didn't answer the question."

"Really?" Zack laughed once. "You're going to make me even later to work for small talk?"

"I just want to know if I should thank you for fixing my tire. You don't have to be such an ass."

"You and Daniel act like you're better than everyone else, but I'm an ass?" He shook his head, his mouth twisting.

The thought of being lumped in with a guy like Daniel made my stomach churn. I opened my mouth to tell him that Daniel and I were so over. "Listen—"

"Spare me your devotion to him, okay?" Zack grimaced. "You guys remind me of this lady when I was a stock boy at Dollars and Deals. She'd come in with her fake blond hair and fake boobs and treat me like her personal slave. Ran me around and never once thanked me."

"Uhm..." I didn't get it. My boobs were real and I wasn't blond. He should've been able to figure out by looking at my car that I wasn't rich either.

"One day, this guy came in and we ended up talking about cars. After a while, he shook my hand and thanked me for my help. All I did was point him to the paper towels."

I frowned, trying to guess Zack's point to the story.

"Turns out he owns all the Dollars and Deals across the country, yet he didn't act like he was better than me. After talking with him, I felt *good* about myself. It made me realize that truly decent people treat others with respect. *That's* what makes them better. Not how many things they own or how popular they are."

I tilted my head, hoping he wasn't saying what I thought he was saying.

"They don't go around *acting* like they're superior and making everyone else feel like crap."

"Oh." I blinked, finally getting it. My mind reeled in outrage. "You mean like what you're doing right now?"

Gina was a hundred times the snob I was—if I was one at all. Why was Zack nice to her? And if Zack was right about me, I wouldn't be friends with John or Ashley.

But seeing him scowl froze the words in my throat. Next thing I knew, Zack had turned his back on me and lithely jumped into his Jeep. As he disappeared beyond the gate, my hands balled into fists.

I couldn't let myself care what he thought.

After texting my mom, saying I was still alive, I hopped into my car and drove. I took the long way home, through windy roads that hugged the edge of the forest, until my anger dissipated.

Once at my house, I found my mom sitting in my dad's lap on the couch.

"Hey," I said. "Dad, were you at my school today?"

"No, why?" he asked.

I shrugged. "Thought I saw you from the back."

My mom smiled. "He was home with me all day."

So who fixed my flat?

After dealing with my ex, then putting up with Zack, I wasn't very hungry during dinner. I ate anyway while doing my best not to think of radioactive spiders and exposure to toxic chemicals.

I couldn't have been the only person in history to have strange powers. There had to be someone I could talk to or somewhere I could go for information. Other than a doctor.

After dinner, I quietly retired to my room and ignored the stream of apologetic texts from Daniel as I continued my research.

† † †

As I drove to school Tuesday morning and thought of Daniel, my blood boiled. His behavior yesterday made civil conversation with him impossible now.

Little quivers of revulsion traveled my body at the thought of him ever touching me again.

Later, when I entered the cafeteria for lunch, he and Gina huddled next to each other at our table. As I made my way through the room, I saw her glance at me. I smiled, but she immediately averted her eyes without even a nod. Did Daniel tell her what happened or was she mad at me again? Whatever. All I cared about was avoiding more drama.

I snagged a tray and stood in the food line, leaning over to peer through the glass and see what they were serving today. My entire body went stiff, sensing who was behind me in line.

Vowing to ignore Zack, I continued to scan the food bins ahead. As I moved forward to close the space between me and the person in front of me, I felt him move up as well. He was so close, I could feel the warmth radiating from him.

I spun when he leaned into me and inhaled. "Did you just sniff my hair?"

His brows rose in innocence. "Why would I do that?"

"Never mind. Just give me some elbow room, would you?" Maybe some distance would silence the fluttering in my belly.

The corners of his mouth curved up. "Flatter yourself much?"

My eyes narrowed. "Now I'm a snob *and* conceited?"

"If you say so." He twisted to face the trays, as if the food was infinitely more interesting than anything I had to say.

I clenched my fists and held my tongue until it was time to collect my food, then wasted no time getting to my friends' table. I'd even found a spot where I couldn't see Zack. As though sensing my mood, John and Maya didn't ask why I'd skipped sitting with Daniel and Gina. As the minutes passed, I chilled and the smiles came easier.

Daniel materialized next to me as I walked to fifth period, grinning. "Hey, babe. Will you wait for me after school? We can do something together after."

I stopped right in the middle of the hallway and turned on him. "Don't act as if nothing happened yesterday," I said, struggling not to slap the smile off his face.

"Oh, I *know* nothing happened yesterday." He snorted.

My palm twitched. "You know what I mean."

He must have realized how truly pissed I was, because the cocky grin disappeared and his gaze dropped to the ground.

"I know and I'm sorry. I was about to apologize, but I'm just so happy to see you." His eyes focused on my chest.

I stared at him, knowing we had less than two minutes before class—not adequate for everything I burned to say.

"Just to be clear, Daniel, we're *over*."

"What?" His mouth dropped open. "Because of yesterday?"

I scoffed. "Yes."

"Oh, come on. I was just playing around." He gave a short laugh. "You're not breaking up with me over *that*."

He was acting like it was some big joke. Whatever.

He'd figure it out eventually. I spun around and rushed to my next class.

At the end of the school day, Maya found me on my way to my locker. "Going straight home?" she asked.

"Almost. I need to talk to Daniel really quick." I dropped the books and a notebook into my backpack and threw it over my shoulder. "I dumped Daniel at lunch and he won't stop texting me. If he has any hope we'll work things out, I need to crush it."

"Wow." Maya's eyes bulged, then her face broke into a grin. "That's a pleasant surprise. Details, please."

"Sure. But later, okay?" I wiped my moist palms on my jeans.

She grinned. "Alright. I'll walk with you for moral support, but we need to stop at my locker first."

As I shadowed Maya down the corridor, I noticed Trevor and Zack approaching. "Now's your chance. Don't forget to smile," I whispered. "And slow down, so we don't have to screech to a halt in case he looks like he wants to talk."

Trevor's eyes moved to Maya and her face lit up.

"Hey, guys," she said.

Trevor looked like a speeding freight train was headed straight for him.

"You can do it. Just stay friendly," I whispered in her ear. "Ask him how he is."

"How's it going?" She smiled at them.

Trevor nodded, still staring. Zack nudged him in the ribs. When Trevor still didn't move, Zack dragged him forward by his arm.

Maya didn't miss a beat. I wondered if she'd ever taken acting classes.

"How was the party last Saturday?" she asked Trevor.

Trevor flinched when he got another jab in the ribs. "It was okay."

Zack's lips moved, but with the mob in the corridor and locker doors banging, I couldn't make out the words.

"I didn't see you there." Trevor shoved his hands in his pockets and inched toward Maya, his eyes darting around. Definitely not the usual confident Trevor I'd noticed. Zack punched Trevor in the arm and took off.

"I didn't go. Daniel's bashes are too much like what I imagine frat parties must be like." Maya wrinkled her nose.

"Can't say I blame you." Trevor smiled, looking a little steadier. "What did you end up doing?"

"I have to go," I whispered.

She nodded emphatically. I left, glancing back to see them smiling at each other. Maya would be just fine.

I exited the building and traveled the concrete path toward the asphalt parking lot. At the last second, I decided to go to the restroom first to check my face. If I was going to dump Daniel once and for all, I wanted to be cute while doing it.

The football field bordered the parking lot and beyond that was a building with another bathroom, which was almost always empty. As I walked the stretch of grass, students became scarce. But, of course, there was Zack about a hundred yards to my left, talking with Coach Hanson.

The bathroom door was propped open. As soon as I walked in, I spotted a pair of converse high tops facing two cute, pink stilettos together in one stall. They were identical to the heels in my closet at home. Wait. No, Gina had borrowed them a month ago.

I was about to back up to avoid Gina when I heard a male voice.

"Mmm. That's nice."

Daniel.

Gina in a bathroom stall with my boyfriend? Well, he wasn't my boyfriend anymore, but only Maya knew that.

Even though I didn't want to know what they were doing, it was as though a giant magnet stuck me to that spot. Leaning against the wall, I melted into a shadow.

"No, not here," Gina said between moans.

"You didn't mind small spaces Saturday night."

My body froze. Saturday night before I'd dumped him? That wasn't a shock, but with *Gina*? Just because I'd wanted to ease up on the whole bestie thing didn't mean our friendship had meant nothing. My throat swelled with her betrayal. Feet rooted to the tile floor, I wrapped my arms around my waist to silence the trembling.

This little scene explained why Gina wouldn't spill about her new guy. And why she didn't acknowledge me at lunch. She hadn't been saving me from Daniel. She was saving Daniel for herself.

Well, she could have him.

The high tops backed up and the door swung open. Daniel came into view, laughing like someone had playfully pushed him. Gina came into view, giggling and lunging for him.

"Yeah, I didn't mind then, but now sharing is getting old," she said, her bottom lip thrusting out. "You've been stringing me along for a week."

A *week*?

"Aw, don't be like that, baby." Daniel got a handful of Gina's butt and she hooked her fingers around his collar, yanking him against her. "You know how I feel about you," he cooed.

Their mouths met and the smacking sounds made me want to vomit. Slipping out unseen would've been easy. I'd just slide against the wall and slip through the door. However, if I caught them in the act, they couldn't try to weasel out of it later by saying it was my imagination or not what I thought.

I stepped forward. "Really, you guys?"

They vaulted from each other like I'd sprayed them with a fire hose.

"Autumn." Daniel wiped his mouth with the back of his hand.

Gina stared at me, bug-eyed.

"My boyfriend and my friend." I struggled to keep my voice from shaking. I couldn't bear for Gina to know how much she'd hurt me. "Such a cliché."

Gina's eyes were cautious, shifting from him to me. "Autumn, I—"

"Save it." Another emotion blended with the fury—disgust. "Daniel and I were over anyway, although you wouldn't know it by all the *I love you* texts today."

I whipped out my phone and thrust the screen at her. "You guys are so perfect for each other."

My face fell as soon as I turned away. How *could* they? I'd finished with Daniel days ago, but the betrayal stung just the same. Gina had a big mouth and could spread word faster than Twitter. She'd be only too happy to twist the truth and brag that Daniel had dumped me for her.

I halted, right in the middle of the field, as if paralyzed. Everyone would be talking about it, whispering to each other and feeling sorry for me. Whether I stayed in town two days or two weeks, being the victim of gossip still sucked.

My eyes stung. I looked back to see if Gina or Daniel had followed, but they hadn't. Maybe they were relieved to end it, too.

Turning back toward my car, I trudged on. When I glanced up, I saw Zack heading right for me.

I slowed. Had he seen anything? Was he there to gloat?

"You okay?" he asked.

"Yeah." I nodded, surprised he'd stopped to ask.

He narrowed his eyes. "You don't *look* okay."

"Like you care." I wanted to tell Zack the truth, although I had no idea why. I gave a watery laugh as hot tears burned my eyes. "I just walked in on Daniel cheating on me."

Zack sighed, shaking his head. "You shouldn't drive when you're upset. I'll take you home. Can you get a ride back in the morning?"

I grabbed my backpack out of my car, tossed it in the Jeep and hiked up into the front seat. Zack to the rescue again. With his habit of saving me, he had to have been the one to fix my car.

"So you just happen to have a pump in your car, so you can fix flats during lunch?"

Zack sighed. "It's a compressor, actually. Figured it would be faster than doing it after school when it'd be completely flat and you'd be there to distract me."

Why did he have to be such an ass about it though?

"Well, thanks." I sniffed, trying to erase the image of Gina and Daniel from my head.

"Who'd you catch him with? Anyone you know?" he asked, navigating the Jeep onto the street.

He'd find out soon enough, but drawing any more attention to how disposable I'd become as a friend and girlfriend was not something I wanted to discuss with *Zack*. "No one important. Why are you going out of your way to give me a ride?"

"You didn't seem in any shape to drive. If you died on the way home and I could've prevented it, I'd feel bad." He checked over his shoulder to make a turn. "Daniel is scum. I think that's a rotten thing to do to anybody, whether they deserved it or not."

"Are you implying I *deserved* it?"

"What?" His brows shot up as we passed through an intersection.

I'd had enough of people who thought I wasn't worth treating right. I'd certainly had enough of Zack's crap. I'd rather walk than spend one more second with him and his attitude. No matter how beautiful he was.

"Stop the freakin' car," I hissed. "I don't need your charity or your attitude. I can walk back to school and get my car." The Jeep still hadn't slowed. "Stop the damn car," I growled.

"Okay, okay. I'll drive you back." He groaned as he turned the Jeep around. "Whatever."

That last comment just pissed me off more. Zack drove through the school gate and I reached for the handle before he'd even stopped. As my limbs vibrated with fury, I tugged on the door, but it wouldn't budge. "Damn thing is stuck."

He reached over and flipped the switch, unlocking the door. He froze, his arm touching mine, and stared at me. He inhaled quickly twice.

This time, he couldn't act like it was my imagination. "You just *sniffed* me." I gave him a look of loathing before flinging open the door and stomping to my car.

Another crappy day. Life just had to get better.

I took extra time driving around the neighborhood to burn off my rage. When I parked in front of my house, I noticed a red Jeep approaching.

What the hell was Zack doing at my house?

CHAPTER SEVEN

I HADN'T NOTICED Zack in the rearview mirror following me, but I hadn't looked either. What was with the guy? He never hid his dislike for me, yet everywhere I went, there he was.

He parked along the curb and skulked around to the passenger side of his car. Scrambling out of my Taurus, I slammed the door.

"What are you doing at my house? Stalking me?" I asked.

Opening the passenger side of the Jeep, he reached in and pulled out my backpack, then stomped over and tossed it at my feet.

"Please stop making me come to your rescue." He turned and thundered back to his car.

I'd been rude to him when he'd gone out of his way to make sure I didn't get in trouble for not doing my homework. I felt small. "Sorry. Thank you!"

Without turning around or acknowledging my existence, he climbed into his Jeep and turned it around. I felt like a super-dork as I watched him speed away.

About a block down, a yellow Corvette pulled away from the curb after the Jeep. That was the second time

I'd seen that car follow Zack. It couldn't be a coincidence. Maybe he owed money to the mob and that's why his job was so important to him. Or drug dealers? Whoever it was, they'd had plenty of chances to hurt Zack and he was still alive. He wasn't in any immediate danger, right?

After picking up my backpack, I trudged inside. The scent of garlic and herbs met me at the door.

"Who was that outside?" my mom asked, snuggling with my dad. "Didn't sound like Daniel."

"Just a guy from school."

"How was your day?" Dad asked.

A yucky feeling sat in the pit of my stomach, but I faked a smile. "Great."

I ran upstairs to get started on my homework and later, returned for dinner—tofu chicken with gravy, mashed potatoes and steamed asparagus.

"Mom, this is so good." I wolfed down the last of it, sighing as I set my fork down.

"Glad you liked it." She took a sip of water, her gaze darting to my dad, then back to me. "Your dad's got several more jobs lined up and they all want him to start right away."

Right away? My breath caught in my lungs.

"The first job's in Arizona, then Montana," he explained. "New Mexico will take longer, so we'll do that last and stay a while."

I'd miss finals and prom. Not that the latter mattered much since I no longer had a date.

"New Mexico would be semi-permanent?" I asked through the buzzing in my ears.

"Yes," Dad said.

"Or you and I can go straight to New Mexico and get settled in." My mom smiled angelically, like she hadn't just squashed all my hopes and dreams.

"My birthday is in six days." I took a quick sip of my grape juice. "I'll be eighteen."

She let out a quick laugh. "I'm well aware of that. I've been bugging you for weeks to tell me what you want for your birthday."

"I know what I want." My foot tapped against the floor as I imagined their reaction to my request.

Dad smiled hesitantly and my mom looked guarded. "What's that, sweetie?" she asked.

"I want you to leave me here. Go do the jobs, then come back."

He shook his head. "No. Not an option."

"I don't want to move again. Dragging me around so I can't even graduate—it's not right."

Mom reached across the table and held my hand, speaking softly. "I'm sorry, sweetheart. We don't have a choice."

I returned her hand squeeze but hardened my tone just a hair. "*You* may not have a choice, but I do. Legally, in a few days, you can't make me go. I'm staying."

Dad narrowed his eyes. "Excuse me?"

I took a deep breath, hoping to steady my heart pounding against my ribs. "The longest I've been away from you guys is overnight for a sleepover." I paused to chew my lip nervously. "Since you won't buy me a new car..."

They sighed in unison.

"Instead, I want to stay here and finish school. You can go without me and treat it like a second honeymoon or something. Or a working vacation. Whatever."

The way they stared, you'd think I'd asked them to hire a male stripper for my birthday. I waited patiently for their response, leaning back in my chair, and folding my arms across my chest to appear tougher.

"No." My dad narrowed his eyes. "We're not comfortable with that. Choose something else."

My confidence faltered. As protective as they were, why had I thought for even an instant they'd cooperate?

"Sweetie, where are you getting these ideas?" She moved the chair out and stood with a hand on her hip.

"Sometimes, I come up with my *own* ideas, Mom." I rolled my eyes and rose to meet her gaze. I leaned against the dining room table to support my wobbly knees. "You guys avoid leaving the house except at night when you go running. If one of you goes on errands, the other stays. I'm almost never alone and when you're not around, you're constantly texting me. I'm being smothered. Don't you see how unhealthy that is?"

Dad's brows furrowed and his mouth dropped open, as if my words were too foreign and terrifying to absorb.

"Whatever you're thinking, stop now. It's not going to happen." My mom moved around the table to stand in front of me, her hands rubbing my arms soothingly. "We have no desire to be away from you, sweetie."

Oh, boy. I loved my parents, more than anyone or anything, but there was something so wrong with how they treated me. "Fine, then don't leave."

"If the idea of moving upsets you that much, your mother can stay with you here."

Her head whipped around to scowl at him, then back to me. "No, that won't work. She's coming with us."

"Mom, in six days, I'll be legal to do whatever I want," I reminded her.

Dad tensed and Mom gasped. "Don't be silly," she said. "How would you survive without money?"

"I'll stay with Maya and get a weekend job."

He narrowed his eyes. "You're bluffing."

"I don't know what's gotten into you." Mom grasped my shoulders, eyes intense. An instant later, her eyes softened and she released me. "When you have your *real* birthday list, let me know."

"It's not going to change, Mom." I'd gone too far to back down now. "Everything you do, from making me budget my allowance to saving up for a car, why bother? How can I learn to fend for myself in the big bad world if you never *let* me?" I glanced from my mom to my dad. "Do you know what it's like with you two worrying incessantly over me? Do you know how stressful it is to worry whether or not you're worrying?" I shook my head. "I'm done with that. And I'm done moving."

My mom paled. I felt bad for upsetting her, but reminded myself this would be good for all of us. "You can always come back and check on me between cities," I said, lightening my tone.

They exchanged looks for what seemed like minutes. I wiped my palms on my jeans and waited, determined to hold out until the bitter end.

Dad bolted from his chair and towered over me. "This is ridiculous, Autumn."

I stood my ground, keeping my tone firm. "No. Playing musical houses is ridiculous. And I'm not waiting for your permission. You have two choices. Let me stay here in this house and help me finish school. Or lose me to Maya. Pick one. I'll be up in my room."

I dashed up the stairs and collapsed on my bed. I couldn't decide if today had been the worst day ever or the best day of my life. I was free of Gina and the pressures of being popular, done with fighting off Daniel's disgusting advances and I just might have a chance at a life in a town with friends I loved.

Regardless what my future held, with everything I'd been through, today still sucked. Exhaustion strained at my peace of mind and unshed tears burned behind my eyes. Burying my face in my pillow, I succumbed to sobs.

† † †

There was a knock on my door as I finished dressing after a shower. "Come in."

My parents stepped into the room, each with their usual lit cigarette between their fingers. I cringed inwardly as the smoke wafted up to the ceiling. Not wanting to throw them off course by complaining, I kept quiet.

"We've decided to turn down the jobs," my dad announced with a proud smile.

It was what I'd been hoping for, but now it wasn't enough. They'd go right back to their extreme hovering and paranoia. "But that doesn't solve the other problem. You guys need to be without me for a while. And I need to be on my own, at least for a couple weeks so you can see that I can do it. I need that freedom."

When they stared speechless, I was pretty sure I had them. "Both of you will go to Arizona. Turn down the others if you want, so long as you stay gone for at least two weeks." I knew they'd negotiate it down.

"Autumn, I'm ashamed of you," my mom scolded. "Two days. That's it."

"Ten days," I said.

"Three days." Dad's eye twitched.

"Seven days." I lifted my chin.

He folded his arms over his chest. "Three and a half days."

"We could do this all night." I glanced at the clock by my bed with exaggerated movements. "I'd rather you enjoyed yourselves for two weeks, but let's cut to the chase. Four days or I'll call Maya and start packing."

My dad's eyes turned to slits before sharing a look with my mom.

"Maybe we were wrong." She tilted her head, studying me. "It's possible we haven't given you enough credit."

Did that mean they were giving in?

"You have yourself a deal," Dad said a moment later. "Four days. Goodnight, sweetheart." He quietly closed the door behind him.

Yes! I did it. They were going to leave me alone for four long, glorious days. No one around to hover or obsess over me.

I allowed myself a moment to revel in my triumph, then sat on my bed and opened my laptop, determined to find something about my new and unusual abilities.

My situation was curious to say the least. Maybe I needed to think outside the box. Myths? Legends? Aside from vampires, werewolves and various other paranormal creatures, information was sorely lacking.

An hour later, I had accomplished just as much as the previous nights. Nothing. My only hope of discovering more about myself was taking the opportunity to experiment as soon as my parents were on a plane. I snapped my laptop shut in disgust and rolled over, drifting off with a vision of my mom and dad basking in the Arizona sun and having the time of their lives—just the two of them.

† † †

When I turned the key the next morning and my car did absolutely nothing, I plopped back against the seat. Right then, I would have given almost anything for a new car.

Hurrying back inside my house, I hoped one of my parents would be presentable enough to drive me to school. Otherwise, I was going to be late.

"Mom. Dad," I called, my voice carrying beyond the empty living room.

"Car won't start?" My mom popped through the

kitchen doorway. She was all done up and completely gorgeous, her long black hair pinned up away from her neck and showing off her exquisite face.

"You're psychic." I smiled.

"Let's go." She found her keys and motioned to the door.

"We've decided to do the Arizona job, then come back here and regroup," she said, once we were on the road.

"Where in Arizona?" I asked.

"Scottsdale." She glanced over her shoulder before switching lanes. "But we're leaving tonight, not Friday. We'll eat dinner early, get ready and go for our run at the last minute. You can take us to the airport."

Sooner? Bonus! But it was so strange, almost too easy. "Why the rush?"

She smiled. "We want to be home for your birthday on Monday. If we leave tonight, we can return Sunday night and would've fulfilled our end of the bargain. If the job isn't finished yet, your father can go back alone."

It was almost too good to be true. Except I didn't love the idea of driving them to LAX on a Friday night up the 405 during rush hour. On the other hand, spending that time with them would be nice since they'd be gone for a few days. "What time is your flight?"

"We're leaving out of Burbank at nine-fifteen."

Going to Burbank airport would save me an hour of driving. Hallelujah.

My mom pulled up to the curb with five minutes to spare before my first class. We'd made good time.

She unhooked her seatbelt and pulled her keys out of the ignition.

"What are you doing?" I wasn't the only student who found it embarrassing for a parent to go inside the school.

"I can't leave town without informing the principal and making sure he knows how to get in touch with me."

"They have your cell on file, Mom. Geez," I said glumly. Why did I think, even for an instant, they could go cold turkey? "You're the only parent who'd speak with the principal in person. No one does that. See, this is a perfect example of why you've been blackmailed into leaving."

She opened the door anyway, then stopped. "Who is that boy? He looks too old to be a student."

I followed her gaze to the wide double doors of the school and instantly deflated. I didn't bother hiding the antipathy in my tone. "That's Zack. And, yes, he's a student here."

Her eyes shot to mine, an eyebrow raised. "Sounds like you don't like him."

"Not particularly." Zack was scrutinizing the crowd. I wondered who he was searching for. "He's an ass."

"I can call the principal later." She closed her door and started the car again.

I didn't know the reason for her abrupt change of mind and I didn't care. It was enough to know she wasn't going inside. "Meet you here after school?" I asked.

She nodded and waved, looking a little preoccupied.

"'Bye, Mom." I glanced toward Zack again, but he'd already left. So had practically everyone else. I needed to hurry or be late for class.

† † †

After fourth period, I took a different route to the cafeteria, hoping to avoid anyone unpleasant. Slipping into the lunchroom through the back door, I scanned for Maya or John. Instead, I saw Daniel. He was in our usual spot talking with Jeff and a couple of his friends. I did a quick visual for Gina, but she wasn't at any of the tables. Zack and Trevor were seated in their usual place. Maya was there too, right next to Trevor.

I wanted to talk with her, but Zack was a major deterrent. So I kept myself busy picking out a walnut salad, minestrone soup and a banana muffin.

Another glance around the room and I found John in the far corner. He waved at me and I waved back. Tray in hand, I took a step forward to meet him as Maya grasped my arm.

"Trevor asked me out this morning." She beamed.

I squealed. "I knew he would."

"What are you doing this Friday?"

"Anything I want." I grinned. "My parents are leaving town for a few days."

Her mouth dropped open. "You're kidding!"

"Crazy, right? I was hoping you were free to hang out." I wiggled my eyebrows.

"Perfect. Because I told Trevor we'd hang out with him and his friends Friday night."

I swallowed hard, feet fixed to the floor and prayed she'd tell me Zack was not part of the equation. "Which of his friends?"

"You and me with Zack and Trevor. Can you believe it?" She said, stepping aside for someone to pass. When she focused on me again, her face wilted. "Are you okay?"

Maya had said *friends*. Plural. Where were the others? But if I told her how badly I wanted to avoid Zack, she'd feel guilty and her plans with Trevor could be ruined. I couldn't let her down.

"I'm fine. That's great you're getting together with him. I'm happy for you." I nudged her with my elbow and motioned with my head to an empty table. "Come sit with me for a minute. It'll give Trevor a chance to miss you."

She giggled as she fell in step with me. "Not a bad idea."

"Have you seen Gina today?" I asked.

"No, she wasn't in second period." We stopped at the nearly empty table and Maya tilted her head. "It's lunch time and you haven't spoken to her?"

"Uhm..." I sat at the vacant end of the table, then glanced over at the guys. Zack stared at me as though he was trying to figure something out. I turned my head, unnerved by his intensity. "I caught her making out with Daniel yesterday after school," I whispered.

"Oh." Maya eased into the chair across from me as air whooshed from her lungs. "I knew Gina was a bitch, but, wow."

"Yeah, wow." But Maya didn't really seem all that surprised. "Did you know about them?"

Maya glanced over each shoulder as though checking if anyone else could hear. "Not specifically, no."

"But you know something. Spill it," I said in a hushed voice, taking the lid off my salad.

"Gina and I were best friends last year," she said. "Back then, she barely knew Trevor existed until I'd told her about my crush. She started flirting with him the next day."

I reached for her hand and squeezed. "That's why you two don't get along? Why didn't you tell me?"

"It was over a year ago. I wanted to give her the benefit of the doubt." Maya's eyes lit up. "You're single again. What about Zack?"

"Oh, no." I shook my head, imagining the wheels turning in her head. "Don't even think about matchmaking. Zack is so not my type. Besides, he can't stand me."

"I don't think that's true."

"Trust me," I said. "He doesn't like me at all."

"If you say so." She rolled her eyes. "I found out from Trevor why Zack had to switch schools so late in the year."

"Do tell." I leaned forward, elbows on the table and rested my chin on my palms.

"Their moms are sisters. Zack's mom has been sick most of her life. An immune system disorder or something like that. Anyway, between school and work, he couldn't be there all the time to take care of her. So she and Zack moved in with Trevor's family where there's almost always someone home."

"Where's his dad?"

"Died when he was a little boy."

"That's awful." My heart ached for him. "How sick is his mom?"

"She gets better, then gets worse. She's on medication that helps but..." Maya shook her head. "It doesn't look good. I guess she's got a few weeks, months at the most. Which is the biggest reason she and Zack moved here. She wanted to spend her last days with family."

My throat constricted. I couldn't imagine losing one parent, much less both. "I'm so sorry for Zack."

"Yeah, so you should try to be nice to him. Get your tray and eat with us. Then we can firm up our plans."

I shook my head, unwilling to press my luck. I would get enough of Zack on Friday. "You go ahead. I'll see you after school."

Maya took off. I was about to relocate to John's table when the bench moved and someone claimed the spot next to me. I knew by his scent it was Daniel.

"Hi, babe." Daniel wrapped his arms around me. What the hell?

CHAPTER EIGHT

"DON'T TOUCH ME," I hissed, wiggling from Daniel's embrace.

He scooted closer. "Just forgive me already so we can kiss and make up."

"Are you kidding me?" I pushed on his chest. He didn't budge, but my butt slid across the bench.

"What's wrong?" Daniel frowned.

"What happened to Gina? I thought you were with *her* now." I scooted further away.

"No need to be jealous. I told her you were the one I wanted." He smiled patronizingly, like he was doing me a huge favor.

"You cheated on me." My eyes narrowed to slits. "And I'm supposed to act like it was no big deal?"

"We were drinking at the party and she came on to me. I didn't know what I was doing." He swept a hand through the air as if to wave it all away.

"Were you *drunk* yesterday too, Daniel, when you were making out on a toilet?"

Daniel sighed. "I'm sorry. It was a huge mistake. But you could be a little more understanding about a man's needs. If you were taking care of me like you shoulda been, it would've never happened. We're in the real world and," he shrugged, "things happen. But I still love you."

I stared at him. "Well, I don't love *you*."

"Aw, grow up, Autumn."

"Oh. Getting *so* drunk that you do stupid things is *really* grown up." I flattened my hands on my lap to steady them, on the verge of making a big, fat scene in front of the whole school. The bell rang and I rose to put my tray away, hoping he wouldn't follow, so I didn't have to smack him.

"You're being ridiculous," he said. "I'm trying to give you a chance to make this right."

I ignored him and kept going.

"This isn't over, Autumn," he called after me.

Forcing himself on me had been disturbing. Cheating on me was vile. But acting like it was *my* fault, then stalking me? Psycho.

"I said I was sorry!" he shouted.

Hoping Daniel would give up on me if I ignored him, I continued at a brisk pace without looking back. At my next class, I slapped my backpack on the surface of my desk and rooted through it for my English book.

A shadow loomed over me. I could tell it was Zack by the warm scent of fresh rain that seemed to be his calling card. "It sounded like he was threatening you," he said.

I spared him a glance over my shoulder and resumed my search. "Just expecting me to blow off the whole incident." When the shadow didn't move, I straightened and turned to meet Zack's gaze. Our arms brushed and I realized how close he stood.

"You're not thinking of forgiving him, are you?" he asked.

"No way." Students brushed past Zack as they filed into the classroom and he shifted toward me to get out of their way. I inched back until my butt hit the edge of the desk. We were still almost touching.

"Good." Zack's face softened. "He's not ready for a relationship."

"He's not ready to mix with people at all." I grimaced.

Zack seemed pensive as his eyes roamed my face. Heat radiated through me as I held his gaze. It was as if Zack emitted an energy which reacted against my own, turning my brain to mush. What were we talking about?

Zack shifted his weight, bringing him closer. "I don't think Daniel's balanced. You should probably avoid him."

Uh-huh. Like I didn't already know that. And if Zack hated me so much, why would he take the time to talk philosophy regarding the guy who'd just cheated on me?

I made myself ignore the sexy dimple in his chin and glared at him. "Make up your mind, Zack."

He gave me a blank face. "About what?"

"About me. Either be all judgy without ever allowing me to defend myself—in which case you don't get to be my friend. Or be nice to me. You can't have both."

His eyes narrowed, then the bell rang and he slipped behind his desk.

I didn't want to give him or Daniel any more thought. They'd already wasted enough of my time.

Instead, I concentrated on what I'd do once I dropped my parents off at the airport, just hours away.

Freedom.

With them gone, I could scrap the Internet research and go straight to experimenting. I couldn't wait to see what else I was capable of.

† † †

When my mom drove me home at the end of the day, I didn't see the Taurus anywhere. "Where's my car?" I asked as she pulled into the driveway.

"We had it towed to the mechanic. You need something to drive since we won't be around to chauffer you." My mom closed the car door and hit the clicker.

"I thought I could use yours while you're gone," I said hopefully.

"Not likely." She laughed. "Yours will be ready later today. We'll pick it up, so you can do your homework and still have time to drive us to the airport later."

"Fine," I said half-heartedly.

True to their word, my parents retrieved my junk-heap just before dinner. They did their run early and when I came downstairs from wrapping up my homework, their luggage met me at the door.

"Oh, good. You're ready." My mom grinned as she bustled and threw things into her suitcase. "I wouldn't want to miss our flight."

She seemed a little too excited about it. "Really? Or are you joking?"

My dad chuckled. "As crazy as it sounds, we're

looking forward to it. Even crazier, we're not afraid to leave you."

"Oh." I blinked. Wow, what a one-eighty.

Mom shrugged. "You've shown some real maturity lately. You'll be eighteen in a few days and legally, well, you'll be an adult. It's time we got used to you not being our little girl anymore."

"Oh," I echoed, too stunned to say more.

"Let's go." My dad nudged me lightly with his elbow.

On the way to the airport, my mom reminded me to do my homework every day, warned me not to throw any parties at the house, then took a moment to stress that they were trusting me and not to let them down. She just had to go one step further by reminding me that the school principal still had her cell number.

They hadn't changed as much as I'd hoped.

While Dad parked at the airport and went in search of a cart, Mom trapped me in a bear hug. Slowly, she released me, then handed me her keys. "Drive home and put these away. Use the Taurus the entire time we're gone unless it's an emergency. Okay?"

Dad collected a cart and began stacking their luggage. "Not having gas money does *not* constitute an emergency."

"Got it," I said, following them into the building.

Once at the security stop, Dad hugged me fiercely, kissing the top of my head. "We'll miss you, sweetheart. Check your email often, huh?"

"I will."

"Just because we've grown as parents these past twenty-four hours doesn't mean we'll never worry again." Mom hugged me, this time even harder. "We love you more than anything. You know that, right?"

I nodded, my throat tightening.

"Time to go." My dad wrapped his hand around Mom's and walked away, glancing back at me periodically, until I couldn't see them anymore.

I drove their car home and directly into the garage. The house was quiet and dark. Lonely. I decided stuffing my face with sweets might take my mind off the emptiness of the house, so I headed to the fridge where my mom always kept goodies. Prepared meals in plastic containers lined the shelves. She'd been busy.

Starting off with a fizzy juice, I twisted off the cap, mindful how much pressure I put on the bottle. I took a sip, enjoying the bubbles forming on my tongue.

Why had I gotten rid of my parents?

Oh, man, I need to stay focused and push away second thoughts. A mere few days wouldn't be adequate to explore my potential. And since it wasn't even nine yet, I could get started on that straight away.

I sprinted out the back door, dying to learn what else I could do. Turning around and backing up, I studied the roof, wondering how high I could leap. If I missed and fell, any injuries would heal quickly. But what if I miscalculated and couldn't jump high at all? I'd end up destroying the gutters or taking out a section of the roof. How would I explain that to my parents?

Jasmine and rose bushes lined the fence around our home. In the middle of the yard stood a giant oak tree. With little light from a sliver of moon, the yard was nearly black. Nobody would see me if I did something impossible.

I scanned the area to make sure no one was around and sprung straight up as high as I could. I soared and, oh my God, my head was level with the top of the tree! Gravity took over and I groped for a limb, but missed. As I began to descend, I remembered how much it had hurt when the glass had sliced through my hand. Regardless of my ability to heal, I bled and felt pain just like everyone else.

Oh, crap.

I crashed into the ground and bit my bottom lip to muffle my scream. It was as if a bomb had exploded in my back. My eyes clouded over in a sea of agony. And then a moment later, I couldn't feel anything at all. Panic tore through me as lay there, my legs bent in an unnatural position.

CHAPTER NINE

WHAT HAD I been thinking?

Even as I prayed that I wouldn't live the rest of my life in a wheelchair, my spine snapped into place. Gradually, the feeling came back into my limbs and I slowly got back on my feet. Moments later, I couldn't wait to run.

How freaking cool.

My parents always lived in rural areas. So long as I'd had my own room, I never cared... until now. In the foothills of Los Angeles County, there were a variety of neighborhoods—from exclusive gated communities to ramshackle little houses. We lived on a quiet cul-de-sac with newer homes and manicured lawns. At the end of the street, a chain link fence formed a barrier between the houses and a field. A little farther, walnut trees beckoned, dwarfed next to giant pine trees stretching as far as the eye could see. Beyond that, a meadow.

I headed out.

Under the cover of dense forest, I inhaled the scent of earth and pine. With my improved vision, I could see the individual leaves at the top of the trees and the tiny yellow eyes of an animal staring at me from a lower branch.

I sprinted, weaving around the raised roots, wayward branches and occasional rock. My legs wanted to carry me faster, but I didn't feel confident yet with the uneven terrain, so I held back. Taking a moment to inhale the smell of the woods, I sensed... a deer?

Scanning the woods, I cautiously moved toward a clearing that was several times the size of our back yard. A deer stood at the far side where the woods began again. He would surely bolt as soon as he saw me, but could I outrun him? I focused on a point on the other side and ran as fast as my legs could go. In an instant, I was there and touching the deer's flank before he scampered off.

My mind reeled from the sheer speed. I wasn't even winded.

Directly in front of me lay a fallen tree. The trunk was probably wider than Zack's delicious shoulders and likely extremely heavy. Bending down, I clamped both hands around a branch and heaved. The tree rose above the ground, but banged into my shins and I dropped it. But I'd lifted it, which meant I could probably bench-press a bear.

I stifled hysterical laughter.

This was just crazy. People didn't suddenly get superpowers. Well, apparently I did, but why? What changed? As I replayed the last few days in my head, I scaled the tallest tree at the edge of the clearing, careful to avoid the sap. Every day for the last week, extreme stress had hit me in one way or another. Perhaps the heightened emotions brought on the physical changes.

No, that couldn't be it. Everyone had stress. Compared to other people's problems, mine were minor. I hadn't been exposed to DNA-altering chemicals and I hadn't been experimented on by some mad scientist. So what was happening to me?

At the very top of the tree, I distributed my weight between two branches, but the tree still swayed beneath me. I gazed at the lights of the city, cars driving in the streets, logs burning in a fireplace through a window of a house.

The world had never been this breathtaking.

Holding very still, I listened. Somewhere behind me a twig snapped and a cricket chirped. Beyond the trees a horn honked and about a half-mile away, a jogger pattered softly along the road.

After inhaling the forest air one more time, I descended. When I landed on solid ground, leaves crunching beneath my feet, I stiffened and sniffed the air. It wasn't a dog... but similar. Coyote?

A moment later, a large black wolf entered the clearing. I could smell him. *Male.* Somehow I knew that scent was definitely male.

He skirted the edges, but stayed close to the trees, his dark green eyes watching me. A coyote probably wouldn't have fazed me, not with what I could do. But this thing—he was enormous. If he caught me, would

I be able to fight him off? Either way, I didn't want to get hurt if I could avoid it.

My body tensed for flight mode, but the wolf stopped several yards away and sat on his haunches, his tongue lolling. Keeping me in his line of vision, the beast yawned and lowered until his belly touched the ground. He didn't *look* threatening. He was still a wild animal though and it would be foolish to let my guard down. Which took the thrill out of being in the woods. Time to go.

I backed away and wove through the thick trees until I hit the open field leading to the houses. While listening for signs of activity, I glanced back occasionally, but didn't see him following.

Wolves in California weren't much of a stretch. But so close to humans? And why was he so damn big?

† † †

Driving into the school parking lot Thursday morning, I tightened my grip on the steering wheel when I saw Daniel sitting in front of the school building where he used to wait for me on the low wall. He spotted my car and jumped off, his eyes following me. Crap. What did he want *now*? Anxious to get it over with, I looped my backpack strap around my hand and climbed out of my car.

He gave me a charming smile, the same one he used whenever he wanted something. "I thought we could talk," he said as I approached.

"I remember when *I* wanted to talk. Instead, we parked and you tried to molest me."

He pretended to clutch at his heart. "Ouch."

"I need to get to class. Say what you have to say." I tapped my foot.

Daniel sighed, his face pained. "I know I don't deserve your forgiveness. I screwed up bad, but... I love you, Autumn. I can't lose you."

He sounded like he meant it, but none of that mattered, because I didn't feel that way about him anymore. "Daniel, I can forgive you, but we're *not* getting back together."

The lines on his face hardened, his eyes darkening. "It's Zack, isn't it? You're with *him* now."

"No. It's *you*. I have zero interest in a relationship with you." Where the hell did Daniel get the idea it had to do with another guy? "I've barely spoken to Zack and I don't even like him."

"You two are always staring at each other."

"Only out of mutual loathing. Trust me." I gave him a quick laugh. "He hates me."

"Don't mess with me." His hand shot out to capture my wrist. "You're playing us against each other."

"You're twisted." He needed to cool off before I accidentally hurt him. "Let me go."

His other hand circled my waist and pulled me against him. "Okay, fine. You win. You cheated on me with him and now we're even."

I stared at Daniel in disbelief, my palms against his chest, ready to shove him into the next century. "I never cheated on you. Now let go." I sensed Zack before he spoke.

"Is there a problem?" Wisps of hair fell around Zack's face, making him look like something out of a magazine. Perfection. My stomach fluttered.

"Stay out of this." Daniel held me tighter.

"Let's ask Autumn what she wants." Zack shifted to me. "Are you enjoying this interaction with Daniel?"

I saw Maya among the forming crowd. Daniel was about to be humiliated beyond belief, but I was done protecting him. I met his eyes and made sure Zack heard me. "No, not at all."

Daniel scoffed. "Okay, you want to play games. Fine." He released me and sauntered off.

"Thank you," I said to Zack.

"Your taste in guys is lacking." He turned to leave.

Since I was wildly attracted to Zack, I'd say his comment was quite accurate.

"What was that about?" Maya asked as he stomped off.

I nodded toward the double doors and we moved in unison. "Daniel expects me to get back together with him."

"Ew." She grimaced, slowing her pace. "You don't want to, do you?"

"No way. But apparently, that doesn't matter to him." I rubbed my wrists where he'd grabbed me. My ex had gone from a jerk to downright creepy.

† † †

At lunch, I found Maya with Trevor and Zack. I tensed. It was either sit with Zack or leave myself open to Daniel. Not that I was afraid of him. Thanks to my new strength, I was afraid *for* him and I didn't want to end up in a position where I had to explain to the paramedics—and possibly the police—how Daniel got hurt. Better to avoid him altogether.

Gina sat with Natalie and some of the same girls she'd scorned all year. That was their problem though. Unlike Daniel, Gina seemed to understand what she'd done was a deal breaker. That or she never cared about me at all. Either way, she was out of my life.

I ate in silence while Maya appeared to be lost in another world chatting with Trevor. Zack stayed at the opposite end of the table, which was easier, because at that distance we weren't obligated to talk.

"I'm hitting the ladies room," I whispered to her when I'd finished eating. "I'll see you after school."

Maya smiled, then returned to Trevor. She used to give me more attention before they'd started talking. But she was so happy, how could I be jealous? I made my way down the nearly deserted corridor. Hearing footfalls, I spun around.

I sighed. "What do you want now?"

"I'm sorry, okay? It's just... you drive me crazy." Daniel stopped in front of me, but he didn't try to touch me. "Autumn, please. Give me a second chance. You owe me that much."

He seemed imbalanced and I didn't want to push him over the edge, but I couldn't let him think it would ever happen between us. "I owe you? What the hell for?"

"Autumn, I still love you." He stepped forward.

I backed up and my shoulders hit the lockers. He pressed his palms low and flat on either side of me, so it would be harder to duck under and get away.

Gazing into his eyes, I saw the pattern. His future. He was the guy who'd treat his girl like garbage, then beg for forgiveness and repeat the cycle all over again. But I wasn't that girl, the type who'd put up with it.

Even though he was kind of freaking me out, I kept my voice steady. "But I don't feel that way about you anymore."

He raised an arm to stroke a finger along my cheek. "Aw, don't be like that. I don't think I can live without you."

I gagged as the warmth of his breath hit me in the face. "You'll have to."

"C'mon, baby, one more chance." He aimed for my lips, but I turned my head to avoid him.

"Get the hell away from me." My hands curled into fists.

"You know you want me back. Why fight it?" Daniel dove for my neck.

I thrust a shoulder up to deflect his mouth. "I mean it. Get off me!"

Zack appeared out of nowhere. "Let her go, Daniel."

"This is none of your business, New Boy. Keep walking." Daniel's gaze stayed on me as if willing me to go along with it.

"I don't think so." Zack took a step forward.

Daniel released me and glared at him. By his stance, it was obvious he'd only let me go to free up his fists so he could pound on Zack. "You think you own her because she sat at your table during lunch? She's *mine*."

Zack moved fast enough to make my head spin, getting right up in Daniel's face. Before that moment, I hadn't realized how big he was, standing about two inches taller than Daniel. "I don't want to *own* her and neither should you. Don't ever let me catch you bullying *any* girl again."

"What are you going to do about it if I do?" Daniel's smirk remained firmly in place.

Zack grabbed him by his shirt, easily lifting him a foot off the ground, and shoved him into the lockers. Daniel's legs dangled as he struggled. Zack slowly eased his grip, allowing Daniel to slide down against the cold metal.

"I won't annihilate you today, no matter how much you provoke me," Zack said. "But only because it would upset my mom."

Daniel straightened his shirt and forced a laugh. I could smell his sweat and knew he was scared. "Mama's boy, huh?"

Scared, with suicidal tendencies, apparently.

"Don't push it, lowlife." Zack raised his brows at me expectantly.

I glanced around at the faces that had gathered. Why did my boy drama always draw a crowd? Cassidy Lieberman never gets a crowd and I happened to know she was dating Eddie and Peter at the same time.

If I left with Zack, everyone would think something

was going on between us. Bad idea. But if I didn't, it would be as good as choosing Daniel. In his mind anyway. So I followed Zack, weaving past kids rushing to their classes. The bathroom could wait.

"You think you can make it through one day without my help?" Zack glanced at me with a bored expression as I walked beside him.

This time, I didn't thank him. His attitude was wearing on me. "Who said I needed your help?"

He whirled around. "That guy is unstable. You got some kind of death wish?"

I straightened my spine. "I can handle him myself."

His gaze traveled over me, from my toes and back to my eyes. "Really? Because where I'm standing, I see a hot girl and a psycho nearly twice her weight. Hardly a fair fight."

Goosebumps prickled my neck. "You think I'm hot?"

He scoffed and shook his head. "That's what you got out of that?" Before I could reply, he'd turned on his heel and gone to class.

† † †

As I left my last class, Gina was waiting at my locker. Figuring I could get my stuff out of it later, I kept walking, but she shadowed me.

"Autumn."

I ignored her.

"I'd like to talk to you. Please."

I stopped abruptly and turned on her. "Between you and Daniel, I can barely breathe in this school."

She scowled. "Daniel's stalking you?"

"I'm amazed you haven't already heard." Word of Zack's rescue should've spread like wildfire.

Her chin trembled. Did she genuinely like Daniel? I hoped not. I wouldn't wish the creep on anyone. Not even Gina.

"Can we talk in private?" she asked.

Gina no longer had the power to hurt my feelings, so what harm could it do? "Sure."

Inside an empty classroom, she closed the door. "What I did was wrong. I shouldn't have let my feelings for Daniel affect our friendship."

I was about to tell her that forgiveness came easily, but trust was a different matter entirely. She didn't give me a chance.

"If you'd gone to the party like you promised," she continued, "Daniel and I would've never had the opportunity to hook up."

Any guilt I may have felt vanished. "And the excuse for making out the other times?"

"You know Daniel. His girlfriend wasn't around and, well, he can be pretty persuasive." She gave me a sheepish smile.

From what I witnessed in the bathroom stall, she could be persuasive too. "Whatever you say. But you and I will never be friends again." I turned to go.

Gina yanked me back by my arm. "I was trying to be nice, because I felt sorry for you. But you blew it." She glared. "And when I'm done with you, not even your geeky friend John will want anything to do with you."

Fury brewed in the pit of my stomach and I raised my voice, my palms itching. "You hooked up with *my* boyfriend and somehow *you* have the right to screw me over? How does that work?"

She gave me a hateful look, the one she reserved for people she loathed the most. "Don't think I didn't notice how you're always staring at Zack. You knew I liked him! You already had Daniel, but you had to have Zack too."

Wow, she and Daniel were made for each other. "You're delusional. Take them both. I don't care." I twisted out of her grasp and shoved her against the wall. "I just want my stuff back—my suede boots and anything else you've borrowed and never returned. Like the pink heels you wore the other day when you were making out with someone else's boyfriend. The leather jacket—" Her gaze fixed on a point behind me, but I ignored it. She was probably faking me out hoping I'd get distracted so she could get the advantage over me. "I want the pink skirt, the black Twilight T-shirt, the—" Her eyes wandered again, and this time the door opened.

I sensed it was Zack without needing to turn around. Crap. The way I had Gina cornered did not make me look good at all. Glancing over my shoulder, I saw Zack quirking a brow.

I shrugged. "She started it."

"Which required bullying?" he asked.

My fists clenched. To prevent myself from looking any worse, I backed up and made a sweeping gesture toward Gina. "She's all yours."

"Thanks, Zack." Gina rubbed her shoulder—which I hadn't even touched—while gazing up at Zack with wide, moist eyes. "I don't know what I would've done if you hadn't shown up. We're still on for Saturday, right?"

"Yeah. I'll see you later. I need a minute with Autumn." He glanced at me, one eyebrow up as though I'd misbehaved.

Gina moved behind Zack where he couldn't see, then smirked.

I wanted to slap her. To keep myself from going after Gina, I focused on Zack. "Why are you even here? You're *always* around."

He shook his head. "Extortion is beneath you, don't you think? Well, maybe not."

"How do you know I wasn't demanding *my* things?" My nostrils flared and I raged inside, my body vibrating. "Never mind. Just get out of my way." I was too incensed to stick around. I stormed past him and down the hall toward my car, praying it would start. I needed to get away before I detonated.

CHAPTER TEN

MUCH TO MY relief, my car fired up right away.

At home, I stomped through the house and tried to think of anything that would calm me down. Wait. Where was my backpack? It contained all my homework.

In my locker at school.

After Gina had distracted me, I'd forgotten about it. I wanted to weep in frustration.

Hearing my phone beep, I tried to remember where I'd left my purse during my fit of fury when I'd flown through the front door. Spotting it on the kitchen table, I rummaged through it. Two texts from my mom.

Sweetie, check your email STAT.

I scrolled to the next message.

Check ur email. Why arent u answering ur txts?

Apparently, I'd been too emotionally distraught to hear my phone go off. My fingers flitted over the keyboard in reply. My poor parents were probably worked into a frenzy imagining all the reasons, none of them good, why I hadn't answered.

I'm fine. Checking email now.

I sprinted up the stairs, raced to my laptop and rapidly scanned my inbox.

Hi Sweetie,

We love Arizona. In fact, we've decided to stay a few extra days past the completion of your father's job. We'd like to see the Grand Canyon and there's an art festival coming up. We plan to come home before going to Montana, but we'll be in touch with the return flight details.

We're very sorry to miss your birthday, but to make up for it, we've decided to buy you that car you keep nagging us for. Isn't that something?

Shocking, actually. But the last thing I'd do was question it and risk them doing a take-back. I eagerly read on.

However, we do have some stipulations.

Of course they would.

We'd like you to hang onto the money you've been saving for a car until we can get together and agree on its use. In other words, don't blow it on a shopping spree.

The second condition is that you not buy a brand new car due to how much it depreciates once you've driven it off the lot.

Mom, always practical.

We don't care what kind of car you buy

Score!

so long as it gets decent gas mileage, has enough power to get you out of a tight jam when necessary and has low miles.

I could handle that.

Our last condition is that the car must be thoroughly inspected by someone at the auto shop. We'd prefer Timothy, but we trust him to delegate it to someone competent.

Oh, almost forgot. We wired fifteen thousand dollars into your account. Use it to pay for the mechanic, the car and whatever else car-related that pops up.

Fifteen grand? Woo-freakin'-hoo.

We trust you to make good choices. Happy shopping. And happy birthday. We love you.

Love, Mom and Dad

Hallelujah! A new car! Who knew blackmail could be so rewarding?

I didn't need to be told twice. I speedily typed in a message full of thanks and telling them I was off to see Timothy. Scooping up my purse, I flew out the door. Memories of my rotten day faded and I could barely contain my excitement as I drove the three miles to the auto shop.

After arriving at the garage, I waited until Timothy finished with a customer, then approached the counter.

"Hi, Autumn. Problem with your car?"

"Not exactly." I explained the situation, the words spewing from my mouth.

"No problem," Timothy said. "When you find the car you want, give me a fifteen minute warning and drive it over."

"I have to bring it *here*?" I squeaked. "And if it doesn't pass your inspection, I have to return it and start all over with a different car?"

"That's the way it's done." Tim seemed like he felt sorry for me, but not enough to give in. "I have too much work to do here at the shop."

"It's just that I don't know the first thing about cars. I could bring you twenty before finding a keeper. I'd be happy to pay one of your employees to go with me." There would still be plenty in the budget for a great car.

"I'm sorry, Autumn." He shook his head. "I wish I could help you."

Oh, no. This couldn't be happening. My parents' behavior was totally out of character and I couldn't blow my chance before they snapped out of it. I mean, hello? Wiring fifteen grand when a week ago they could barely leave me alone for an hour? Who knew how long the aliens would control them?

My eyes teared. "But I know zilch about cars."

"You know what?" Timothy rubbed his chin. "I have a part-time kid I can spare for a couple days or so. Just for you."

That was when I felt it. His presence. Oh, God, please no. As if in slow motion, I turned to see Zack getting out of his Jeep. He'd changed into a navy blue shirt that matched Timothy's.

Could it be that the future of my car was now in Zack's hands?

He approached, eyes narrowed at me.

"Autumn, this is Zack. Zack, you're going to help this nice, young lady find a car her parents would approve of. You're in a hurry, right, Autumn?"

I nodded.

"We can do without you for a few days while you take care of her. Work out the schedule with Autumn." He switched to me again. "You guys are good customers, so I'll only charge you twenty bucks an hour."

Totally doable. "Great."

"Did you want to start today?" Timothy asked, glancing at the clock on the wall. "You've still got time before car dealers close."

Could I handle another dose of Zack so soon after the Gina incident? The answer was clear. If it meant getting my car even one day sooner, yes. "If he's up for it."

Zack groaned, but too low for Timothy to hear. "Isn't there anyone else who can do this?"

Timothy cocked his head, eyes turning into slits. "You're not qualified to advise her on a car?"

"I am, sir, but—"

"Excellent." Timothy jotted an address on a slip of paper and handed it to me. "I suggest Abraham's Auto Sales. They have good, affordable cars and they're close by. At Weatherly, go south and it's right on the corner." He swiveled to his left and looked past me. "May I help you?"

A woman to my right bellied up to the counter.

Reluctantly facing Zack, I said, "You ready to go?"

"Can we take mine as opposed to..." He eyed my car.

"If we take mine, maybe I can trade it in."

"Or sell it privately and get more for it," Zack countered.

"Okay. I just need to lock it up." I headed toward the Taurus.

"Yeah, because there's someone out there who's dying to steal that car."

I turned and glared.

He gave me a sheepish smile. "Sorry. Couldn't resist."

I gave him a look that said I wasn't amused, then forged on. Inside my car, I rolled up the windows, then got out and closed the driver's side. Something didn't sound right. The door hung off kilter, so I bumped it with my hip and it closed fully. I backed up and stared at the indentation my thigh had made. Great. Like my car wasn't unsightly enough.

Willing myself to relax, I jumped into the Jeep and strapped on the seatbelt. The vehicle began to move.

"Want the radio on?" he asked.

Would Zack bond with me over a favorite song? Not likely. But the music might keep my mind off the awkwardness of being stuck with him. "Sure," I said.

He fiddled with the radio until he found a station with The White Stripes and their beats pounded from the speakers.

The ratty soft-top wasn't airtight and the windows were down. Tendrils of hair escaped and whipped me in the face. I gathered most of it into a ponytail with one hand while my other hand stayed busy trying to capture the rebels.

"Would you like the window up?" Zack asked.

I spared him a quick glance. "Uhm, sure."

Without hesitation, he rolled it up. "Want the air on?"

"Why are you being so accommodating?" My eyes narrowed.

"We're not at school, Autumn. This is *work*. Timothy needs to hear I was courteous and professional." He sighed. "I need this job. I have to save enough money, so I'm okay when..." His words trailed off.

My stomach tightened as I remembered what Maya told me about his mom and how she was dying. The thought of him being left parentless made me wonder what were the right words to say.

"Anyway..." Zack shifted in his seat. "Was that a yes on the A/C?"

I quickly averted my gaze. "Yes, please."

He reached over to adjust the air and my eyes drifted to his well-defined forearms. Who knew arms could be so sexy? And he had confidence—the most powerful aphrodisiac known to womankind. He was decent too, always there when I needed him, even if he was a bit reluctant about it. When he was polite, I actually *liked* him. How would he act if he didn't dislike me? That would be interesting.

Oh, God, no! Contemplating being with Zack in any other way than as my mechanic or classmate would lead to disappointment, since he thought I was a snob and all. I couldn't allow myself to crush on him. But wasn't I already doing that? I'd switched from a twisted pervert who loved me too much to an ill-mannered oaf who didn't like me at all.

What was wrong with me? The super-powers had given me some sort of dementia or something. Panic swept through me and I panted, almost hyperventilating. In horror at my physical reaction, I ripped my gaze from him, stared out the window and tried to stay calm.

Zack was so right. I had lousy taste in guys.

I felt his eyes on me. "Are you okay? Do I need to pull over?" he asked.

"I'm fine." My heart pounded and a rush of heat spread through me. "A little nervous about car shopping."

He chuckled. "Driving a new car instead of that deathtrap is cause for anxiety?"

I fanned myself with my hand. "I need to find something that fits my parent's criteria or they might retract their offer."

"What's the criteria?"

"It needs to be reliable without lagging when it should be moving. It has to be good on gas with low miles. Most important, it needs a thumbs-up by Timothy for under fifteen grand."

"Shouldn't be too hard." He turned into a driveway of a super-sized used car lot. "Any idea what I should keep an eye out for? Sedan? SUV? Something sporty maybe?"

"Uhm." I blinked. "I don't know."

He looked at me like I'd just set fire to a wad of cash. "You drive an ancient car and you haven't thought about what you'd rather be driving?"

"I..." My tongue twisted up. "Yeah, I've thought about it, of course. But I wasn't expecting my parents to chip in, so I was working with a much smaller budget and researched accordingly."

Zack jumped out of the car and dove into an ocean of metal and wheels, with me trailing behind.

"Tell me what you *don't* like so we can rule those out."

"Station wagons and mini vans." I had to move faster than usual to keep up with him. "I don't care for sedans either."

Without breaking stride, his eyes swept the lot, then stilled. "Over there." He led the way to a light blue, convertible Volkswagen Beetle. White top, shiny rims. "You like it?" He went to the side window to read about the car, then got inside and poked around.

The sticker price was within my budget, with a little leftover, and I *liked* Beetles. But I wanted to hold out for a car I *loved*. Opening the other door, I stuck my head inside. "It's a little too girly for me."

His jaw ticked as he exited the bug. "Let's look around some more."

We strolled by car after car, but none of them spoke to me. When we'd almost made it to the other side of the lot, Zack said, "Anything here that catches your eye? Anything at all?"

I shook my head, scanning the inventory one last time. Everything I'd seen had been either too big, too boring or too expensive. "Not really."

"Even a vague idea of your preferences would be helpful."

I leaned against a compact SUV. "Do you have any suggestions?"

He forced a smile. "I did, but you shot it down."

As I rolled my eyes at him, my gaze landed on something small and sleek. As if hypnotized, I moved away from the SUV toward a black car. Finally...

Zack's hand wrapped around my arm. "We have to go."

I blinked. "What?"

"We have to go. Now." He tugged and I went along, surprised at how strong he was. Just before we got to the Jeep, a man appeared in front of us, blocking our way.

CHAPTER ELEVEN

I GUESSED THE man around ten years older than us. He wore black boots, faded jeans and a black cowboy hat over a long, brown ponytail. He gave me a friendly smile, but an eerie energy emanated from him, creeping me out.

Over the past few days, I'd gotten used to my crazy extra-sensory perceptions. Most of the time, I barely noticed the volume around me or weird smells unless something specific stuck out. The energy around this man definitely stuck.

"Playing hooky from work?" His too-smooth voice traveled over my skin like a slimy film.

"No." Zack's hand slid to my wrist, then he positioned me behind him, making me think he felt the threat too. With his free hand, he pointed to the emblem on his shirt with the auto shop name. "She's car hunting."

Warmth spread through me as I noticed the crisp cotton of Zack's shirt tickling my arm and the oddly soothing effect of his skin against mine.

She's a pretty little human. Girlfriend?

I jumped back, breaking contact with Zack. It

was as if the words were said out loud. Except they weren't. I was positive the man's lips hadn't moved. Was I hearing voices now?

"No," Zack said.

No what? Had there been a question?

They stared at each other for what seemed like minutes. Then the man tipped his hat and smiled. "Be seein' ya." He nodded at me, then strolled toward... a yellow Corvette that looked exactly like the car I'd seen tailing Zack the last few days. The man climbed inside and drove away a minute later. I had a feeling he wouldn't stray far from Zack though.

"What just happened?" I demanded.

Zack busied himself with the car next to him, nudging a tire with his shoe, then reading the fact sheet. "You were there, same as me."

"Uhm." I mulled over his reply, which hadn't told me a damn thing. "I've seen that car before. He's been following you. Are you in some kind of trouble?"

"No." He moved onto the next car, eyeing the fact sheet.

I sidled up beside him. "A creepy guy is keeping tabs on you and that's not a problem?"

Zack whirled on me. "Wasn't there another car you wanted to check out or are we done for the day?" He nodded in the direction I'd been heading before the man had arrived.

Resigned to Zack's reluctance to explain that guy, I forced my mind back to car shopping. "I thought we had to go."

"No, we're fine."

"Whatever. I saw something interesting that way." I hadn't forgotten about the shiny black vision. I marched off, stopping directly in front of the sleek, black car to absorb its beauty.

"This?" He looked incredulous, like I'd just asked him to marry me.

"What's wrong with it?" I reverently skimmed my fingertips along the sloped hood.

He laughed. "These things have no guts. And they're known for breaking down."

"But it's so pretty." I wondered if the interior was leather.

"It wouldn't meet your parents' criteria." He sighed. "See anything else you like?"

I shook my head dejectedly.

"C'mon. There's another dealership a couple miles away."

I reluctantly turned away from what was now my fantasy car, climbed into the Jeep and strapped myself in. "Zack?"

He checked over his shoulder, then steered onto the street, blending with the flow of traffic. "Yeah?"

"Maya said you and Trevor were the same age, but you seem so much older than him. And not many high-schoolers could lift a big guy like Daniel off the floor so easily."

He gave a small shrug. "Genetics, I guess."

Seemed like a logical explanation, but I sensed something more. My eyes drifted from his wide shoulders to his cut forearms. "So you're honestly only a few months apart?"

"Yeah." A slow smile spread over his face. "Were-wolves mature faster than humans." He winked at me, a lone dimple appearing in his left cheek.

His comment gave me an eerie chill, but I gave a fake laugh. "It's all so clear now. I was thinking maybe you were a vampire, but that couldn't be it, not with how much you're in the daylight. Werewolf makes *much* more sense," I said, rolling my eyes.

"Of course, it does." Zack took his eyes off the road long enough to grin at me.

He acted like he was kidding, but everything he'd just said freaked me out. Especially since my new abilities defied the norm. Still, the idea of werewolves was absurd. A few extra muscles, sure. But changing from human to a completely different life form?

I stared at him, my irritation escalating. Soon, my thoughts returned to the man in the cowboy hat. "That man at the dealership. It was like you two had an entire conversation that didn't really take place."

"So?" His eyes remained focused straight ahead.

"What am I missing, Zack?"

The muscle in his jaw ticked. "Autumn, let it go."

The episode was too weird to forget. "If you're in trouble, maybe I could help."

"Even if I was, I wouldn't tell *you*," he said.

"Fine," I replied, shifting in my seat to stare out the window, annoyed that he still wouldn't give me a chance. If we didn't find a car today, then tomorrow, I'd find someone else to help me. Someone who hadn't already convicted me.

At the next dealership, Zack killed the engine and drew in a long breath, his hands tightening on the steering wheel.

I reached for the door handle.

"Wait a sec." He studied me a brief moment. "I'm sorry for snapping. You didn't deserve that. I'll be better."

That was an improvement and I didn't want to waste time finding anyone else to help me. "Okay."

Leaping out of the Jeep, I scanned the inventory, spotting a car identical to the one I'd just been drooling over. Except this one was red. I nodded toward it. "I don't suppose there's a chance that car would be the exception."

He followed the path of my eyes and shook his head. "If Timothy found out I let you buy one of those, I'd never work in this town again."

I sighed and walked between the rows of cars, stopping at a shiny, dent-free blue car with a sunroof. The price on the window was marked well within my limits.

"This one gets decent gas mileage." He began reading the statistics. "No warrantee, probably because it's got over a hundred thousand miles on it."

"That much?" I shook my head and moved on.

Zack shadowed me, then paused in front of a blue mustang. "What do you think of this?"

I tilted my head. "I like these, but they're such boy cars."

Zack glanced up at the setting sun. "How about we call it a day, then you go home and search the Internet? Get an idea of what you like. Check some sites that have classified ads of used cars. Find one and we'll check it out tomorrow."

"Brilliant plan." I brightened and smiled.

"That's what you're paying me the big bucks for. Let's go."

I happily drove off with Zack, thinking about our shopping tomorrow. Wait. That was when we had the get-together with Trevor and Maya. After school, would I have time to car shop and still shower? "We're all going out tomorrow night."

He looked pensive a moment. "Trevor made dinner reservations for seven, so we're not picking you up until six thirty. If you can get ready in an hour, we can still car shop if I drop you off at five thirty."

That didn't leave much time, but even an hour would be worth it. "I could meet you at your house after school."

"It's a deal." Zack pulled into the lot of the deserted auto shop where I'd left my car. "Except I'll pick you up at your house."

"Sounds great. I'll see you at school tomorrow." I smiled, getting out of the Jeep.

Zack waited until I started my car before driving away. His bad attitude aside, he had great manners. Gentlemanly. Protective. But I couldn't let his good side get to me. Not only because of his negative feelings for me, but also because I hadn't forgotten he was seeing Gina on Saturday.

As soon as I arrived home, out of habit I automatically searched for my backpack to do my homework, then remembered I'd left it in my locker earlier when Gina derailed me. Damn. I'd have to arrive to school extra early tomorrow and get everything done before my first class.

I was dying to get out and feel the wind against my face. To run. The woods called to me, but it was still light outside and I didn't want my neighbors to see me leaving. They might tell my parents, who didn't need to know I was stealing away all by myself into the forest. They'd only worry. Even in the dark, I'd make sure to run fast enough that no one could identify the blur.

Common sense told me to stay home, away from mysterious wolves and anything else that lurked in the night, but the urge to stretch my legs triumphed. So, shortly after dinner, I changed into sweats and slipped out the back.

With more strength came better control of my body. I made only the faintest of sounds with each movement, which could be mistaken for a raccoon or some other small animal. I leaped over fences, sprinted through back yards and across the field, slowing when the trees appeared in front of me. The run had invigorated me, like my body hungered for it.

I scrambled up a tree trunk for a better view of the woods, then stopped, sensing a presence. Wolf? Peering down from a branch up high, I spotted a huge black wolf below and wondered if it was the same one as the night before. How many black wolves of that size could there be?

The wolf raised his snout and tested the air, which seemed fitting since my trail ended at the tree. I remained motionless above to not alert him of my presence. He seemed fairly tame last time, but for all I knew, he hadn't gone after me because he'd just fed.

What if he was hungry now?

After what felt like an eternity, he trotted off. Thankfully, not in the direction of my house. I seized the moment and dropped from my spot in the trees. Tomorrow, I needed to find a place to hang out that wasn't inhabited by an oversized wolf. In the meantime, some wolf research was in order.

At home a few minutes later, I lounged on the sofa, my laptop resting on my thighs while the television blared to keep me company. The Internet offered endless information on wolves, so I easily found what I needed.

Sizes varied widely, depending on the type of wolf, with an average of forty to one hundred and twenty pounds. However, there were occasions, although rare, that wolves had been discovered in Canada, Alaska and Russia weighing up to two hundred pounds. Comparing my size to the wolf's, I guessed he probably weighed at least that.

But it's not like we were far enough north to warrant a two-hundred pounder. So, what was a big wolf his size doing so close to a Los Angeles suburb?

† † †

Friday morning, I arrived at school earlier than any sane student. Luckily, the diligent staff of Verdugo Hills Academy got started well before their pupils, opening the doors and giving me access to my locker. Retrieving the neglected backpack, I took it back to my car and powered through my homework.

I'd wrapped up the last of it when someone tapped

on my window and I flinched. Zack pointed at the building, then disappeared. I checked the clock on the dash. Damn. If I didn't hurry, I'd be late for my first class. Zack to the rescue again.

During lunch, before Trevor had a chance to monopolize Maya, I cornered her to plan the logistics of the upcoming evening out. Zack and Trevor had already arranged to pick up Maya, then me. I suggested that we all meet at a designated spot, but she insisted that Trevor was adamant about seeing us home safely. Great, so I'd be trapped with Zack and unable to leave anytime I wanted.

Zack had put the constant scowl on hiatus, but he wasn't exactly friendly either. Knowing I'd have more than enough of him later, I hung out with John during lunch.

Gina and Daniel didn't sit together. I wondered why. But if she and Zack had a date on Saturday, why would she want Daniel? I hoped Zack had a platonic explanation for their Saturday meeting and that he had better taste than to get involved with Gina.

But I was used to disappointment when it came to Zack.

At the end of the school day, Gina met me at my car. She shoved a bag at me and smirked. "Out with the old and in with the new." She strutted away.

I peeked in the bag containing my clothes she'd borrowed, then hurried home. If I made every minute count, there would be enough time to car shop and get super cute before the weird double date. I'd feel better about the whole thing if I looked fabulous.

Having a chance to relax would be a good idea too, since being harried and uptight could counteract any results of the hard work beautifying myself.

When I got home, I had a powerful urge to get out and feel the wind, see the stars. It was a shame the sun still shined and Zack would arrive any second. I'd have to wait until the evening was over before giving in to that need.

Hearing a knock, I darted to the front door. "Hey," I said as I shut it behind me and locked up.

"Did you search for cars on the Internet last night?" He asked as we headed to the curb. He rounded the hood of the Jeep and got in.

Crap. "No." I strapped myself in. "I meant to, but got involved in something else. Sorry."

He lifted one shoulder and dropped it, steering away from the curb. "No worries. I know another dealership with a huge used inventory. You can search there as easily. Not as efficient, but we can still make progress today."

Why wasn't he annoyed that I hadn't done my car homework? Was he finally softening toward me? Or just enjoying the fact that the more time he spent with me, the more it would cost me?

We arrived at the dealership a few minutes later and I blindly followed Zack through the giant car lot, since I had no idea where to start. Nothing caught my eye until I saw the black Porsche buffed to a high gloss.

Zack chuckled. "Way out of your budget."

"I can dream, can't I?" I peered through the window at the interior.

Feeling an energy, I turned. A man in black stood by a silver SUV, his eyes trained on us. Zack stepped sideways to partially shield me from the man's view.

"I'm under Charles' supervision," Zack said.

The stranger furrowed his brows. "Charles?"

"Yes," Zack replied.

A moment later, the man smiled at me. Though he seemed less imposing than the cowboy, his too-smooth demeanor gave me the willies. It was as if an underlying ruthlessness itched to break free.

Like the episode with the cowboy, Zack and the man in black eyed each other intently for several seconds, then the man gave a curt nod and left.

Zack put a hand up. "Don't ask."

"Not like I get any answers when I do. I just hope you're not mixed up with drug dealers or have huge gambling debts." Zack and I would never be friends, but that didn't mean I wanted him to end up in cement shoes.

"Right. Because between work and school and my family, I have *so* much free time to get high and play poker. Let's get you home."

Zack dropped me off at my house and I raced into the shower. After debating several minutes on what to wear, I remembered that Trevor had made reservations, which meant a nicer restaurant. So I curled the ends of my hair and slipped into a plum-colored halter dress that pushed up and squeezed, giving me much more cleavage than anyone had a right to. It hugged my waist and gently draped over my hips, flaring just enough to create soft folds that clung to my thighs.

After a touch of powder, a quick brush of mascara and a light coat of lip-gloss, I stepped into a pair of slip-on heels with tiny crystals covering the arch and backed up for an overall view. Not bad.

Zack would probably be wearing something nice, too. He might even smell good. Even the thought of him made my cells vibrate like flashing lightning. What the hell was wrong with me? So he had hot muscles, smooth skin and good God he smelled like freshly cut grass and wet earth after a storm. I had to remember not to breathe him in or I'd forget I was supposed to hate him. Zack was a guy who didn't like me. I needed to return the favor.

I checked my cell for the time, then peeked through the curtain to see his Jeep pull up to the curb. I ran my fingers through the soft waves of my hair to fluff it and flipped my head back. I was making a couple of adjustments with a few wayward tendrils when the doorbell rang.

I flung the door open, a wide grin waiting for Maya.

Zack took a step back like I'd blinded him. "We're... Y-You..."

Did he just stutter?

CHAPTER TWELVE

"UH..." ZACK BLINKED, then his lips moved again, but no sound came. He looked phenomenal in black pants and a dark gray sweater pushed up to expose his forearms. His hair was disheveled as though he didn't care what anyone thought. Why was his lack of concern for his looks so sexy? "We should get going," he finally managed to say.

I gathered my cool and pulled it close, forcing a smile. "Hi, Zack."

He flinched, abruptly spinning and heading to his car. I followed him out and met him at the passenger side of his Jeep where he opened the door for me.

"Thank you." Peeking inside the Jeep, I saw Trevor and Maya in the back.

"Hey, Autumn," Trevor said.

Maya grinned, looking like she was going to burst.

"Shouldn't one of them be in the front seat instead of me?" I asked Zack who was still standing beside me. It felt way too much like a double date with us separated into couples. Maya and Trevor made no move to rescue me.

"They wanted to sit together." Zack made a motion for me to climb in.

I reluctantly settled in the passenger side.

"You look hot," Maya said as Zack got behind the wheel.

"Thanks." Finally a compliment after all my hard work. I beamed.

"Yeah, you look really nice, Autumn," Trevor chimed in.

Zack made a noncommittal sound, engrossed in the stereo knob and finding a station. I really needed to lower my expectations where he was concerned. I turned in my seat, chatting with Maya and Trevor, until we stopped a few minutes later. Facing the front again, I saw a restaurant. Italian. My favorite.

We waited while they cleared a table for us. Maya and the boys didn't have a problem hanging out in the waiting area, claiming a section of the bench right away. But I felt awkward with nothing to do.

"Ladies room, Maya?" I asked, still standing.

"Sure." She jumped up, glancing back at her date. "We'll be right back."

We snaked between tables and dodged waiters as we made our way through the crowded restaurant. In the restroom, we went straight to the mirrors.

"Did you see the way Zack looked at you?" Maya giggled. "I think he likes you."

I stared at her with my mouth open. "Are you kidding? He hates me."

She tilted her head. "Really? I thought I felt a spark between you two."

I laughed. "It's called *loathing*. You don't notice, because you're too busy making goo-goo eyes at Trevor."

"Isn't he amazing?" She dug out her lipstick and opened it. "Zack's pretty nice too. You'd see that if you gave him a chance."

It was too complicated to explain, so I gambled that she might not notice a subject change. "You look great, by the way. Can't go wrong with a little black dress."

Maya glided the color over her mouth. "I just bought it. I got a few other things for our next get-together too. You think our table is ready yet?" She smacked her lips together and dropped the tube in her purse.

My eyes flared at the idea of another uncomfortable double date-ish night. "Let's find out."

The restaurant had become even busier during our short stint in the bathroom. Zack and Trevor were seated at a half-circle booth in the far corner. As Maya and I carefully weaved past tables and bodies, I wondered what the boys were talking about. If I tuned out the music coming from the speakers, the clanging of silverware and the din of other voices, could I focus on only *their* voices? I zeroed in on them and concentrated.

"What about you and Autumn?" Trevor asked.

Zack gave a short laugh. "She's not my type."

Trevor nodded thoughtfully. "Smokin' hot isn't your type?"

"Oh, she's hot alright." Zack laughed. "More than that—she's freaking beautiful. But, dude, she's way too high maintenance. She's..." He shuddered. "Scary."

"Autumn? She's sweet. Maybe she's only scary with *you*. Maybe she likes you, but she's trying to hide it, because you behave like such a dog around her."

Zack's brows raised. "You think she likes me?"

I wanted to run screaming, but I squelched the urge when they noticed our approach. They scooted out of the booth, standing on either side of the table, so we could slide to the middle and be trapped. Lovely.

Maya slipped in on Trevor's side, which left me next to Zack. I settled in and mulled over this new information. They thought because I wasn't nice to Zack, I *liked* him? How horrifying. I'd have to rectify that as soon as humanly possible. But how? I could pretend not to care, act like nothing bothered me and be nice, no matter what. But not *sweet* nice. *Casual* nice. And a little emotionally remote. That would do it.

"We have friends from A to Z," Trevor told Maya with a grin. "Get it? From A." He pointed at me. "To Z." He wagged his index finger at Zack.

"The alphabet has things in the middle. With her and me, it's just A and Z. Nothing between us." Zack picked up a menu and eyed it.

Ouch. "Careful, Zack," I said coolly. "If you're mean, people will think you like me." I grabbed a menu and checked out the entrées. "What's good here?"

Zack squinted. Probably trying to decide if I'd somehow eavesdropped on their earlier conversation. He could stew in it for all I cared.

"They have some good vegetarian stuff," Trevor answered. "Cheese ravioli, tortellini and veggie pizza."

"You're a vegetarian?" By Zack's expression, you'd think I'd just announced I was converting to communism.

"Yes. What's wrong with that?" Oops, my voice was too sharp for the *casual nice* I'd been going for.

Zack's eyes shifted and he moved away ever so slightly.

I glowered at him. "It's not illegal, you know."

"I think I'll have a double cheeseburger with bacon," Zack said.

Hamburger at an Italian restaurant? He was trying to bait me. Now was the time to apply my philosophy. I removed all traces of irritation from my face and smiled. "That's great. Hamburgers are high in protein."

"Autumn, what's the deal with Daniel and Gina?" Maya asked. "I thought I'd see them all kissy-kissy after Monday, but I haven't."

"Why would you think they'd hook up?" Zack asked.

Exactly what I wanted—for the uber-hot new guy to know I'd been dumped in the worst possible way by both my friend and my *boyfriend*. My humiliation with Zack was almost complete. My front teeth scraped my bottom lip, removing the last of my lip gloss.

"Because Daniel cheated on Autumn with Gina. I thought everyone knew that." Maya paused, glancing at the boys, then back to me. "Did she return your stuff?"

I nodded, sensing Zack's gaze on me. By the tingling at the back of my neck, I had a hunch he was annoyed. But if he'd given me the benefit of the doubt at the time, he wouldn't feel like such an ass now.

"Ooh. Could I borrow that leather jacket?" she asked. "It'll go great with some shoes I just bought."

"Sure." I kept my eyes trained on the menu and ignored Zack. Maybe he'd been upset to hear about Daniel and Gina because he did like her and their Saturday gig really was a date. Ick.

A busboy came by and set a tray of hot bread on the table. "Your server will be right with you."

"Thank you." Trevor smiled at the server.

"That was *Gina* with Daniel?" Zack snagged a piece of bread and slathered butter on it. "And when I accused you of extortion, you were really asking for your *own* things back?" he asked.

I lifted my chin and made an effort not to get irritated. "Yeah, right after she tried to pull my arm out of its socket. You have a knack for misreading my situations."

His fist tightened on the butter knife. "You should've told me."

"I did, but you were too busy being a jackass." I dropped my bread and stared at him.

He stared back, one corner of his mouth lifting. "I thought you were totally into jackasses. Daniel's proof of that."

Damn, but he was sexy when he smiled like that. I wasn't falling for it though. "Well, at least you admit what you are."

"Okay, you guys." Maya giggled nervously. "Let's play nice, huh?"

132

A pretty brunette appeared at our table. "Are we ready to order?"

No one spoke up and my stomach was so empty, I thought it might make good on its threat and implode. "I'll have the cheese ravioli in the pink sauce," I said.

After everyone else ordered, Maya and Trevor talked animatedly about movies, which left Zack and me on our own. Now that we'd gotten everything out in the open, maybe we could get past it.

"What got you interested in cars?" I asked.

"Necessity."

His terse reply wasn't helpful in keeping the conversation going. "So it's just a job?"

"I like seeing how things work and figuring out why they don't." All annoyance had vanished from his voice. I wondered how long that would last. "What was so interesting yesterday that you didn't have time to research cars?"

"I saw a giant wolf last night when I went out for a walk. Actually, it was the second night in a row." I twirled the handle of my fork between my thumb and middle finger. "So I researched wolves instead of cars. But I'll do the car stuff in the morning and still be ready when you pick me up."

"Hmm. What did you find out about the wolves?" he asked, angling toward me and narrowing his eyes.

A tingle crept up my spine. "Most wolves are usually under a hundred pounds, give or take, but they've been known to get twice that size."

He nodded. "You shouldn't be out in the woods alone."

My fingers stilled. How did he know I'd been alone?

CHAPTER THIRTEEN

"I NEVER SAID I was alone..." My voice trailed off as alarms pealed in my head. "And what makes you think I went into the woods?"

Zack sighed as if I were trying his patience. "You said *you* went for a walk and the forest is practically in your back yard. Where else would you see a wolf?"

I glared at him. "Can't you be nice for one evening?"

He took a bite of the bread, then returned it to the small plate. Inhaling slowly, he lifted his chin and sniffed the air. He repeated the act two more times.

I struggled to keep my voice level. "You're smelling me again, Zack."

"Yeah." He must have been totally oblivious to how much he was pissing me off, because he sniffed me again. "You smell unusual."

"Gee, thanks." The disgust had to have been evident in my tone. Just when we were getting along. Sort of. "Thanks for letting me know," I said with a sarcastic edge.

"No, not in a bad way. You're a mixture of..." He inhaled again, long and deeply. "Lavender and vanilla and a little bit earthy."

"Earthy?" I'd been called many things, but never that. "Whatever. Just stop sniffing me, okay? It's weird."

"Autumn," Maya interrupted. I'd forgotten she was next to me. "There's a carnival next weekend. We should go."

That would be a nice break from all the drama in my life. And refreshing not to have Zack there. "I'd love to."

"You're coming too, right Zack?" Maya asked.

My mouth dropped open.

"Uh..." He stared at me with wide eyes, but I couldn't think of any way to rescue myself, much less come up with an excuse for him. He turned to Maya again. "Sure, if I'm not working that day."

Trevor shook his head. "You don't work on Sundays."

"I might be car shopping," Zack explained, his eyes darting to me.

Trevor waved him off. "Not at night."

I tuned them out. It was bad enough we spent our afternoons together without donating my play time to him.

"Maya told me about your mom," I said once Maya and Trevor were absorbed in each other again. "How's she doing?"

"Hanging in there." He stared into the plate in front of him. "I'm not seeing much of her these days."

And I was sucking up his extra time by car hunting. "We don't have to shop over the weekend if you don't want to."

"No, it's fine. If I stay home too much and hover over her, she doesn't like it. She wants me out living life, meeting girls." He shook his head. "But if we could meet at Trevor's place tomorrow, that'd help."

"I'm so sorry about what you guys are going through," I whispered. "What rotten luck."

"She's had *great* luck, actually. She wasn't supposed to live past eighteen." He toyed with the little bread plate. "But she went into remission and had me, kept me safe after my dad died and made it to my eighteenth birthday. I'm lucky to have had so much extra time with her."

I dropped my gaze as my eyes misted. I cleared my throat, willing myself not to get choked up. "So I'll meet you at Trevor's. What time is good for you?"

"About one o'clock?"

"I'll be there." The food arrived and I attacked it, shoveling it in while still maintaining a ladylike veneer.

Lord, Zack's dinner smelled unbelievable. I tried to ignore the aroma, but that only made it harder to enjoy my own food. Half way through my pasta, I set my fork down and watched him with his big, juicy burger. Sauce dripped out and onto his plate as he bit into it. The delicious aroma made me crave his food instead of my own.

My mom had lectured me for years on the food industry—how animals were treated and the hormones they were given. And it had worked. Until now. What was up with this sudden need for meat?

"What?" Zack finished chewing and swallowed. "Is it bothering you to see me eat an animal?"

"Not at all." I stared at the burger, saliva pooling in my mouth.

"Do you want a bite?" he asked.

I froze, my eyes wide. What would my parents say if I turned carnivore? "I've never eaten meat before."

He thrust it at me. I took the juicy burger, licked my lips and sunk my teeth into it. As I chewed, the flavor melted on my tongue and my taste buds rejoiced. I started to hand the burger back to Zack, but before he had a chance to take it, I swallowed and brought the burger back to my lips. Opening wide, I shoved it in.

Zack chuckled. "Should we order another one?"

Heat rushed into my cheeks and I pushed the food toward him. "Sorry."

His eyes danced with amusement, the dimple in his left cheek appearing. "You can eat that and I'll order my own. It's totally fine. I think you need it more than I do."

"No!" I finished chewing the stolen bite and swallowed, so I could talk. "I don't know what came over me."

"The movie starts in forty-five minutes," Trevor reminded us.

When the check arrived, Trevor insisted on picking up the entire tab. It didn't feel right, since it wasn't a real date. But since he'd snatched it up and left the table to pay, I had no other choice.

Maya beamed when he returned to the table. "That's so sweet of you."

Zack and I led the way to the Jeep with Maya and Trevor lagging behind. Arriving at the car, I turned as they strolled toward us. Trevor looked at her adoringly, stopping to capture some stray hairs that had fallen over her eyes. She paused too, smiling up at him shyly. Gently, he brushed them off her face.

I wanted someone to look at me like that. The same way my parents looked at each other. I knew I was still young and didn't *need* to settle down yet. But my age didn't stop me from dreaming. I didn't want to kiss a bunch of frogs first or compromise ever again.

† † †

In the dark theatre, Trevor and Maya sat in the middle with Zack and me on the ends, all loaded with popcorn and soda. The movie was an unimpressive action flick, but it provided cover where I didn't have to do anything but take up space next to Maya. When the movie finished, we called it a night, but I would've loved to stop for a burger.

When Zack dropped me off and said goodnight, he was strangely pleasant as he walked me to my door. He didn't scowl at me or anything. "No walking in the woods alone tonight. You're safer at home," he warned.

I rolled my eyes. "I'll be fine."

"All alone with wolves? Really?"

His show of concern made me want to agree. "I'll consider that before I do anything rash. I promise."

"Good." He waved, then jumped into his Jeep and drove away. Maya and Trevor waved goodbye from the back window.

At home, I zoomed up the stairs, already stripping off the dress. Once in my room, I tossed it on my bed and kicked off my heels. I couldn't wait to be in the woods and wasn't planning on taking time to find a different forest without strange wolves. Throwing on sweats, a T-shirt and some sneakers, I tore out of the house.

The wind on my face soothed me and I lifted my chin to see the glowing twinkles in the darkness above. With my heightened senses, I drew in the night scents of pine and earth. My ears picked up the chirps of crickets and a small animal rustling in the nearby brush.

I'd never felt better in my life.

What undiscovered powers did I have? With my body's ability to heal rapidly, could I be killed? Would I require a stake through the heart like a vampire or a silver bullet like a werewolf? Werewolves, vampires and leprechauns... I chuckled softly to myself at the absurdity of my thoughts as I raced past my neighbors.

Like lightning, I charged through the forest, with furry little animals scampering in my wake. As my lungs effortlessly took in air, a familiar scent wafted toward me and I slid to a halt, bits of dirt spraying the nearby shrubs.

Wolf.

He came into view beyond a clump of trees, dark and magnificent. A few yards away, he hesitated, almost as though he didn't want to scare me. I can't explain why I suddenly felt comfortable with this wild beast, but I did.

"I'm not in danger with you, right?"

He sat on his haunches and swung his head side-to-side as if answering no. I was *not* going to make anything out of *that*. He couldn't possibly have understood me, nor could he know sign language.

I took his cue and sat on a nearby boulder. "So what's your story?"

He rose, then slowly edged a few feet toward me. About a yard away, he sat again, his eyes alert. This was the closest I'd ever gotten to him, close enough to see into his deep green eyes and admire how the moon glinted off his dark fur. Beautiful.

I'd already been out for a while and the need for speed had subsided. "I should get going. See you here tomorrow?"

He barked once, then stood on all fours when I rose from the boulder.

"Such a gentleman. You know who you remind me of?" I giggled. Yeah, as if the wolf cared. But I had a captive audience and Maya wasn't around to talk to. "This new guy at school. Total douche. You're not a jerk like him, but you're both *so* pretty." A vision of Zack when he'd met me at my door earlier flashed through my mind. "You should've seen his face when he saw me tonight. He actually stuttered."

The wolf whined and dropped his head to the ground, burying it under his paw. At that moment, my feelings for the wolf and Zack were similar too—I wanted to pet them both.

I laughed. "Goodnight, sweet wolf."

† † †

By the time I'd made it into bed, I'd been exhausted. But, wired from my brush with the most glorious thing ever to meet my taste buds and my strange wolf friend, sleep didn't find me until around two a.m. Five hours later, I popped up, wide awake and well-rested.

Which was odd since I'd always been an eight-hour girl. Maybe because I healed so fast, my body recharged quickly now too.

Several hours remained before I had to be at Zack's house. First order of business: fulfill Zack's homework request. I did enough online car shopping to make plans to see an FJ Cruiser. I doubted that a decent one would be in my budget, but maybe by some miracle while I was there, I'd find something else that would work for me.

Done with the Internet for the time being, I shut down my laptop, then stood and sniffed the air. Rancid smoke and nicotine. Ugh. Maybe if I cleaned, I could enjoy the house stink-free for the duration of my parent's absence.

After opening all the windows, I made the kitchen and bathrooms sparkle, swept the hardwood floors and polished the furniture. My olfactory system still picked up the smoke that had seeped into the paint and wood, but the air quality had improved dramatically.

After a shower to rid my body of the chemical and disinfectant smell, which was almost as bad as the smoke, it occurred to me that I didn't have Zack's address or phone number. So many opportunities and I'd never asked him for either. I'd have to call Maya for that, but didn't look forward to listening to her gush over Trevor. It only made me realize how much my own love life was lacking. I wrapped a towel around myself and dialed Maya.

"Hello?" a sleepy voice croaked.

"Maya, it's me. Did I wake you?" Of course I did. "I need Zack's address or phone number."

She yawned. "I was so excited after Trevor kissed me goodnight, I couldn't fall asleep."

I grinned. My annoying semi-date with Zack was definitely worth seeing her dreams of being with Trevor finally come true. "I'm so happy for you."

"Yeah, me too. I don't know their address, but they live two blocks down on the same side of the street. Right before it curves."

"On what street?" I asked.

"Your street, silly. But towards Foothill Boulevard, not the forest. It's the yellow house with the white picket fence. You can't miss it. Can I go back to sleep now?"

"Sure. We'll talk later. Sleep well." Who knew Zack lived so close?

Wearing snug, faded jeans and a white tank top, I slipped into some flip flops and headed out. I didn't bother starting the Taurus, opting to walk there instead.

His house had yellow clapboard siding with white-trimmed windows. A bicycle, Frisbee and other play items littered the yard, spilling into the driveway. Potted plants hung from either side of several steps that led up to a wide front porch. Homey.

I knocked and a pretty, dark-haired woman answered. I could hear boys shouting in the background as the door opened wider. She smiled and waved me inside. "You must be Autumn. I'm Cara, Zack's aunt." Beyond her, a boy darted by.

I stuck out my hand. "Oh, you're Trevor's mom.

Nice to meet you."

She shook my hand, then closed the door behind me. "You too. Zack's around here somewhere."

Cords and gadgets littered the coffee table and the overstuffed couch, stretching across the muted blue-green rug to connect to a wide flat-screen TV. Zack came into view, following a boy who looked about ten-years-old. "I demand a rematch, Brian," he said.

A gleam came into the boy's eye. "If you want to lose again, how can I refuse?"

"Cool," Zack said solemnly. "Hey, maybe you could show me one more time how to do it."

"Yeah, whatever." Brian smirked and sauntered off down the hallway.

"You shouldn't let him beat you *all* the time, Zack," she whispered. "I want him to learn he has to work things out for himself."

Zack shrugged. "But it makes him so happy."

I stared at him, little butterflies invading my belly, warmth and fuzziness washing over me. Why did he have to do such a sweet thing for his cousin? It made me wish he didn't save his surly self for me.

"Hey, Autumn." He shifted his weight to his other leg as his gaze made a circuit around the room. "My mom wants to meet you."

Warm and fuzzy turned to cold and prickly. What if his mom didn't like me? "Why?"

"I don't know. She just does." After a moment, he turned and I followed him down the hallway, since anything else would've been rude.

He tapped twice on a door, then opened it and motioned me to go ahead. The room was light and sunny, the curtains riding the wave of a light breeze. Sunflowers greeted me from a vase on the nearby nightstand.

The woman in the bed flicked a remote and silence filled the room. Pallid complexion aside, she had the kind of timeless beauty that required no makeup. Long, dark brown hair, olive skin a shade darker than her son's and catlike eyes that crinkled in the corners from her welcoming smile.

"Ah, *tesora*, come closer." She patted a vacant spot next to her on the bed. "It's so rare Zack has a girl over."

"Mom, I told you. We're just working together. She's not a *girl*."

Ouch.

Favianne's brows rose. "She looks like a girl to me."

"I meant she's not my girlfriend." He sighed. "She's paying me to help her buy a car. This isn't a social call."

"It's nice to meet you, Mrs. De Luca," I said, offering a tentative smile.

"Call me Favianne." She beamed at me. "What are your plans today?"

"We..." My eyes shot to Zack, hoping he'd save me, but he only stared back. "We're going car shopping."

"Sounds exciting." She grinned.

Her enthusiasm and graciousness permeated my body, calming me. "It is. I'm still not sure what kind to get though. But I won't keep him out long."

She waved a hand at me. "Borrow him as long as

you want. When he's home, he mopes around. Especially lately." Favianne switched to Zack. "Did you two meet at school?"

"Mom. Stop," he moaned. "It's not a date."

His mom tried to hide her smile. I felt oddly connected to her and she was so sweet, I had an overwhelming desire to see her happy.

I just couldn't resist.

"Actually, we met a little over a week ago. He's really been there for me—helped me with my car when it broke down. One thing led to another and last night, we double-dated with Trevor and my best friend." I snuck a peek at Zack whose mouth had dropped open.

Favianne beamed. "When you're done car shopping for the day, you'll both come here for dinner."

Oops. Zack was going to kill me.

CHAPTER FOURTEEN

"THAT WAS LOW, even for you." Zack rocketed down the steps of his house and marched across the lawn, trampling an innocent plant before jumping into the Jeep.

Mindful of the flowers, I followed suit and strapped on my seatbelt. Was I sorry for what I'd done? I recalled the way Mrs. De Luca's eyes lit up. No, I wasn't. I'd only just met her and already loved her. And Zack... well, I was never going to please him anyway.

"What? It was a double date. Sort of." I shrugged.

"I can't believe you stood there and lied to her." He exhaled sharply and the tires squealed as he steered the car from the curb. "It's my life, *my* family, Autumn. Mine."

"I didn't lie to her. Everything I told her was the truth."

"It wasn't a date." His eyes shot to me, wide and wild.

Poor guy. He was pretty worked up. "Not to us. But technically, since it was us and another *couple*, you guys picked us up and paid, it *was* a double date." I let that sink in, before speaking again, but in a softer tone. "I'm sorry it upset you, but I'm not sorry for making your mom so happy. Did you see her face?"

Zack eased up on the accelerator and the Jeep slowed, his shoulders relaxing. He blew out a breath. "If you could let me do most of the talking over dinner, I'd appreciate it," he said stiffly. At least he was calmer.

"I'll try, but if someone asks me something, they'll think I'm an idiot if I don't answer."

"Eat dinner. Then go. The sooner you leave, the less trouble you'll get me into. Where are we going, by the way?"

"There's a dealership I want to check out on Palm and Brand."

He changed lanes to make a left turn. "Did you quit smoking?"

"What?" I stared at him, my eyes bulging and my jaw slack. "I can't *quit* something I never started." I wondered if that was why Zack sniffed me sometimes.

"Normally, you smell like smoke. Not today."

God. I hadn't realized the stench of the house had followed me. I shrunk in my seat and gazed out the window. "My parents smoke inside," I mumbled toward the glass. "They're out-of-town and I cleaned this morning. There wasn't as much stink to cling to me, I guess." Why hadn't anyone ever told me?

A few minutes later, Zack parked and I made a beeline for the Cruisers.

"These are good cars. Gas mileage isn't great, but not horrible either. Built for off-roading, so they'll move when you need them to. They're not cheap though." He stopped to scan the rest of the lot. "I don't see any other used ones except these."

"None of them are in my price range." My whole body deflated and I sagged against a silver FJ. "I'd have to get one that has something seriously wrong with it or super high miles. Either way, my parents won't like it."

"Let's see what else they have." He nodded his head for me to follow.

I trailed after him. He occasionally stopped at a car and raised a brow, then I'd shake my head. When we'd gone through the entire used inventory, we returned to his Jeep.

"Did you Internet shop like I suggested?" he asked.

"Yes, but it's hard to tell. You can't walk around a picture or get inside it. I researched a bunch of SUVs and found the Cruiser. I really liked it but, well, we know how that turned out."

"This isn't life or death, Autumn. Relax. We'll find you the perfect car. Come on."

"You don't know my parents," I said, climbing back into his car. "It's a miracle they've come this far. I need to seal the deal before they realize what they've done."

He chuckled softly. "Duly noted."

We drove a little further and stopped at a Honda dealer.

"These aren't cheap either," I pointed out.

"The idea is to see the real thing, not pictures. Walk around the car and get inside, like you said. We'll go to several dealerships today and you're not allowed to buy anything. When we're done, we can regroup and decide what to do next. In the meantime, we're window shopping, okay?"

That didn't ease my anxiety at all.

"Are you trying to get this done before your parents come back to town? Less interference?"

"Exactly."

"When do you expect them?"

"Not sure." I shrugged. "A few days maybe."

"Then there's no pressure. We have all day today and tomorrow too."

Except that would be two more days with Zack, torturing myself with someone who could never be mine. But what choice did I have?

When we were done with Hondas, we did the same thing at two more dealerships. We were examining the fact sheet of an SUV when Zack gave a man-nod to someone outside my line of vision. I turned to see the man we'd met before. Except this time he wasn't wearing a cowboy hat. I glanced at Zack. "Do we have to leave?"

"I don't think so." Zack carried on, business as usual, but kept the man in his view.

I already knew not to invade his personal bubble. "What time does your family usually have dinner?"

"Around five-thirty, since my mom usually falls asleep early. We should get going."

"Good. I'm starving." I snuck a peek at the man, but a quick scan told me he'd taken off.

On the drive to Zack's house, he frequently checked his rearview mirror. I wondered if he was making sure we weren't being followed.

"How was your date with Gina? Or is that later tonight?" Not that it was any of my business. I fully expected Zack to shut me down.

"Date?"

"The other day, she asked if you two were still on for Saturday. You said yes. Remember?"

He waved a hand. "It's not a date. We have Science together and need to work on our project."

"Oh." Gina had been at his house, sharing his family with him? I struggled to ignore the jealousy gnawing at me. "Your mom must have been excited for you to have a girl over."

He snickered. "My mom didn't like her at all. She doesn't see Gina as settling down material."

His mom didn't like Gina, but she liked me. I turned away and smiled smugly.

Wait... did that mean she thought *I* was settling down material? Sure, I lusted after Zack—okay, I lusted after him a *lot*—but settle down with him? "At eighteen, she wants you *settled*? What does that mean? Engaged or married?"

"She married at our age." He shuddered. "She's old school."

"Gina told me you already have a girlfriend." I peered at him from under my lashes, trying to act casual.

"She said that?" He glanced at me briefly before returning his eyes to the road.

"Yep," I said. "On your first day at school."

"The subject never even came up. I think Gina's a little insecure. By making me unavailable to you, she eliminates the competition."

"I'm hardly competition. You and I haven't exactly gotten along."

He stopped for a red light and glanced my way. "Yeah, but Gina didn't know that."

Gina, the sneaky witch. "You spend a good amount of time with her at school."

"Gina's pretty." He made a face. "But she's not the kind of girl I'd get serious with."

"But the fact that you're nice to her at all..." I cocked my head. "She's a bigger snob than I could *ever* be."

"I pegged Gina the second she opened her mouth. No surprises there. But you..." He blew out a breath. "I wasn't expecting you to kick me to the curb when Daniel made an ass of himself."

"Yeah, well, I scolded him, but you'd already left."

Zack seemed to absorb that. "Gina's always trying to hook up with me."

"Why don't you go for it?" We were having a real conversation and it wasn't unpleasant at all. Yay. "You don't have to marry her."

"The other day she asked me if I liked *girls*," he said, but I noticed he hadn't answered my question.

I'd never thought about the possibility of Zack playing for the other team. "It's a valid question, I suppose, since no one at school has seen you, uh, *interact* with anyone."

He squinted, tilting his head as if he couldn't believe I'd said that. "I've been going to that school for a *week*."

"Oh, right." I shook my head. "So, *do* you like girls?"

He laughed, low and deep. "Funny."

Zack hadn't answered that question either. Whatever. I wasn't going to date him, so it didn't matter.

But since he seemed open to conversation, why not pry? He may not answer all of my questions, but he might answer some. And I just couldn't get past how mature Zack looked for his age. "How much older are you than Trevor?"

"Two months."

An answer, finally. "Did you two grow up together?"

"Yeah. Since I don't have any siblings, and Aunt Cara didn't have Brian until years later, Trevor and I were raised like brothers."

I was an only child too. That was one thing we had in common. But I was envious, because Zack grew up with a good substitute. My parents hadn't stayed in a city long enough for me to develop a relationship like that. Or any relationship. "Your mom said something to me in another language. Do you know what she said?"

"*Tesora*. It's Italian for darling."

"So you're Italian."

"Partly." Zack nodded as he turned down our street. "My mom is full-blooded, but not my dad. He was German, but grew up in Italy. That's where they met. She was educated here though, which is why she doesn't have an accent."

"Like me." I loved this talkative side of Zack. "My mom's half Italian and my dad's parents were English."

He parked in front of his house. "Let's go in and say hi to my mom." He sighed. "Please just stick to facts and not give her any ammunition."

I gave him an innocent look. "I'll try."

Trevor was on the couch playing a video game with his two younger brothers. "Hey Autumn," he said as I stepped over the threshold.

"Boys," Cara called from the kitchen. "Dinner in five."

"Yes, ma'am," Zack replied. "Let's go get my mom."

I shadowed Zack. At his mom's door, he knocked twice, then opened it.

"Did you two have any luck?" she asked, looking even prettier than last time I'd seen her. She wore a white blouse with a high neckline and puffy sleeves. She'd pinned up her hair, which reminded me of women I'd seen in old photos.

"No," I said while Zack answered the opposite.

"Yes and no," he clarified. "She didn't buy anything, but we set out to window shop, which is exactly what we did."

"Oh." Favianne gave a sly smile. "So you have to go out again tomorrow?"

"We are. Right?" he asked me.

I would've been okay with not car shopping, so Zack could enjoy a day off. But the idea of having him all to myself again appealed to me. I needed to get a grip. "Uh, I hadn't thought about it. I assumed you had other things to do."

"I could use the extra money."

And... crashing back to earth. "Of course."

His mom sighed and shook her head at Zack. "Let's not be late to dinner or Cara will be annoyed."

Zack reached behind the door and pulled out

a wheelchair. He pushed it up against the bed and leaned over to scoop up his mom.

Favianne swatted him away. "I can do it, *Tesoro*. You all treat me like an invalid. I can still walk when I need to." She dragged her legs over and scooted off the bed. Zack repositioned the chair so the seat touched the back of her knees and she slowly lowered to the chair. He wheeled her out of the room to the dinner table.

Whatever Cara was cooking, it smelled heavenly. Garlic, basil and bell pepper. Mmm. Something else too. Sausage?

Cara and the two younger boys occupied one side of the table. Both ends were vacant until Zack wheeled his mom to one of them. He pulled out a chair for me next to her and sat on my other side. "Aunt Cara, did you cook the meat separately? Autumn is a vegetarian." He glanced at me as an afterthought. "Or have you gone carnivore?"

I chuckled. "Still vegetarian. So far." A giant bowl of salad sat at the other end of the table, but I'd skip that today. I got plenty of that kind of food at home.

"It's mixed into the pasta and cream sauce, but they're big pieces. You could easily pick it out. Unless you don't like the juice either." Cara bit her lip and furrowed her brows, but it wasn't her fault no one told her I didn't eat meat.

"It's totally fine. I don't mind picking it out. Thank you." It smelled so heavenly, I wanted to eat it right then, meat and all. But considering how I'd devoured the hamburger, I didn't want to open myself up to anything new just yet. At least, not in front of Zack and his family.

Cara went around the table with a large bowl and a pair of tongs, filling everyone's plate with the pasta.

I stared down at my serving. It smelled mouth-watering and I determined to hold out until everyone had been served.

"Uncle Mac, this is Autumn," Zack said.

I'd been too wrapped up in the aroma of the food to notice the big man with massive shoulders and light reddish-brown hair who now sat at the other end of the table. The red explained why Trevor and Zack's coloring were so different.

"Nice to meet you." I smiled.

"You too. Welcome." He returned my smile, then eyed his plate. "Smells great, babe."

Cara finished serving him, then returned to her chair. Once he took the first bite, everyone else began eating. We didn't do that at my house, but there were only three of us. The bigger the family, the more rules, I supposed.

"Did Maya get a hold of you?" Trevor asked me.

My phone hadn't rung all day. If it had, I would've heard it. "I think my cell is at home. Why? What's up?"

"We're going to Santa Monica Pier after dinner. Wanna come with us?"

If Zack didn't go, I'd be a third wheel. If he did, it would be an awkward double date again. Or maybe not so awkward. Zack had been well-behaved the last few hours. "Uhm."

"You're coming, Zack?" Trevor asked.

"Sure. I'll walk Autumn home after dinner to get her phone and we'll meet you and Maya back here."

I didn't remember agreeing to go, but when Zack was being nice, saying no was much more difficult. Seeing his mom's face, I realized resistance was futile. Not that I wanted to put up a fight, but I hoped his mom wouldn't be too disappointed when he didn't marry me. "This is yummy, Cara. Thank you so much for having me over," I said, trying not to think about Zack's sweet side and all the things it could lead to, but probably wouldn't.

When everyone finished eating and dispersed, Zack began clearing the table. I thought he was going to set everything on the counter or in the sink and then bail. Instead, he dumped the leftovers down the disposal and loaded the plates into the dishwasher.

"I can wipe everything down. What should I use?" I asked.

He tossed me a sponge. I snuck a peek at him now and then as I cleaned. Even though it was hopeless, seeing him be domestic upped his market value. He even loaded the dishwasher *correctly* with everything orderly. By the time I finished, he'd started on the pots and pans. Impressive. And incredibly sexy.

With everything in its place, he washed and dried his hands. "Let's say goodnight to my mom before we go."

Visiting her at bedtime seemed more intimate than daytime. I hesitantly shadowed him anyway. Zack tapped the door twice and went in. Leaning over, he dropped a kiss on her cheek. "Goodnight, Mom."

"'Night, *Tesoro*." She turned to me. "Come visit again soon."

"Thank you. I will." I gave her an awkward wave.

We said our goodbyes to the rest of his family and walked at a leisurely pace down the sidewalk to my house.

"Zack?" I glanced his way to see him watching me. "Why are we hanging out again? You could've said no."

"Yeah, but did you see my mom's face? You were right. I don't have much time with her. Whatever she has left, I want to see her happy."

I was oddly disappointed *she* was the only reason he hung out with me. I stopped in front of my house and faced him. "Right. But..."

"But what?"

"Well, you've been awfully pleasant today."

He laughed. "Are you complaining? We might have a few more days together. Why make it harder than it has to be?"

That sounded good. But not safe. If he was polite *and* hot, how could I not crush on him? This could be bad.

When I turned and resumed walking, he grabbed my hand, forcing me to meet his gaze. "Autumn, I don't have a girlfriend," he said. "And I *do* like girls."

CHAPTER FIFTEEN

"GINA WILL BE happy to hear that." I laughed nervously, but my mind was screaming, "Oh, my God."

Zack gazed into my eyes as he inched closer.

My heart thumped in my chest as I imagined that he might kiss me. As every nerve ending in my body went on red alert, I held my breath.

He shook his head and released my hand. "Uhm, when my mom is gone, whether it's weeks from now or months, Aunt Cara will probably want me to stay. But I wouldn't feel right imposing on her any longer than we already have."

I couldn't be sure why he told me that, but my mind was even more muddled by my great disappointment over him not kissing me. I was sure he'd been about to. I struggled to focus. "Maybe your aunt loves you and won't consider you an imposition."

He nodded. "But I can't stay. I have no idea where I'll go. Mexico. Canada. Maybe I'll go to Italy. When I'm on the road, I don't know how often I'll talk to Trevor and I'm closer to him than anyone."

I got the picture. He wasn't going to be around and

wanted me to know that once he left, I'd never see him again. Don't get emotionally attached. "So you're saying that you don't want to form any ties that can't be easily broken?"

Zack exhaled in relief, nodding. "Exactly."

If he felt the need to tell me, I must've given myself away somehow. Maybe when I'd been waiting for him to kiss me. God, how obvious I must have been. "Thanks for letting me know," I said lightly. "That's nice of you, Zack."

I let us inside my house and he waited downstairs while I ran to my room to change. Leaning over the bed, I steadied myself with my palm flattened near the edge of the mattress. Damn it. He was just a guy. And a grouchy one at that. Nothing special.

Except that he was helpful, gentlemanly and totally gorgeous.

Getting pathetically infatuated with a guy who didn't want me was stupid, stupid, stupid. And even if he could muster up some feelings for me, it didn't matter, because he wasn't sticking around.

I dashed downstairs and into the family room to see him holding a picture of me when I was about five-years-old. "I think I'll pass on the beach," I said. "You guys can go without me."

"And me be the third wheel? Not on your life." He refocused on the shelf of photos as if the matter was settled.

Like his word was final. I wanted to stand my ground, but I knew Maya would be disappointed if I didn't go. "Fine. I'll be right back."

I returned to my room and wiggled out of my tank top, replacing it with a T-shirt. Nights could get chilly even in Los Angeles, more so at the beach. I stopped at the bathroom to double check my hair and makeup, then went to find Zack. He wasn't in the family room.

"Zack? Where are you?" I followed his scent to the living room where he sat on the couch, staring. "What are you doing?" I asked.

"Nothing." But he had a strange look on his face, like he'd just received some bad news. He got up and handed me my cell phone. "This is yours?"

"Yes, thank you." I took it from him, then snagged my purse, pausing when I thought I heard him taking a long, slow breath. Was he smelling me again? I couldn't be sure. "What's wrong?"

"Nothing." He jerked his head toward the front door. "We should get going."

I pulled my sweater off the back of the couch, tied it around my waist, and led the way to the front door. On the way to his house, he was quiet. Too quiet. For someone so talkative earlier, it seemed odd. Why would he encourage me to come if he wasn't going to talk to me?

I really needed to stop obsessing on him. We would all go out together, have fun, then go home and I'd get to the woods as fast as possible to work off my frustration.

When we arrived in Santa Monica, we went straight to the boardwalk and got ice cream, then took off our shoes and walked on the beach. It was pleasant and relaxing, even though Zack had almost nothing to say. Why the switch?

After a while, we got bored of the shops and piled into the Jeep.

"Bigger Burgers is up the street here." Zack pointed ahead to his right.

Oh, yeah, that sounded good. I turned to face Trevor and Maya in the back seat, swallowing the excess saliva, so I could talk without showering them. "You guys hungry?"

"For Bigger Burgers? Always." Maya grinned. "Those are so good."

The restaurant didn't have a drive-thru, which was extremely disappointing to me, since going inside took more time. Further, everything was made fresh, so I'd have to wait even longer. We went inside and the boys claimed a booth in the far corner. As expected, Trevor and Maya sat next to each other on one side, leaving Zack and me to sit together. At least this time the guys went in first, which allowed the girls the possibility of escape. Not that I was going anywhere. I wanted that burger.

A busboy stopped to see what we wanted to drink.

"We're ready to order," I said.

"We are?" Maya asked, her brows flying up.

Trevor blinked.

"Sorry." I dropped my gaze to the table, heat rushing into my cheeks. "I'm hungry."

Maya giggled. "I guess so."

On my left, Zack zeroed in on me. "We just got

here. We don't even have menus yet."

"Right." I nodded, hoping our server would get to that soon.

After a few minutes, a young man delivered our drinks. An eternity later, a woman arrived, wearing an apron and holding a pen and small tablet.

I hadn't seen the menu, but since it was a burger place, I didn't need to. I already knew what I wanted. Holding myself back, so I didn't seem like a starving lunatic, I waited until Maya gave her order. My foot swung back and forth under the table. Finally, it was my turn. "Double cheeseburger with everything and fries."

I fidgeted, feeling Zack's eyes riveted on me as he gave his order. Why was he staring? Being hungry wasn't a crime.

Maya tended to her phone after a series of beeps. "Oh, my God," she mumbled, furiously texting as more messages came in faster than she could reply. Minutes later, Maya closed her phone.

"Get this." Her eyes enlarged and her tone grew solemn. "Daniel was attacked by a wolf last night and dragged into the woods. Police couldn't find a body and no one's seen him since."

Silence settled around the table like a thick fog.

My stomach knotted. Just because Daniel was a monumental tool didn't mean I wanted anything bad to happen to him. "How do they know it was a wolf?"

She gestured to her cell. "That was Janine who spoke to a friend who overheard her dad talking—who's a cop. It's true. Jeff made a report at the station."

"That's... hideous." I gaped at Maya, not knowing what else to say.

"I never heard of wolves in the area. Coyotes maybe, but not wolves," Trevor said. "Can anyone else backup Jeff's story?"

"Not that I know of," Maya said. "Apparently, it was only the two of them. Jeff said they were camping."

"And drinking, no doubt." Trevor's mouth set in a hard line.

"Maybe Daniel wanted some alone time," I said. "And Jeff was too drunk to remember where Daniel went, so he made up a story to save his own ass. Or maybe something else happened and Jeff is covering it up by blaming it on an animal." I didn't think it was a wolf to blame. Certainly not *my* wolf. He'd never attack a human or he would've already hurt me.

"What did the police say?" Zack asked.

"Jeff called them right away. By the time they got there, Daniel was long gone. They searched the woods and couldn't find a body or any evidence of foul play. For now, they're assuming it's a prank and waiting to see if Daniel shows up."

"His parents must be going nuts," I said, thinking of Mr. and Mrs. Austin and what pain they must be going through with their son missing.

"I can imagine," Maya agreed.

"Jeff's parents have loads of money and influence," Trevor said. "Daniel's too. I bet they'll make sure it's the sheriff's top priority."

Could a wolf really have gotten Daniel? Maybe there

were other enormous wolves in the forest. After all, he came from somewhere, right? He could be part of a pack of oversized wolves. Weirder things have happened. I was proof of that. "Did Jeff say what color the wolf was?"

"It wasn't black, Autumn," Zack said quickly.

I turned to him, staring. "What makes you think I thought it was *black*?"

"Well..." He stared at the table. "Uh..."

"Your ex-boyfriend gets attacked by a wolf and you two are debating what *color* it is?" Maya narrowed her eyes at me, then Zack. "Seriously?"

"It's pointless to talk about it at all," Trevor added. "There was no wolf. You know how big it'd have to be to drag someone Daniel's size? I don't think so. I'm betting Jeff and Daniel were playing some dangerous games and things got out of hand. We'll probably never know what really happened, because Jeff and Daniel's parents are rich enough that anything damaging to their family's reputation would be covered up. In any case, I don't think we'll be seeing Daniel again."

Zack waved his hands. "Stop. Too much speculation. Ten bucks says Daniel shows up at school Monday denying there was ever an incident involving wolves."

Trevor grinned. "I'll take that bet."

The plates arrived and the subject was dropped.

Had my wolf attacked Daniel? Or was there some rabid wolf around? Maybe Zack was right and I shouldn't be in the woods alone, especially if the new wolf was as big as the black wolf.

I set the napkin in my lap, aware of Zack's eyes on

me. Slowly, I picked up the burger and took a dainty bite. I chewed, swallowed and took another.

The sauce was scrumptious, the pickles divine. I immediately went for another bite, moving the meat around on my tongue, reveling in the juices. I took note of the tomatoes and onions, grateful I'd ordered it with everything.

I got lost in the flavors, the people and things around me vanishing. Mmm. So good. As I opened for another bite, my gaze landed on Trevor and Maya. They were staring at me, their jaws slack and their eyes wide. Beyond them in the next booth, the occupants had twisted around to gawk at me. I closed my mouth and forced my hand to set the burger down. "What's wrong?"

"Uhm..." Maya averted her eyes and mashed her lips together. The group at the next table behind Maya and Trevor were still ogling me.

I raised my brows and my voice to reach the eavesdroppers. "What?" I asked them. They quickly returned to their own meals.

Zack put his own burger aside and twisted to face me. "You were growling and making other... feral noises."

Maya nodded in confirmation, her eyes still big.

On my list of life's most humiliating and awful moments, this would be at the top. But they didn't need to know the depths of my embarrassment, so I rolled my eyes and faked confidence I didn't have. "Oh, is that all. Geez, you act like I'd grown an extra head. Lighten up, guys."

Trevor and Maya laughed and I returned to my food, but made a point to set the burger down and make conversation between bites. It took all my concentration to remember we were in a public place and not slip into another world.

When Zack pulled up in front of my house, he tossed Trevor the keys. "Take care of Maya. I'll walk home."

He could've stopped home first, then let Trevor drop me off like last time. Hmm. I waved goodbye and took my time walking to the front door in case my hunch was right. Zack had something to say. Or *do*. My shoulders tensed, then I shook it off. Yeah, right. As if he would kiss me. Surely, if a guy planned to make a move on a girl, he wouldn't act weird and distant all night. Even a guy totally inept with girls knew you had to try to impress them.

I heard the Jeep drive away.

"Autumn."

I spun to face him. "What's up?"

"Good burger, huh?" He studied me.

I laughed. "Yeah, it was great. Thank you."

"Are we shopping tomorrow?" He took a step closer.

What did he want? I backed up with an eerie feeling. "If you're up for it."

He nodded, his face expressionless. "What time?"

"How about first thing in the morning?" I imagined having all day to shop. With Zack. Yum. "Nine?"

"I'll pick you up." Zack smiled, but it was strained. He held out his hand. "I'll unlock the door for you."

Body language said he wasn't trying to hook up with me. So, what was up? Total gentleman or serial killer? If he meant harm, I could put up a good fight. My instinct told me, though, Zack wasn't a creep. I dropped my keys in his hand.

"I wanted to talk to you about something. Do you mind if I come in?"

"Uh, I guess not."

Once he unlocked the door, he swung it open and stood in the doorway. I squeezed past him as his nose neared me and he inhaled.

"You did it again." I shot him a dark look, my hands on my hips. "Do you know how weird it is to have some guy constantly sniffing you? You have a fetish or something?"

"Autumn..."

"What? Spit it out already." The anticipation was making me crazy. His proximity was not helping. Sadly, I was getting worked up enough that I *really* wanted him to kiss me.

"You don't smell like other people," he whispered.

I froze, a blind fury brewing. "Excuse me?"

He backed up. "I mean, you don't smell like a normal person."

"Your clarification is *not* flattering." Here I was, feeling foolish and love-struck waiting for his goodnight kiss, maybe even a make-out session, and that's what I got—an insult? Oh, I wanted to wring his neck. I wanted to pound on him, smash him to itty bitty pieces. "You convince me to go out with you guys, ignore me all night, then insult me? I smell *not normal*? You've been rude before, Zack De Luca, but this beats them all. I'd like you to leave. Now."

He stared at me like he was surprised. Or confused. He'd told me I stunk. Did he expect me to get turned on, because my smelling offensive made *him* irresistible?

"Autumn, that's not what I meant."

"So I *do* smell normal?"

"Well, no—"

"Out." I glared and pointed to the doorway.

"Wait. Let me explain."

"Is English not your first language?" I growled, my jaws clenched.

He held up both hands in surrender and backed away, through the door and down the steps. I slammed the door and peeked out the window. He was still staring at the house.

Damn it. I was so furious my arms and legs trembled. My stomach twisted up and I wanted to howl at the sky. I bolted upstairs to change into my running clothes, needing to get out before I exploded.

Dressed, I flew down the steps. With my hand on the doorknob, I stopped. Zack hadn't said I smelled *bad* but that I didn't smell like a *normal person*. Strange choice of words. When I kicked him out, he looked stunned, not angry. Did he know something about me? If so, what?

And how the hell did he know about the black wolf?

Closing my eyes and inhaling deeply, I took a moment to calm myself before peeking out the window. Zack was gone. I needed to talk to him, but pounding on his door this late and waking his mother wasn't an option. She needed her sleep. Besides, whoever answered might assume I came for a booty call. Unacceptable.

I would go for my run, email my parents, then get to bed. Tomorrow, I'd have plenty of opportunities to grill him.

Or kill him.

CHAPTER SIXTEEN

I RACED TO the meadow, my head swimming with thoughts of Zack and freaky scenarios. Impossible things were happening with my body, so how could I believe those kinds of impossibilities belonged only to me? Someone, somewhere could be going through the same thing. Maybe even Zack.

Earlier at Bigger Burgers, he hadn't seemed shocked like the others over the rumor of Daniel and the wolf. Plus, his sense of smell was awfully good and he seemed unusually strong for his age. In fact.... he behaved eerily similar to my black wolf and I couldn't ignore the fact that he'd joked a few days ago about actually being a werewolf.

Was it possible he was a werewolf? Could were-wolves exist in real life?

I stood immobilized in the center of the clear-ing, balling my fists. No, there were no such things as werewolves. Trevor's theory was probably right and Jeff had made the story up to avoid getting into trouble. Or he had an alcohol induced hallucination.

Or maybe my special abilities gave me an unusual scent and Zack had a very good sense of smell. It could be as simple as that. I closed my eyes again, feeling nature around me and inhaling the fragrance of moss and pine.

Yes, that's it. Zack was a normal teenager and there were no creatures that went bump in the night.

I sensed him before I saw him. He came into view, my black wolf, approaching me slowly. About a yard away, he sat in front of me.

"You didn't attack Daniel, did you?"

He whined and lowered his belly to the ground.

"No, of course you didn't." Such a strange creature. My mind reeled, but I was tired of thinking. I needed to get on with my run and get home to bed. "Race you around the meadow?"

I took off, darting along the trees that bordered the clearing. After a couple laps, I dashed through the forest and leaped as high as I could. I soared, skimming the top of a tree and landing on the other side of it, then rocketed back to the clearing and skidded to a stop several feet from the wolf.

He hadn't moved. Standing on all fours, his ears stood straight up, tail down, eyes trained on me.

Holding out the back of my hand for him to sniff, I slowly moved toward him. He nearly touched my hand, blowing out quick breaths and warming my skin. I held very still as he edged even closer, dragging his wet nose up my arm and around my waist, circling me. Then he stood on his hind legs and laid a gentle paw on my shoulder, burying his muzzle in my neck and hair.

Holy crap. I had a wild wolf all over me.

He sucked in a long breath and exhaled at the back of my neck. I imagined that's how Zack would sniff me. If I let him. Chills danced on my skin and tranquility washed over me as I ran a hand over his shoulder, my fingers reveling in his silky fur.

I stared at the wolf who was still eye level with me. "Oh my God."

Zack was not a werewolf, damn it. He wasn't. It was absurd to consider such a thing. Having superhuman strength was one thing. Morphing into a completely different form was absolutely preposterous.

I stepped back and created distance between me and the wolf. "I have to go," I mumbled, backing further away. Once in the trees, I hit the dirt at a dead run.

† † †

At nine o' clock sharp the next morning, Zack rang the doorbell. He wore jeans and a work shirt, his sleeves pushed up, hair messy. He'd never looked better.

I flung the door open and folded my arms over my chest. "I don't want to talk about it."

His mouth curved up. "Talk about what?"

"What I smell like. Besides, by now, you already know." I took in a slow, deep breath. Yeah, I'd wanted Zack to explain himself last night, but since my most recent encounter with the wolf, I already suspected I was going insane—I didn't want it confirmed. Not just yet anyway. "We'll car shop and when we're done for the day, we'll go our separate ways."

"What will I tell my mom and Aunt Cara when they ask why you declined their dinner invitation for tonight?" He smiled smugly.

I could feel my eye twitch. "What's Cara making for dinner?"

"Spaghetti and *meat*balls." He lifted one brow.

Bastard. "Fine. After dinner, we're done."

He gave me his lopsided grin, displaying the lone dimple. "Are you ready?"

"Yeah." I grabbed my purse and we jumped into his car. "What's with the shovel on the back of the Jeep?"

"Never know when you'll need to bury a body."

I stared at him.

"I'm teasing, Autumn." He gave a quick laugh. "These vehicles are made for off-roading. Sometimes you need to dig yourself out of a ditch."

I could totally picture Zack doing something like that, all rugged and manly. "Doesn't seem to be helping you dig yourself out of the pile of crap you fell in last night."

"If you'd let me explain—"

I held up a hand. "Not necessary. Really."

At a stop sign, he held up a piece of paper, then set it on the dashboard and drove again.

"What's that?"

"The address to a car I thought we'd check out. It's close by."

"What kind?"

"Mustang."

I made a face. "A muscle car."

"I guess so. They're not known for being great on gas, but they're not too bad and the miles on this one are low." Checking to make sure the road was clear, he switched lanes. "Give it a chance. You never know what you'll like unless you try."

Several minutes later, we pulled up to a curb. A small yard artfully crowded with lush shrubbery and colorful blooms surrounded a little brick house. I'd been uneasy about buying a car from a private party, feeling safer getting something from a dealership that checked and rechecked their cars for quality. In theory anyway. My worries dissipated as I inhaled the fragrance of the flowers. Anyone who put this much care into their garden wouldn't neglect a car, would they?

We knocked and moments later, a gray-haired man opened the door. He was so old that you could no longer tell his age. Seventy? Ninety?

"Mr. Peters?" When the man nodded, Zack continued. "Hi, I'm Zack. We spoke on the phone earlier this morning?"

Wow. Zack must have called before he came to my house. Calling that early on a Sunday? Impressive.

"This is Autumn. She's the one looking for a car."

The man smiled, but his eyes seemed sad. "Hang on. Let me get the key."

Mr. Peters returned and took his time leading us to the side of the house. He held out a remote and the garage door slowly opened.

I couldn't see what was under the cover. The old

man shuffled over to the rear of the garage and lifted a corner of the giant stretch of gray cloth.

"Let me help." Zack hurried over to the other side and, inch by inch, they unveiled a silver convertible Mustang.

There had to be something really wrong with it, because it was too pretty to be within my budget. Freakishly high miles or a missing engine?

Mr. Peters popped the hood and disappeared behind it with Zack, who fired off questions. I had no idea what they were talking about, so I amused myself by examining the body. The top was already down and I could readily see the interior, which appeared clean. Circling the car, I noted the shiny rims and glossy paint. In the bright morning sunshine, I saw a sprinkling of chips in the paint. My Taurus was riddled with that sort of thing, most likely caused by spraying gravel. You couldn't miss them. On the Mustang though, it wasn't noticeable unless you examined it closely.

"What year is this?" I asked.

Zack peeked out from behind the hood. "It's five-years-old." He vanished again.

I slid behind the driver's seat and poked around. It had forty-two thousand miles on it. Working my way back to the front and under the hood, I listened as Zack asked about the engine modifications and horsepower. Mr. Peters replied, but his words meant nothing to me. Zack seemed impressed, nodding and raising his brows.

"Can we take it out? We'd like to drive it to make sure she likes it. Then me, to see if it's sound." He gazed down at the engine. "Although I don't think that's going to be a problem."

"Why are you selling it?" I asked.

"It was my son's. He loved this car." The man's eyes moistened, his gaze dropping to the concrete floor of the garage, chin quivering. "He doesn't need it anymore."

Zack just stared without speaking.

His son must have died. Or something else terrible. How awful.

"No need to look at me like that, young lady. It's not *all* bad. My son left me two wonderful grandchildren." Mr. Peters patted my hand, then slowly moved several feet to the passenger side and got in. "C'mon. Let's take this baby for a spin."

I lagged behind, tugging on Zack's arm. "How much is this thing?" I hissed.

"You'd been saving up for a car before your parents chipped in, right? Use some of that."

I gasped. "What? You dragged me out here for a car *over* fifteen?"

"Sshh. He's selling it for exactly fifteen, but I know some of your money is going to the shop. I was hoping to negotiate, but now I know something happened to his son, it would feel wrong." He nodded toward the driver's side. "Come on. You're up first."

Damn. Even if I liked it, I couldn't buy it. Unable to resist, I climbed in anyway.

The car rode like a dream and the longer I drove it, the easier I imagined owning it. My hair whipping around and tickling my face didn't bother me at all, like I'd thought it would. In fact, it made me feel free, like I was running through the woods.

I slowed to a stop at a red light, noting the smooth braking. When it was green, I gunned the engine and watched in the rearview mirror as Zack's head snapped back. "Sorry," I told Mr. Peters who sat to my right.

He chuckled. "You like it?"

"Yeah, I do." I sighed and pulled over, then switched places with Zack.

His test drive was shorter than mine, maybe because he'd worked on and driven enough cars to know what to be wary of. He gingerly backed into the old man's garage and we got out.

At the front steps of the house, Zack asked Mr. Peters, "Do you mind if we consult for a minute?"

"No problem. Holler when you're ready." He leisurely made his way back to the car, opened the passenger side and got in.

"Seems like a fair deal considering its condition and low mileage. What do you think?" Zack whispered when we'd gotten a few feet away, his expression guarded.

I glanced over at the silver beauty and gnawed on my thumb nail. "I'm a little nervous about going over my budget. My parents made me promise not to tap into my savings. I can't break my word." This was so wrong. I finally found a car I wanted and it wasn't buyable.

Mr. Peters climbed out of the Mustang and walked the few feet to stand in front of us. "When you get older, things start to go. Eyesight's not so good anymore. Don't have the stamina I had at Zack's age." He glanced at Zack, then me. "But my hearing's good. What's your budget, dear?"

My eyes shot to Zack. Something felt so immoral about making this nice man bring the price down. I had a feeling it was already too low. "About fourteen-five."

Mr. Peters took my hand, covering it in both of his. "Sold for fourteen. Use the leftover to take this nice young man out to a proper dinner."

"But—"

"No buts." He shook his head quickly and decisively. "I'd rather sell it for less and know it's going to a good home. My son would've liked that."

I swallowed, my lashes suddenly wet. "Thank you."

"Sir," Zack began. "It's Sunday and the banks aren't open. Will you hold it for us until after school tomorrow when we can make it to the bank?"

"We can give you a good faith deposit," I offered.

The man waved a hand. "Not necessary. I'll hold it for you, but if you change your mind, call me."

We shook his hand and said our goodbyes, promising to be there the next day.

I hopped in the Jeep and nearly squealed. That beautiful machine was going to be mine. I flashed Zack a grin. "That was amazing."

He chuckled.

My stomach growled. Guess the cereal I'd eaten for breakfast had been amazingly inadequate. Maybe my body needed more fuel for its mysterious new abilities—which I was no closer to finding the reason for. "Early lunch? It's on me."

"I can always eat. If we get burgers though, we're not eating in public." Zack suppressed a smile.

I felt my face flush. "Thanks for finding that car. I love it. It's perfect."

He turned toward me and grinned knowingly. "I had a feeling."

The ride to the burger place was spent listening to Zack explain in the most painful detail each modification that had been done to the car. After he'd found it for me though, I was big on forgiveness.

Zack pulled up to the drive-thru. "Double cheeseburger with everything?"

I nodded, handing him some cash. He put in our order and as soon as the bag of food passed through the window, my mouth watered. My driving need for meat raged through every cell in my body.

"There's a park close by. We might find a spot in the shade." By the time he finished the sentence, I'd already taken my first bite. He laughed and pulled over.

We ate in silence. I held myself in check, but devoured the last morsel and licked my fingers, vowing to eat my next burger in private where I could be as uninhibited as I wanted.

Once he'd dropped me off at my house, I called Maya to tell her about my new-to-me car.

She went on a roll about Trevor. "I was about to go inside when he kissed me again. He's an amazing kisser, by the way." I heard her breathy sigh. "Anyway, I was reaching for the doorknob to go inside when he asked for exclusivity. I can't date anyone else and neither can he. I feel like I'm in a dream and I have *you* to thank for that. If you hadn't pushed, I'd still be a stalker."

I laughed. "I'm sure you two would have gotten together eventually."

"Maybe. We're going bowling tonight. You and Zack should come."

"Oh, I don't know, Maya."

Zack had been so nice all morning, I'd forgotten what a jerk he'd been the night before. When he was pleasant, we got along quite well. That was dangerous because I liked him. Too much. I'd been insulted enough and didn't want rejection on top of it. I desperately searched my mind for a valid excuse to get out of bowling.

"Come on, Autumn. I want to see your new car," Maya said, distracting me from creating a good fib.

Whew. Now I didn't have to make up anything. "I'm not picking it up until tomorrow."

"Then I want to see *you*."

Other than my parents, Maya was the only other person I'd gotten to know well enough to truly love. Saying no was nearly impossible. "Okay."

Since Zack had found me a car, his services were no longer needed. He could go back to being his grumpy self. Hopefully, he wouldn't be too annoyed when he realized he'd be hanging out with me again after dinner.

He might even say no to bowling. A part of me felt empty at the thought.

† † †

Either Zack had lied about what Cara planned to make for dinner or she changed her mind. Meatballs seemed too similar to hamburger, so it was probably for the best. Regardless, the food was fabulous—chicken marinated in lemon and rosemary with scalloped potatoes and steamed asparagus. After a couple bites of chicken and coming close to sensory overload, I opted to resist the meat and stick to veggies.

I decided I loved Zack's family almost as much as my own. I liked that they used 'please' and 'thank you' liberally while passing food around the table. I loved how they waited to eat until everyone had food. Good manners were appealing. Not that we were Neanderthals at my house, but Zack's family made etiquette an art. Best of all, they treated me like I belonged there.

Much to my relief and surprise, Zack went bowling with us. We teamed against Maya and Trevor, winning the only two games—probably because their minds weren't on bowling. I wondered why they invited us when they could've spent time alone.

At my house, Zack tossed his keys to Trevor. I walked to my front door, Zack shadowing me. At the top of the steps, he held out his hand for my keys. I gave them up, but hoped we weren't going to have a repeat of last time he walked me to my door.

Zack turned the key in the lock and swung around to face me. In order for me to enter my house, he needed to move out of my way. Instead, he raised a hand to lift a lock of hair, rubbing it between his fingers.

"Soft. I like your hair like this."

I gave a shaky laugh, thankful I'd taken the extra time to curl the ends of my hair before dinner instead of pulling it into a ponytail like I'd been tempted to do. "It's a ton of work to make it wave like this."

His hand slipped over my shoulder, his thumb catching on my tank strap. "You should wear a top like this every day."

He inched closer. Though he barely touched me, my entire body sizzled in anticipation.

CHAPTER SEVENTEEN

ZACK'S EYES FIXED on my mouth and a wave of heat coursed through me.

I shifted forward just a hair and tilted up my chin to meet his lips. "Maybe I'll wear it tomorrow."

"No. Don't wear it to school," he said, his gaze roaming my face. "It's not safe."

A tiny part of me couldn't help asking, "What's not safe?"

Zack blinked, shook his head and took a step back, signaling the end of our moment. Damn. "Well, you know what they say about guys," he said. "They only want one thing."

"You're a guy." A hot guy, I wanted to add. "Does that rule apply to you?"

"It applies to Daniel, who's already proved himself very annoying. And you weren't showing nearly this much skin." He swung around and sprinted down the steps. At the sidewalk, he stopped and pointed at my house. "Go inside."

My stomach sank, but I managed a nod before closing the door and locking it.

If that had been about to turn into a kiss, why did I have to ruin it by talking? Deep down, I knew if Zack genuinely liked me, there would be other opportunities. Still, I took little comfort in having blown a perfect one.

† † †

The black wolf met me in the meadow and ran with me. I didn't run at full speed, because I didn't think he could keep up. He moved pretty damn fast though. Maybe because of his size, his long legs covered ground more quickly. Whatever the reason, having his company was comforting—it felt *right*.

Once I'd gotten the run out of my system, I slowed and he lagged behind, nipping at my calves and ankles.

"Stop it, Wolfie." I laughed and kept going, but he did it again. This time, he playfully snapped at my shoe. His teeth hooked on the heel of my sneaker and I stumbled. Trying to regain my balance, I twisted and fell backward. The wolf leaped on top of me, his paw on my shoulder, his muzzle edging toward me. The weight of him pressed me against the dirt and compelled me to stay down, but I didn't feel in the least bit threatened.

My fingers ran through his soft, silky fur. "You're so sweet," I said, offering him a small smile. "Want to spend the night at my house? I'd love your company."

He froze, his eyes meeting mine and I couldn't shake the feeling that there was something he wanted to tell me. His eyes... they reminded me of Zack's. Clearly I had too much of Zack on my brain because this was a wolf, not a human.

Without warning, he vaulted off me, ran toward the trees and disappeared.

† † †

My mom emailed me what they'd been up to and the nice time they'd been having. I replied, telling her about the Mustang. Then I deleted it. What if they told me not to buy the car? I'd have to start the search all over again. Instead, I told them about the promising lead to pursue tomorrow after school. All true.

Ten minutes before I planned to leave for school the next morning, there was a knock at the door. Zack, looking as delicious as always. "Oh, hi." My stomach dipped. "What brings you by?"

"It seemed smarter to drive together. After school, we can go directly to your new car. Otherwise, we'll end up with an extra vehicle."

Couldn't he have said he needed more time with me? That an entire night away was more than he could bear? Was that really too much to ask?

I sighed and motioned him inside. "Great idea. I'll be ready in a few minutes. You can wait here or I can go to your house."

"I'll wait here." He'd already turned his attention to some family pictures on the wall. I dashed upstairs to get pretty.

When we pulled into the student parking lot twenty minutes later, I noticed Daniel right away. He sat on the wall, extremely alive—not eaten by a giant wolf—where he used to wait for me. Even though I didn't like him, not even a little bit, it was good to know Jeff had imagined things after all. Daniel's eyes shot to mine as I jumped out of Zack's Jeep and closed the door. Zack and I exchanged glances as we met at the bumper of his car.

"You were right," I said. "He's just fine."

"Yep. Definitely not dead." Zack squinted as he studied Daniel. "Not so sure about the *fine* part though."

Yeah, there was something different about Daniel. An energy. I felt a tingling in my toes, but not the good kind. The kind that told me to steer clear. Zack's comment made me think he sensed it too, that Daniel was even less balanced than before.

"If I walk you to class, he'll be less likely to bother you."

"Thanks." I was pretty sure I could take Daniel down, but I didn't need the hassle. Besides, no way would I refuse Zack if it meant more time with him. Being around him felt safe. And kind of like I was his girlfriend. Not a bad thing, except I knew the truth.

Zack escorted me to class and when it was over, he was waiting outside to take me to my next class. He showed up after that class too and the next one. We silently walked side-by-side, his eyes alert, body tense as he moved. How he knew my classes, I didn't know or care.

He'd stopped making idle chitchat the moment he'd seen Daniel that morning, like he was saving his energy and attention for something bigger. As the day progressed, I became more convinced that Zack sensed the change in Daniel too. Did other people also sense it? If only Zack and I could tell, that might mean Zack was like me, maybe not-quite human.

What were the chances? My mind kept taking me back to werewolves, but I knew they didn't exist. But what if they did? If Zack was a werewolf, was I one too? And what about Daniel? If he really had been dragged away by a wolf...

My brain nearly exploded with the impossibilities.

At lunch, Zack entered the huge cafeteria with me at his side as eyes fixed on us from all over the room. He was a master of cool, confidently guiding me through the throng of students and warily avoiding Daniel, until we sat next to Trevor and Maya.

"I owe you." Trevor handed Zack a ten-dollar bill.

Zack stared blankly. "For what?"

"Daniel returned to school. Apparently, Jeff was delusional, like you said." Trevor's eyes searched the lunchroom, finding Jeff at one corner and Daniel at the other. "Not sure what's up with Jeff's random story, but I haven't seen them together all day."

"It's definitely odd," I said, watching Daniel out of the corner of my eye.

Zack had a bead on Daniel, too.

Maya and Trevor, on the other hand, were too absorbed in each other to notice our lack of interaction. Before lunch ended, Maya scooped up a little gift bag and ushered me out of the cafeteria and into the girl's room.

The bathroom door closed and she thrust the bag at me with a big smile. "It's girl stuff, so I knew the guys wouldn't care if we did this without them. Happy birthday."

"You remembered." Grinning, I plucked at the decorative tissue and peered inside. "You've been to Mathers. Thank you." Reaching in, I sifted through bottles and bottles of nail polish.

"Has he kissed you yet?" she asked.

"Who?" As I scrutinized each bottle, my mind was vacant as to whom she could possibly be referring to, since Zack wasn't in the realm of possibilities. Unfortunately.

"Zack. Duh."

I didn't want to get into the complications of Zack, so I checked my face in the mirror to avoid Maya's eyes. "It's not like that with us."

"He's hot. You're hot. It's basic chemistry. Didn't he walk you to your door the last two nights and drive you to school this morning?"

I swiveled to face her. "It's just a work thing and it made sense to take one car. If we each take our own, then pick up my new one after school, we end up with three. Nothing else to it."

She wagged a finger at me. "That doesn't explain why you two are joined at the hip between classes. I know he's walked you everywhere today. And now you're barely talking. You two have a fight?"

"He's very platonically looking out for me and wants Daniel to think we're together, so he'll stop harassing me." I checked my face in the mirror, hoping she'd buy my lie-on-the-fly and leave it at that. After all, Zack's disinterest in me wasn't exactly a happy topic.

She narrowed her eyes. "There's something you're not telling me."

I blew out a breath. "Look, I hate to break it to you, but Zack's had opportunities to kiss me and hasn't taken them. Now, since it's my birthday, can we please change the subject?" Hoping she'd move on, I examined a bottle of Black Cherry nail polish. But my thoughts strayed back to Zack. He didn't seem to hate me anymore. If he did, he wouldn't be shielding me from Daniel. But did he *like* me?

"Ha! You *do* like him. I knew it." A grin spread over Maya's face. "I can totally tell by your expression."

Busted. But I kept up the ruse and rolled my eyes. "Let's get to class." I headed out without waiting for her reply.

† † †

Zack wasn't waiting for me after my last class. I stood outside the door and wondered how long he'd be delayed and whether I should stay put or meet him at his car. By the time I realized Zack wasn't going to show, only a handful of people milled about. Being the last one in the hallway all alone didn't seem smart.

Without warning, the energy around me shifted. The back of my neck tingled and I had the creeps in a big way. After one last scan for Zack, adrenaline pumping, I made a beeline for the exit. The urge to get far away from Daniel drove me as I focused on the double doors at the end of the corridor. Careful not to speed and attract attention, I kept a brisk pace.

The double doors loomed ahead a few yards. As I rushed past a classroom, a hand snaked out and clamped onto my arm, knocking me against the doorway and dragging me through. I knew it was Daniel by his scent, which was much stronger now, but different somehow.

My heart beat faster and my legs trembled with the certainty that something was really wrong. The kind of wrong that gave women nightmares and made them take self-defense lessons or buy mace.

With more force than I was prepared for, Daniel shoved me into the corner of the empty room, flattening my back against the wall and pressing his hand over my mouth. His lips curled and his face twisted into a sneer. Surprised by his iron grip, I turned mute. Not that I could talk anyway, since his hand worked well as a gag. When did he get so strong?

"Finally, we can talk in private. I've missed you, baby. God, you smell good." He buried his nose in my hair and inhaled at my temple. "I'm going to remove my hand now, but if you try to scream, I'll stop you before you even get started. Understand?"

"Mm-hm."

Daniel exuded power, an unmistakable energy, very much like Zack. Why hadn't I realized something was odd about Zack before? That was why I always knew when he was around. It was a particular energy he alone emitted. And now Daniel.

My breathing came in quick gasps when Daniel slowly freed my mouth. If I tried to escape, could I?

Or should I wait for a better opportunity? I had no idea how strong Daniel was or if he could kill me.

"Don't be scared, Autumn. I won't hurt you unless I have to. Zack, on the other hand, well, that also depends on you." His moist breath coated my cheek and ear lobes. "I love you so much, Autumn. We can be happy again if you just stop fighting me and let it happen." He cupped my face, his eyes pooling.

He loved me? In a seriously twisted way, maybe. "Daniel, you don't want to do this. You don't want me."

His chin quivered a moment and he smiled sadly. "You're all I think about."

"What you're asking is impossible. I can't give you what you want and you can't make me happy. I'm sorry."

"Then we'll be miserable together." He rested his forehead against mine. "I told you before, no one else can ever touch you again."

Daniel was really scaring me now and not fighting wasn't getting me anywhere. I clenched my fist and struck, aiming for his stomach. But at such a short distance, I couldn't build up any real momentum. He grunted on impact and scrambled to capture my hand. When my limbs evaded him, one of his hands wrapped around my throat, cutting off my air, while his other hand snaked under my skirt and up my thigh.

My vision darkened and just when I thought I was close to passing out, he loosened his grip around my neck. I gasped as oxygen rushed into my lungs.

"Be a good girl now." His lips descended toward mine.

"Daniel," I heard Zack growl.

Oh, thank God. I'd never been so happy to see Zack.

"You need to leave." Daniel scowled over his shoulder at the intruder. "Getting rid of me won't be so easy this time."

"Hang on a sec." Zack held up his hands, palms out. "You're right. Things aren't like they were before."

"I said, get out," Daniel hissed.

"Not gonna happen." Zack kept his voice calm and even. "You'd put up a bigger fight, but I'd still win. I'm like you, but I've been this way a lot longer. The older you are, the stronger you get. Didn't the guy who made you tell you that?"

"You're bluffing," Daniel said.

"You don't believe I'm like you?"

Daniel snorted. "That's not what I meant, moron. I don't think you can take me."

Zack nodded thoughtfully. "I don't think *you* could take *me*. I guess we'll have to find out. But what if I'm telling you the truth and I beat you? No matter who wins, a couple guys like us fighting in a small space like this, we'd trash the place and reveal our true nature."

Our true nature? What did *that* mean?

Daniel laughed again and his grip loosened, then he turned to me, sneering. "He's only delaying the inevitable. We'll be together again soon. I promise." He kissed me on the mouth, mashing my lips against my teeth. Finally, he broke contact. Then, without taking his eyes off Zack, he slipped out the door, which closed behind him.

I squeezed my eyes shut, a light tremor invading my body. "I tried, but he had me pinned. He was too strong."

In a flash, Zack wrapped his arms around me.

I circled his waist and clung to him as I laid my head against his shoulder. The heat from his body washed over me, comforted me.

"It's okay now," he said. "I'm so sorry I wasn't there to meet you. Gina got a hold of me and I'll bet Daniel put her up to it."

My eyes pooled, but I refused to let the tears fall. If I cried, Daniel would've won in a small way. I couldn't allow that.

"Better?" Zack pressed his lips to my forehead, then he moved to my temple where he dropped a feather-light kiss.

His lips almost made me forget how Daniel had freaked me out. "Yeah." I sighed, a faint moan escaping me.

Zack stiffened against me and let one of his arms fall to his side. "We should go."

Yeah, away from Daniel. But in case he was still lurking, I needed to pull myself together. Chin high, I nodded and led the way.

Daniel's Audi still sat in the parking lot and I involuntarily shivered and glanced around the courtyard for him.

Zack opened the passenger door and I climbed in. After rounding the Jeep, he fired it up and backed out. "You can't let him get you alone like that again. You're not strong enough to stop him if he..."

I froze, the implication of Zack's words making me feel like I needed a shower. "You mean if he tries to rape me?"

Zack's voice steeled as he peeled out of the school parking lot. "He could get away with it if he said you'd given yourself willingly, which wouldn't be hard for others to believe since you guys were together."

My breath left my body in a whoosh. My eyes burned and I felt strangely uncomfortable in my skin. "We dated, yes, but I never slept with him. Ever." The entire event had been horrific and I felt sufficiently violated. Explaining my situation only added to the humiliation. I started shaking uncontrollably and all I wanted was to run it off. "Pull over and let me out."

"I can't. We need to get you home." He spared me a glance. "Autumn, stay with me. You can't morph now. Focus on me, Autumn."

Morph? What the hell? I stared at my arms that were vibrating into a blur. What was happening to me?

"Autumn, look at me." He squeezed my hand, pulling my attention to him. "If you just relax, it'll be okay," he murmured.

It took every ounce of my will to stay with Zack and push thoughts of Daniel, and how he'd nearly assaulted me, out of my mind. My body had an odd floating sensation, but the tremors had stopped.

"I didn't sleep with him." A sob burst from me. I didn't think Zack cared about my sex life, but I still wanted everyone to know that I hadn't done *that* with *him*.

"I believe you. Hang on." Zack kept a hold of my hand while negotiating a turn. Seconds later, he pulled into the driveway of my house and killed the engine.

I sat there, numb and unable to move. My lids were heavy, and I fought to keep them open. Why was I so tired?

"My first almost-morph wiped me out too." He slid an arm under my knees and the other around my back, scooping me up.

I didn't think I'd asked out loud why I was so tired. But with the fuzz in my head, I couldn't know for sure. I yawned. And what did he say about morphing?

At the front door, he put me down so I could rummage through my purse for the keys. In a fog, I handed them to him and he let us in, then I staggered to the sofa and collapsed.

"What's happening to me, Zack? What happened to Daniel?" I had so many more questions, but was too spent to stay awake for the answers.

† † †

Heavy paws pounded through the forest as the pack chased me, gaining ground. My heart slammed against my ribcage as I ducked through the brush, only to come face-to-face with a wall of rock. Their growls sounded behind me.

I sucked in air to scream, bolting upright. My heart pounded and adrenaline roared through my veins. Slowly, the room came into focus and I realized I was home. There were no wolves hunting me.

Zack sat on the sofa at my feet. He placed a warm hand on my ankle. "Bad dream?"

"Yeah." I reached a hand to my forehead. "When I was younger, I used to have nightmares about wolves. It's odd I'm having them again."

"Autumn, don't you know why you were shaking so much in the car?"

"No. Do you?" As much as I liked Zack touching me, I sat up straight and dropped my feet to the floor.

"How can you not know?" He narrowed his eyes as if willing me to say what he wanted to hear.

"Because I don't. But apparently you do, so why don't you clue me in?"

"I'll do my best." He rose and held out a hand for me. "But we'd better get to the bank first."

"What time is it? How long have I been sleeping?" I stretched and stood, feeling much better.

"Half hour or so. We still have time, but we should get going. When we get back, I'll answer all your questions."

"Okay." Locating my purse, I made sure I had my ID and reached for the doorknob.

"Wait." He moved some strands of hair from my face.

My eyes lingered on his lips as I stood rooted to the floor. The other night, I'd thought Zack would kiss me, but I'd opened my mouth and ruined it. In the class room earlier after Daniel left, Zack had been holding me. When I'd sighed, he'd withdrawn. Maybe this time, if I didn't make a peep, I wouldn't interrupt him from kissing me.

Alas, Zack spun around, picked up my keys and opened the door.

Giving in to my *feelings* for Zack was a terrible idea anyway. Obviously, he was emotionally unavailable. I mean, he'd had so many opportunities to hook up with me and hadn't. I needed to face facts that Zack just didn't feel that way about me.

At the bank, I handed the teller my ID, Zack by my side. After studying my picture, she handed my ID back to me with a smile. "Happy birthday."

"Thank you." I returned her smile, but inside I couldn't believe that once Maya had presented me with the nail polish at lunch, I'd completely forgotten it was my birthday. Not that it mattered since my parents were gone and we hadn't planned a party.

As we left the bank, cashier's check in hand for fourteen grand, my stomach protested. I wanted a burger. "I'm hungry."

"Me too."

"Uhm, I think I'll go back to being a vegetarian though."

"Why would you do a thing like that?"

Why, indeed? It was nearly unthinkable. "I don't like what it does to me. It's weird losing control over food."

He chortled. "But you enjoy it so much."

"Whatever. I've survived my whole life without meat." I groaned anyway.

Zack laughed. "Atta girl."

I ordered a bean and cheese burrito while Zack got

tacos. I did my damnedest to ignore the aroma of the beef while we ate. After we made the exchange with Mr. Peters, we headed to my house, me in the Mustang and Zack in his Jeep.

The top was still down and the breeze whipped around me. It felt almost as good as my nightly runs, free and unchained. I lovingly steered my beloved car into the driveway and Zack pulled in right behind me. Locking the Mustang, I tossed the keys into his waiting hands. As I walked with him to the front stoop, his eyes scanned the area. For Daniel, I assumed.

Once inside the house, I dropped my purse. "Thank you for everything today. You keep rescuing me." I tilted my head and shifted my weight from one leg to the other, my gaze meeting his. "Except for John, I've never been friends with a guy who didn't hit on me."

Zack's lips curved. "Who says we're friends?"

Irritation crept up on me. I opened my mouth to tell him how right he was and that we weren't friends, but he cut me off by holding up a hand. "Just kidding. Speaking of hitting on you, whatever possessed you to date a guy like Daniel?"

Backing up, I sat on the couch and took off my shoes, folding my legs under my butt. "Daniel could be charming when he wanted to be."

"There's nothing charming about him now." Zack sat on the other end and turned to face me.

"Agreed." I pursed my lips in thought. "So, why are you helping me?"

"When I went through this, I was alone and it sucked."

"Went through what?" I asked.

"What *you're* going through. You're changing. You're stronger, your senses are heightened and you heal almost instantly. Right?"

"Yes," I whispered, wondering how he knew. "Why did I change? In the library, you told Daniel that you and he were the same. I'm like you guys?"

He shook his head. "No."

"Then what am I?"

He sighed. "I'm not a hundred percent sure. But you're definitely not like us."

Great. He didn't know what I was. But he knew what *he* was and he knew about the black wolf. I wanted my theory ruled out once and for all. "What are *you*?" I held my breath.

His gaze fixed on me. "I already told you the other day."

CHAPTER EIGHTEEN

HE'D SAID HE was a werewolf. If he was just mess-ing with me, I didn't want him to think I half believed him. I narrowed my eyes. "Tell me again."

Zack glanced at the window. "It's dark. Let's go for a walk."

"Why?"

"So I can show you." He rose from the sofa.

We left the house together and I walked with him in silence, trying not to think about the reason for our outing. Why was I even going with him into the woods when the whole idea was absurd?

He led me to my spot in the clearing and stopped in the center. How did he know where to go? The little hairs on my arm stood at attention as chills swept over my body. No, it couldn't be. "How did you know I was changing?"

Zack bent one leg with the other bearing his weight, hands in his pocket. "For days, I kept catch-ing a hint of something extra when I got really close to you, something not human. Since it was so faint, I kept thinking it was my imagination. I found myself following you, just to see if maybe I could catch you doing something superhuman."

That explained why Zack always seemed to be everywhere. He'd been watching, but not because he liked *me*. He'd probably never like me. My throat tightened.

Oblivious, as usual, to my inner turmoil, Zack continued. "Every time I tried to go in for a better whiff, you were onto me. I couldn't satisfy my nose without you thinking I was a perv. So when I walked you home after dinner last night, I poked around while you went upstairs. Your sweater was draped over the couch, so I sniffed that and anything else I could find. I still wasn't sure, but I had a feeling. Like, I just knew."

"Knew what?"

"You're not human."

Considering my strength and other abilities, not being human wasn't a stretch. I took a shaky breath. "And you're not human either?"

"No. I told you about that our first day of car shopping." The corners of his mouth lifted. "But you didn't believe me."

"Of course I didn't believe you." Werewolf. Werewolf. Werewolf. The word echoed in my head, but the idea was too crazy for me to fully let it in.

"Oh, and I forgive you for laughing at me," he said dryly. "But, in all fairness, you looked way hot that night and I'm still a guy." He gave me a lopsided smile.

Right. I'd told the wolf about Zack stuttering when he'd seen me.

"You're the black wolf," I said, trying to make myself believe what I'd just said. I covered my face and squeezed my eyes shut, disappointed that the connection I felt with the wolf probably wasn't felt by Zack. Wait, was I going to buy into this and believe in werewolves? I took a step back. "This is getting out of hand. I'm not sure about this whole supernatural thing. It's too much. I think... I think I need to go."

"You want to see me change into a wolf?"

No, because then it would be real. "Y-yes."

"Damn." He pointed to his pants. "When I morph, I'll leave a pile of clothes. When I turn back, I'll be naked. Before I become human again, I'll bark twice so you can turn around."

"You're going to morph right now?"

He closed his eyes and spread his arms like wings, his body shimmering. Then he disappeared. That lasted a split second before the black wolf stood on all fours, a pile of clothes at his paws.

There he was. My wolf. With his beautiful green eyes. I had to be losing my mind. But Zack just changed into a freaking wolf, which meant werewolves existed and I was perfectly sane. How was that possible?

He barked, but I only stared. He barked two more times. Still, I couldn't move.

The wolf locked the pants in his teeth and dragged them into a clump of bushes. A moment later, Zack emerged wearing them, still naked from the waist up. Since his boxers were still on the ground, I knew they weren't on him. At a time like this, I really didn't need to know he was going commando.

A spattering of hairs over Zack's chest made a narrow trail leading into the waist of his jeans. His chest was well-defined; above his hips, the muscles at his sides flared up and out. I swallowed. At that moment, I couldn't think of anything more beautiful than him.

Plucking his boxers off the grass, Zack shoved them into his back pocket, then slipped his arms through the shirt, leaving the front unbuttoned. "You were supposed to turn around."

His voice distracted me from his washboard stomach and brought me to the present.

Oh. My. God. Zack was a werewolf. It had been him, the black wolf, every night in the woods. The werewolf theory fit with Jeff's story that Daniel had been dragged away by a wolf, before Daniel's drastic change.

"We ran together. I talked to you as a wolf. Trusted you. All this time, you knew and I didn't. You should've told me." I glared at him. "You sneaky—"

"I *couldn't* tell you." His voice rose, matching mine in volume, his hands balled into fists. "You were a human."

"According to you, I'm *not* human."

"I didn't know that at the time. Besides," his muscles relaxed, a smile forming, "I *did* tell you."

"You were joking and knew I wouldn't believe it." We were getting nowhere and I was no closer to finding out about myself than before.

"We don't reveal ourselves to mortals. The penalty is death. When I realized you weren't human, I tried to tell you, but you shut me down. You weren't ready."

I searched my memory for anytime he'd hinted, then gasped in disgust.

"Informing me that I *stunk* was your way of telling me you were a werewolf? Are you kidding me?" I breathed deeply to keep from slapping him.

He opened his mouth, but shut it when I held up a hand.

"Never mind." I squeezed my eyes shut for an instant in an effort to wipe away the frustration. Now was the time for prying information from Zack, not arguing. "Let's move on. You said we can't reveal ourselves to mortals. Where does your mom fit into all this? Does she know?"

"No. At first, I thought I was coming down with something and didn't want to worry her. By the time I figured it out, I didn't want to burden her with all the things that went with it. Then I learned some werewolf law and realized I couldn't tell her because she's human." He gave a quick laugh as he bent down to put on his socks and shoes. "All this time, I haven't been able to tell anyone."

He'd been all alone in his weirdness, unless... "So someone bit you? Is that how you turned?"

"No, my mom had no clue she was marrying a werewolf."

Which of my parents were supernatural? Did the other know? Maybe it wasn't hereditary in my case. For all I knew, they could be human and I would be alone in this, too. Except for Zack, but he wasn't exactly a friend. More like he was just fulfilling a duty.

So what was I? My head spun with too many questions that weren't going to get answered tonight. Suddenly, my limbs sagged and I just wanted to crawl into bed. "Do you ever wish you were just a normal person?"

"It is what it is. I deal." He slipped on a shoe and glanced up at me. "And so will you."

But I didn't want to anymore. Not tonight. "I'm going home." I turned to leave.

Zack leaped up, leaving his laces untied. "What?"

"Maybe I just need a good night's sleep." I shook my head, my throat aching.

He grasped my hand and pulled me to face him. "It's a lot to absorb and you're confused. You'll get through this, just like I did."

I nodded, staring at his chest. His beautiful, smooth chest.

He pressed me closer and stroked my hair. "Soon, it'll all be second nature and you'll wonder how you ever survived as a mere human."

"Why don't you like me?" I mumbled into his shirt.

Zack chuckled softly in my ear. "I just morphed into a wolf right in front of you and you ask *that*?" He gently pushed me away, turning around to tie his shoe. "It doesn't matter if I like you. I'm not staying here and wherever I go, you can't come with me."

"Why?" I sounded pathetic, but at that point didn't care.

He stood and stepped toward me. "I don't have much experience with... whatever you are—none, actually. I suspect you're a shifter. If I'm right, couple months from now, you'll be lucky if you're still alive."

CHAPTER NINETEEN

"LUCKY IF I'M still alive?" I squeaked.

"Yeah, you're in enough danger without hanging out with a werewolf."

"How would I be in danger, just because I'm a shape-shifter hanging out with you?"

Pacing a few feet from me, he ran a hand through his hair, then spun and faced me again, his expression solemn. "I don't know for sure *what* you are."

"But you have a pretty good hunch I'm a shifter or you wouldn't have suggested it."

"Yes." He surveyed the forest. "We should finish the conversation at your house. Daniel could be lurking."

Back at my house, we settled in my living room, me on the sofa with my legs curled underneath me and Zack in the recliner.

"Why is it dangerous to be a shape-shifter? Explain," I demanded, locking my fingers together so I wouldn't chew my nails.

"Werewolves don't get along with shifters. We either hunt them for sport or use them as slaves. Which is why you can never let Daniel get close to you again. He didn't figure it out today, because your scent is still so light. He probably doesn't even know about shape-shifters yet. But if he pulls something and you fight back, he'll see how strong you are and know something's up."

I'd been feeling like a wuss for getting pinned by Daniel, but now relief washed over me that I hadn't struggled more. He would've figured it out and I'd be toast right now.

"The man in the cowboy hat and the guy in black—the ones we saw at the dealerships? If we see either of those guys again, you have to remember to stay away from them. If they smell you..." Zack pressed his lips into a straight line.

"I could become a slave?" I cut him off before he could finish. "If you have no experience with shifters, how do you know they're slaves? It's ridiculous to think slavery would still be going on in this day and age."

"There's always been slavery of one kind or another throughout history. Besides, werewolves are old-school. They still have a king and they follow werewolf law above human law."

A chill ran up my spine, imagining one of those guys taking me prisoner. "They're creepy. I'd avoid them anyway, even if you didn't say a thing."

"Good. Your scent will probably get more noticeable as you get older and stronger. So long as you keep your distance, you'll be fine. I think. If Daniel figures it out and tells the scouts about you—"

"Scouts?" So much to learn.

"Both those men were scouts." He rose to sit on the arm of the recliner, probably so he didn't have to crane his neck to see me. "They search for new blood, more men for King Mortimer's army. Young werewolves like me aren't allowed to be on their own. We're either part of a pack where we can be observed or we become scouts and do the king's bidding. He runs a tight ship. Do you have anything to drink?"

"Yeah, sorry." I jumped up and made a dash into the kitchen. "Why such control over everyone?" I asked as I disappeared behind the fridge door.

"I guess any stray wolf is seen as a potential threat who could start his own pack and rise up against him one day."

"Root beer?" I asked.

"Sure."

I didn't like where this conversation was going. "So they're going to take you away to be part of a pack?" After snagging a can from the fridge door, I headed back to Zack.

"That's the plan. I'm eighteen, which means I'm under the king's rule now."

I handed him the soda and began to pace. "Sounds like werewolves aren't free either. We're *all* subject to the werewolf king, right? Except some are treated better than others."

He popped the can and took a sip. "True, but at least I have *some* rights and privileges. You'll have none. For instance, as far as I know, there's no werewolf law preventing Daniel from hurting a shapeshifter. It's totally legal for him to kill you."

I swallowed. "Thank God for human law and that

he thinks I'm human, huh?"

"Yep." He pushed himself off the recliner arm and relocated at the fireplace. "Let's keep it that way."

I'd been so pissed at my parents for carting me from city to city, but that seemed so trivial now. Potential slavery was a much bigger problem. My eyes stung and I averted my gaze. "So if they knew about me, I'd be taken from my family and forced to work all hours and live in squalor?"

He nodded, his expression gave. "Best-case scenario, yeah."

I wanted to weep at what the worst-case scenario might be. I couldn't think about that though. I had to learn everything I could in order to survive. For that, I needed to know everything about werewolves. "So what now? You're eighteen. Why haven't they taken you already?"

"We're allowed to finish school and I'll be able to spend some time with my mom after that. But once she..." He trailed off, leaving the sentence unfinished.

I chewed my lip. I wouldn't want to be in Zack's predicament, about to lose another parent. "You handle the situation with your mom well."

"What choice do I have?" He stared down at his feet a moment, then back at me, his eyes red-rimmed. "Charles—the cowboy you met—wasn't too bad. He said I could stay until my mom's gone, hang around a few days after the memorial service. The other guy, William, wanted to take me now."

"Leave a mother without a son during her last days? That's disgusting," I said, anger rising on Zack's behalf. I flopped back onto the sofa.

"I told him to talk to Charles. I don't think he appreciated that. I'm pretty sure he's the one who bit Daniel so he'd have someone here on his side. Someone at school to spy on me."

Right. They could multiply anytime they wanted. Just great. "To spy?"

"Yeah." Zack's eyes darkened as he picked up a vase from the mantle, then set it down. "Or to steal me from Charles and take credit for me as a new recruit. I don't know. Werewolves have anger issues and they're prone to fighting, but they still have laws they have to follow. The more likely theory is that William's planning something and didn't want to get his hands dirty. An experienced scout can't break the law, but the king is more lenient on new wolves."

"So turning Daniel gives William someone to do his dirty work?" I asked.

"Exactly." He returned to the recliner and sat on the edge of the seat.

"And he turned Daniel of all people," I said. "Anyone else wouldn't be obsessing on me and I wouldn't have to worry about being discovered." It felt like the walls were closing in on me. The more I learned, the less room I had to live any kind of a normal life. I clenched a fist, my jaw tight. "Is there anything good about being a shape-shifter? Anything at all?"

Zack shook his head. "Other than versatility in shape, no."

I glared at him. "Seriously? That's all you got? Could

you make this anymore depressing or harder for me?"

"I'm trying to help." He crushed the now empty can of root beer. "Don't kill the messenger."

"Sorry." I pressed my fingertips to my temples in hopes of holding off the threatening headache. There had to be a way for me to get out of this mess alive. My thoughts drifted to the first time I'd seen that man at the dealership.

"Can you guys talk telepathically?" I asked. "Is that why you and Cowboy Hat just stared at each other?"

"Yeah. We had an entire conversation right there."

"I knew something was up." While I was immensely relieved Zack hadn't gotten involved with drug dealers, the scouts didn't seem any nicer. "Could you talk telepathically with me?"

"Most likely."

As much as I would've loved to try it out with Zack right then, there were more important things on my mind and I didn't want to be distracted. I waved a hand to dismiss the subject. "Let's do that later. I'm more concerned with the scouts and you."

If they were all like Charles and William, we didn't stand a chance. My stomach sank.

"I'm okay for right now. You, on the other hand..." He pressed his lips together for a moment. "We need to get you figured out. See if you really are a shape-shifter. If so, you need to get used to morphing. If someone comes at you, you'll need to be a bear or something to fight. That ability is probably the only thing that will save you."

"I just change into a bear and that's it?" Could it be that easy?

He lifted a shoulder and shook his head. "I don't know. We have all the other superhuman abilities you have, except we're stronger. At least as a bear, you stand a chance. Maybe. In your human form, Daniel will easily overtake you. From now on, you go nowhere without me. Understand?"

"Okay." But what would I do once Zack left town? Maybe the other werewolves would leave too. Maybe they'd take Daniel with them.

"You can't sleep here alone. Either you spend the night at my house or I stay here." He groaned. "I'll have to explain it to my mom in such a way that she doesn't start making wedding plans."

I gave him a dirty look. "Because being stuck to me is so terrible?"

"No." Zack shook his head. "I just don't want to lie to her."

"Then tell her the truth."

"What?" His eyes bulged.

After dealing with my parents' paranoia for so many years, I'd become the expert on spinning the truth. "Tell her my parents are out-of-town and my ex-boyfriend is stalking me. It's all true."

"And what are we going to do with you when I'm at work?"

I mulled that over a moment, tapping my lip with my index finger. "If your mom knows my situation, maybe she'll be okay with me hanging out at your house. After I finish my homework, I can help Cara and your mom with whatever they need."

"When your parents come back, you'll stay with them. You'd be safer among humans. We tend to avoid anything that might bring in the police and expose us."

"Wait. Why do you assume my parents are human?" I tried to think how that could be possible. "If I was born this way, wouldn't they be shape-shifters too?"

"Well, my mom is human. My dad was a werewolf and kept it from my mom. It's possible your mom is human and your *real* dad is a shape-shifter." He hesitated and watched me warily like I was a corn kernel about to pop. "If she had no clue, then this man you think is your father wouldn't know either."

"What?" I rose from the sofa, my gaze riveted to his. "My dad is my dad." He had to be. "I don't have a *real* one too." I knew that as well as I knew my favorite color.

"Relax." Zack stood too, holding up his palms in surrender.

"Don't tell me to relax." My hands balled into fists at my side. "You just told me he's not my real dad."

"Autumn. I'm just throwing out theories. I'm not God and I'm not the werewolf king. I didn't create the universe or turn shape-shifters into slaves. Don't get mad at *me*. I'm telling you what I know. That's what you wanted, right?"

I fell back onto the sofa, staring at the wall ahead of me.

"If your parents were anything, I would've smelled it on their belongings, the photographs, his jacket hanging in the closet and anything else they've touched here. Which means you can never tell them. Autumn?"

Right, because revealing myself to a mortal carries the penalty of death. "I'm tired," I said quietly, still focusing straight ahead.

"We have to go to my house, so I can talk to my mom and pick up some things. Then you can go to bed."

"I want to be alone," I said in soft voice. "Go home, Zack."

He stood in front of me and held out his hand. "I'm not leaving you. But once we get back and I've made sure your bedroom windows are secure, you can do whatever you want."

"If my window is locked, you think that'll stop a werewolf?" I asked doubtfully.

"No. It'll slow things down and they'd make noise. I'd be upstairs before Daniel got to you." He stuck a hand in his pocket and pulled out his cell to eye the screen. "It's getting late. I'd like to get home before my mom falls asleep."

It wouldn't be right to make him miss a visit with his mom because I insisted on being a big baby. Though Zack had to be wrong about my parents, he was trying to help me. So I sucked it up and gave him a smile. It was a weak one, but the best I could muster.

Zack found my keys, ushered me out and locked the door behind us.

"So you realized only yesterday that I wasn't human?" I got in the passenger side of Zack's Jeep and closed the door.

"Around then, yes. I would've found out sooner, but I was too busy not liking you." He started up his car and glanced my way. "After our first dinner and movie with Maya and Trevor, I suspected I'd judged you too quickly."

"What you really mean is you realized what a dumb-ass you'd been." Teasing him helped pull me out of my funk.

"That's one way of looking at it." He snorted. "Anyway, after our trip to Bigger Burgers and you ate meat the same way I ate it when I hit maturity, I was almost positive. You confirmed it when you raced around the meadow that night."

At Zack's house seconds later, we hurried inside to see his mom. "Hi, Mrs. De Luca," I said, shadowing Zack into her room.

"Hello, sweetheart." She gave me a sleepy smile. "And how are you enjoying your new car?"

"Love it. Although by the time we picked it up and had dinner, I didn't have much time to play with it."

"Mom," Zack said. "Autumn has a situation. Her ex-boyfriend is harassing her and her parents are out-of-town. She shouldn't be alone in that house. I'm going to grab a few things and spend the night there."

"To protect her?" Mrs. De Luca's looked doubtful. "Shouldn't you report this to the police?" she asked.

"They can't act on anything unless he does something, right?" I asked.

"True. Using *your* reasoning, Autumn's even safer with us, because there are more people here." She smiled and patted his hand. "She'll take your room and you can sleep on the couch."

"Yes, ma'am." He looked at me pleadingly as if I could figure a way out.

"My parents are out-of-town the rest of the week. I've already imposed on your hospitality enough." It was all I could come up with.

His mom glanced from me to him. "Are you sure this isn't an excuse so you two can have some *privacy*?"

Zack gaped, his eyes huge.

CHAPTER TWENTY

"MOM, HER EX *really is* harassing her. He cornered her today at school. And it's not a matter of *privacy*," Zack said. "I'm eighteen now and it would be nice if you didn't treat me like a child."

"Fine." She smiled at him, a smile full of a mother's love. "I trust you. Sleep at Autumn's, but call me in the morning."

"I will."

"So how was your day?" she asked him as though he wasn't about to go spend the night alone with a girl.

Zack answered, but I itched for a run in the woods and wished we'd taken advantage while we were in the forest earlier. I hoped the chitchat ended soon.

A chorus rang out as Favianne's bedroom door opened. "Happy birthday to you," they sang. Cara, Mac, Trevor and the two boys each held up a cupcake with a candle, their lips moving in unison.

By the time they finished, my eyes were wet. "How did you know?"

"I heard the bank teller tell you happy birthday." Zack grinned, but I wasn't sure if it was from joy at celebrating my birthday or if he took pleasure in embarrassing me.

"That was hours ago," I said stupidly.

He snorted. "I don't have short-term memory loss, Autumn."

Duh.

Twenty minutes later, his family had gone and I tossed the last bite of a second cupcake into my mouth. "That was nice of your family. And you," I added. "Thank you."

"You're welcome." He dropped a duffle bag on his bed and threw clothes in it.

I pointed at his bag. "You need help?"

"No, I'm good." He zipped it up and hefted it over his shoulder. "If you want to drive around in your car the next few days, I can leave the Jeep here and give my keys to Trevor."

If we went anywhere, Zack would be stuck with me. I'd have him all to myself and he'd be at my mercy. I tried to act nonchalant as my anticipation mounted. "Sure. Trevor would like that."

Zack collected a few more things and we headed to my house where I changed into sweats.

"You seem like you're feeling better. You still want to be locked up in your room after our run?" Zack asked.

If only he had plans for me. Plans that involved making out on the sofa. I inwardly sighed and focused on answering him. "I'm okay, but I have more questions for you when we get back."

I held my index finger vertically against my lips,

then let us out the back and locked the door. We made no more noise than the wind as we soared over the fences and through the neighbors' yards. Finally, the forest closed around us.

"Are you going to turn into a wolf?" I asked.

"I need to, yes. When I morphed earlier, it wasn't long enough."

"You *need* to?" I asked. Zack made it sound as though he had little choice.

"Shape-shifters have more control, which is why they can reproduce," he explained. I must have looked baffled, because he chuckled and continued. "With any shape-shifter or werewolf, once they morph, the unborn baby dies. Our urge to shift is overwhelming. The only way we can increase our population is for a male to mate with a human, like my dad with my mom. Or we turn them."

"Like what happened to Daniel."

"Right," Zack said. "If shape-shifters stay in their human form, which is easy for them, they can carry to term."

"You explained that so officially. I swear, Zack, sometimes you sound like an old man."

His brows furrowed. "What do you mean?"

"You talk so adult-like."

Zack swooped to pick a twig from the ground and absentmindedly studied it. "I started taking care of my mom when I turned sixteen and got my license. Before that, I helped with the grocery shopping, cleaned. I even helped pay the bills. So I've been on my own for a while. Responsibility catches up with you after a while, I guess."

"Oh." I felt bad for bringing it up. "But if you have no experience with shape-shifters, how do you know so much?"

"Books." He perked up, a smile forming. "My dad left me a box of things and made my mom promise to keep them forever. It was a whole box of stuff—old yellowing pages with drawings of werewolves, stories of legends and werewolf law. I think my dad knew there was a chance he wouldn't be around and wanted to make sure I had everything I needed. I loved those books. Not because they represented a world I could escape into, but because my dad left them for me."

I followed him as he weaved through the trees. "And when strange things started happening to your body, you realized everything you'd read in the books was real, that your dad left them to guide you."

Zack glanced over his shoulder, smiling. "Yeah. There's info on shape-shifters too, but I didn't study that as hard, since it didn't apply. Tomorrow, after school, I'll drop you off at my house and you can read them while you wait for me to come home from work."

I giggled. He made me sound like his wife. "Yes, honey."

"Let's run." He leaped, turning into a wolf in mid-air and leaving his clothes behind. I chased after him.

† † †

"Next time I bark twice, that means *turn around*," Zack enunciated slowly. "I'm tired of dressing in the bushes."

"Sorry." I dropped the house key on the kitchen table. "I thought you were trying to tell me something."

He blew out his breath. "I was!"

I suppressed a giggle. "Sorry. I'll remember next time."

He turned the deadbolt on the front door. "Stay here and I'll check the house."

Zack moved so fast, my eyes barely kept up. He made a blur as he zoomed upstairs, stayed there for several seconds, then downstairs again to zip from window to window.

"All clear." He stopped in front of me. "It's late. We should get to bed."

Bed. Zack. Bed. "Okay." I stared at him.

"Maybe you should show me where I'll be sleeping?" He looked at me expectantly.

"Right. My dad's office has a futon that might give you more room than the couch."

He mulled that over. "Where's your dad's office?"

"Across from my room." Maybe Zack would be tempted in the middle of the night...

"I'll take the sofa," he said quickly. "Got a blanket?"

No stranger to disappointment where Zack was concerned, I found a sheet, a couple pillows and a soft, clean blanket in the hallway cabinet. I brought them to him and pointed in the opposite direction. "You can use the bathroom down there."

"I remember where it is." His eyes fixed on mine.

I shifted uncomfortably. "Well, I guess it's goodnight then." I paused a moment and turned to go.

"Autumn."

I stopped and turned back, my chest swelling with hope. "Yes?"

"Don't lock your door. Don't even close it." Our eyes met and the seconds passed. "If anyone comes for you, I need to be able to hear. Goodnight."

Fear nipped at me. How would I be able to sleep thinking Daniel might come after me? I nodded and headed up the stairs.

In my bed, I stared at the ceiling and prayed sleep would come. Anytime I heard a noise, my head flipped toward my window to make sure nobody was trying to break in. Plus, I kept expecting Zack to sneak into my room. Actually, I wasn't *expecting* it to happen. I knew him too well to think he was that easy.

But I hoped.

† † †

The smell of unwashed wolf closed in on me, fur tickling my skin and fetid breath in my face. I trembled, hot tears burning my eyes. The wolf snarled and I scrambled back as he leapt toward me.

"Autumn. Autumn, wake up." Zack pulled me off the pillow by my shoulders.

I lifted my head and rubbed my eyes, trying to wipe away the mental fuzz. But I was aware enough to notice my comforter wasn't anywhere near us, certainly not separating me from him. I must have kicked it off during my nightmare.

"Are you okay?" Zack was sitting directly in front

of me, his thighs straddling mine, heat from his bare skin radiating through me.

I nodded.

He exhaled in relief and leaned back to sit on his heels. "Heard you scream and I ran up here. Been calling your name over and over, but you wouldn't wake up. Scared me for a minute there."

I'd been having that same dream where I was being chased. "I was running from wolves."

He brushed a finger down my cheek. "It was just a dream."

"More like a nightmare," I whispered, my gaze locking onto his. He wore nothing but a pair of boxers. As my ragged breath slowed, I realized the only other thing between us was my threadbare tank top and skimpy panties.

"Autumn." His breathing quickened and he growled so low it sounded like a purr. Then he tilted my face to meet his and drew closer until I felt his breath on my skin. "You're too beautiful."

CHAPTER TWENTY-ONE

I WANTED TO scream for Zack to kiss me, but I held my breath, afraid if I said anything or moved, he'd go away again. When I met his gaze, every nerve in my body came alive. Slowly, he moved toward me, then his lips brushed mine and lingered for a brief moment. He drew back just a hair and gazed into my eyes as an almost inaudible moan escaped him.

Then his mouth was on mine.

My lips parted and when our tongues tangled, I savored the taste of him and his sweet, earthy scent. Way better than anything I'd ever imagined. I felt his hands at my sides, his fingers splayed at my waist and his thumbs just under my ribs. Our lips separated and his gentle pressure eased me backward until my head rested against the pillow. The mattress gradually took his weight as he lay over me.

Heat seared through my limbs.

I sighed as his mouth met mine again. My fingertips made a feather-light trail up his spine, then back down. I was rewarded with a shiver. As he cradled my face in his hands with his fingertips at the nape of my neck, his thumb grazed my temple. He gently turned my face and his mouth followed the curve of my jaw, the tip of his tongue burning a path to my ear.

With my palms against his lower back, I brought him closer. A low growl reached my ear and he buried his face in my neck.

"Oh, God, Autumn. I can't do this."

"Of course, you can," I said and a breeze from Zack's quick departure hit the bare skin of my legs.

"I'm sorry," he said from my bedroom doorway, then disappeared.

My limbs trembled and my heart was still pounding. I curled up in a ball, wishing for the ache to go away. What had I been thinking? I'd known him a little over a week and was already giving myself away to someone who'd rejected me over and over. I needed to get a grip.

But I'd gotten my kiss and it was everything I'd fantasized about.

† † †

"Autumn. Wake up. We have to leave in a half hour and I need to stop at my house. With all the Daniel drama yesterday, I forgot my homework."

Rubbing my eyes, I glanced over my shoulder at Zack in the doorway wearing only boxers and tousled hair. I lay curled up on my side, still without my comforter. He stood almost behind me, which gave him a clear view of whatever my skimpy panties didn't cover.

As if realizing he'd entered dangerous territory

with me, he backed up and bumped into the doorway. Righting himself, he yanked the door shut behind him.

I chuckled. Served him right after the kiss-and-dis the night before.

After showering, I quickly got dressed and dashed to the fridge to get a snack for later. But I'd pillaged it over the last few days and there was nothing edible left. If Zack would be staying here, I needed to go shopping.

"Autumn? You ready?" Zack called from the front door.

I grabbed my backpack and followed him outside.

"Do you mind if I drive?" he asked.

I tossed him my keys and climbed in the passenger side. Once we were on the road, he took a deep, meaningful breath.

Uh-oh, here it comes.

"About last night." He snuck a peek at me, then focused on the road ahead.

"Yeah?"

"You're *really* pretty. Any guy would be insane not to want to hook up with you."

I felt another rejection coming on.

"Sorry." The Mustang slowed as it hugged the curb. Zack gave me an apologetic look. "I'll be fast."

I waited in the car, while he dashed inside the house to get his homework. About a minute later, he flew out the front door and down the steps, then jumped into the driver's seat without opening the door.

"You were saying?" I prodded, wanting to get it over with.

Zack inserted the key in the ignition, but didn't start the car. He swiveled in his seat to face me. "My mom is getting worse every day and I'm not going to be here once she's gone. I can't stay. You know that."

Right. I'd forgotten about all that. Zack, on the other hand, lived with the knowledge every day. What must it be like to know that your parent could die at any time and nothing could save her? I'd probably avoid attachments too, then bail first chance I got.

"It was late," Zack continued. "I was groggy. You were wearing so little and you made me forget. But I can't forget again. You're a nice girl, Autumn, but with my mom's situation and work and school and the scouts, there's nothing left of me. You deserve better than that."

I wanted to tell him that I deserved *him* and the feelings between us. But my pride went with, "Fine. Whatever."

Zack took a deep breath. "We need to concentrate on getting you through your first morph, educating you on shape-shifters—with what little info we have—and making sure you're safe."

I nodded and stared out the window, my eyes stinging.

The engine roared to life and the car began to move, but I barely noticed. I had this amazing guy who liked me—at least enough to make out with me—and he could never be mine. Where was the justice?

I needed something to take my mind off Zack and how I couldn't have him. "Why don't you turn your mom into a werewolf? Then she'd be strong and healthy, right?"

"I can't turn her for the same reason my dad couldn't. She's too frail. If we bite someone and they're weak, the wolf virus kills them. If they're strong, they fight the virus and develop an immunity of sorts. Except it's more like a *unity*. The healthy human cells meld with the wolf cells, creating a powerful human that's also a wolf."

Zack found a spot close to the school entrance and handed me the keys. "I've been thinking. Daniel might give up on you if he thinks we're a couple."

Sounded interesting. "So we should act cozy?"

"Yeah." His eyes darted away.

"I can pretend if you can." But I hoped it wouldn't be too painful for me once the charade was over. I reached for the door handle.

"If anything happens and I'm not there after your last class, leave without me."

I spun in my seat. "No. Because this time, Gina won't be in the way and you'll be waiting for me. I'm not going to desert you, so you end up walking home. Or worse."

"Fine," he mumbled, opening his door.

Students gaped as we got out of my car together. Zack rounded the hood and walked by my side, his arm protectively draped around my waist. Gina glared at me from near the bike racks. Standing next to her, Daniel looked like steam would billow from his ears at any moment. I spared him a glance before spotting John who gave me two thumbs up.

It felt comfortable and safe with Zack by my side touching me. And yummy. I had to remind myself we weren't really a couple.

"She has to go to the bathroom. Now." Maya faced Zack as though daring him to challenge her.

He laughed. "I'll be waiting."

Yes, he would. Right outside the bathroom door. He'd probably even listen in with his super-human hearing. I'd have to be careful what I told Maya.

Dragging me through the hallway, she eyed a girl going into the bathroom ahead of us. There went our privacy. She stopped right outside the door, position-ing us in the corner. I spotted John approaching. He huddled up with us.

"What is going on with you two? Trevor said Zack spent the night at your house," she whispered.

Word traveled fast.

"He did?" John asked. "Your taste in guys has im-proved."

"It's not like that," I said.

She folded her arms over her chest. "Liar."

"She likes him," John said.

"Did he kiss you yet?" she asked.

"If he spent a whole night alone with her and didn't try to hook up with her, he's clearly gay," John said.

I laughed and held up a hand to stop further prob-ing, though good-natured and well-deserved. "I'm not denying he's gorgeous or that I like him. But guys," all humor left my voice, "he doesn't want a relation-ship. When his mom is gone, he will be too." I lowered my voice. They didn't need to know all the details, but I didn't want to have to pretend with my closest friends. Plus, they could help keep an eye on Daniel.

"Zack stayed over, because Daniel..."

"What?" Maya asked, eyes narrowed.

"He cornered me yesterday after school," I answered. "I was a little freaked out, but I don't think he's dangerous. Zack is just being overly cautious."

Her head rocked up and down, eyes bigger than usual. "I knew he was a pig, but I didn't think he'd stoop that low. I'm so sorry. But you got a night with Zack." She grinned. "All's well that ends well."

"Maya, you are so bad." My mouth dropped open as I playfully slapped her arm.

"So, did anything happen last night?" she prodded.

"Uh, that's my cue to leave." John grimaced. "I don't need the gory details. See ya."

"'Bye." I shot John a smile as he took off. Sensing Zack close by, I chose my words carefully. "I spent the entire night in my room and he slept on the sofa." There. I'd told her the truth and implied exactly what Zack would want—without the little extras.

"That sucks."

"What's the point of wanting someone who doesn't want me back?" I couldn't have Zack thinking I was pining for him. "How are things with you and Trevor?"

"Heavenly. We've only been dating a week or so, but it feels like we've always been together."

I smiled. "I'm glad one of us is in a normal relationship."

"I can't believe it finally happened." She sighed. "See you at lunch."

Maya rushed off to class and Zack ushered me down the hallway. "You better not make me late. Nicely done, by the way," he said.

No remark at all on my comment about not wanting him, but that was just as well.

† † †

At lunch, I invited John and Janine to eat with us. Where I sat, I could see Daniel. Jeff sat with him again, along with Gina. She and Daniel huddled up next to each other, Gina frequently brushing up against him.

Daniel's eyes cut to mine. As he held my gaze, he kissed Gina. So they were out in the open about being together. Poor Gina had no idea what she was getting herself into.

I shuddered.

Maybe having Gina at his disposal will keep Daniel off you.

The words came into my head and I jumped. But they didn't come in through my ears. It was like an *impression* of words, like when you hear something and replay it in your head another time. A slow smile spread over Zack's face.

You heard me. Good.

Can you hear me? I asked.

Zack grinned. *Very good, Grasshopper.*

Rumors are already starting that we're together. If we keep talking like this, people will think we're making eyes at each other. I snickered inwardly.

You don't need eye contact to mind talk.

I focused on the other end of the room.

I don't care what people think, do you? He threw a balled-up napkin at me. *I say we give them something to talk about.*

John leaned over and whispered into my ear. "He's *so* into you."

Knowing Zack heard that, I laughed and elbowed John. I'd missed him.

† † †

After school, Zack dropped me off at his house and stayed parked at the curb until I went inside. The place appeared deserted, but I heard distant noises, like kids playing in the backyard.

Something delicious tickled my nose. I followed the scent of garlic to the oven and peered in at the casserole. It reminded me that I needed food at home. If I left now, I'd have the groceries put away and maybe have time for homework before Zack got back.

Since his family didn't know I'd arrived, they wouldn't miss me if I snuck out. I sprinted to my house, stopping in front of the Taurus. Zack had my new car, which meant I'd have to drive the old nasty one. So wrong.

Inside my house, Zack's scent rushed me. It was strong enough to make me wonder for a split second if he was there. If my parents came home, and if they were shape-shifters, they'd smell Zack all over the place. Not only would they ground me the rest of my life for having a boy overnight, but they'd forbid me to hang out with a werewolf. I shouldn't take any chances.

I gave the place a quick scrub, wiping down the sofa where he'd probably been sweating, as well as the kitchen countertops and table. Then I made my shopping list, thankful I hadn't spent all the money my parents had wired.

An hour later, car loaded with groceries, I neared my house. As the lawn came into view, I noticed an unfamiliar car sitting in our driveway. I parked and cautiously approached the front porch. A shadow appeared beyond the screen door just before it opened.

CHAPTER TWENTY-TWO

"DAD!" I LEAPED into his arms and he swung me around, laughing. When my feet touched ground again, I hugged my mom fiercely. "I'm so glad you're back. I've missed you guys." I hadn't realized how much.

My mom released me, but kept my hand. "We missed you, too."

Dad scanned the immediate area, his eyes landing on the Taurus. "Where's that new car you emailed us about?"

Uh-oh. I couldn't tell them that Zack had my car or about the whole Daniel situation. Why make them worry? Zack and I were officially going nowhere and, besides, I had everything under control.

"The mechanic has it." Which was the truth. "You'll see it tomorrow. I thought you were staying in Arizona a few more days. Why didn't you tell me you were coming back?"

"It's all good," my mom said, squeezing my hand. "Your father heard from one of the other jobs. They're in a bigger hurry than we thought and the pay is substantial enough to make us speed things up. It's a small job in Montana, so we thought we'd go there and come back in a couple weeks."

"You're *both* going?" Without being blackmailed into it?

"Is something wrong? You sounded happy in the emails, so we thought you'd like a little more alone time." She studied my face and pressed a warm palm to my cheek.

I smiled. "I really missed you guys."

"Everything going okay?" my dad asked.

"School is still tolerable and I have a new car. Couldn't be better." And it was all the truth. So long as I had Zack in my life, I knew everything would be fine.

"You think you can do without us for a couple more weeks?" he asked. "It might end up being a little longer, but not by much. If it's a problem, your mother can stay."

I missed my mom and her cooking, but Zack's aunt's cooking kicked ass too. Plus, I still needed to learn to morph and if they were human, I couldn't have them around while I practiced. If they were shifters... Since they weren't grilling me at the moment, they probably had no clue a werewolf had been in their house.

If only I could ask them what they were.

"I'll be fine," I assured them. "I'm glad you guys will be together. When you're not working, you can sight-see in Montana together. Like an extended vacation."

Mom pulled me close. "That's what we thought. But did you *want* to come?"

As much as I'd love to be with them, no way was I leaving. "Prom is coming soon. Last year I missed it, because Dad got a job and we moved."

Now that I thought about it, why was prom so important when I didn't have a date? I couldn't imagine Zack taking me. Even for pretend. It would be far too personal for him—and too much like a real date. But what if his feelings changed up the road and he asked me?

"You can stay." Dad ruffled my hair. I loved his playfulness, but not that particular gesture.

"How soon are you leaving?" I asked.

Mom checked her watch. "In about forty-five minutes."

"Seriously?" My mouth dropped open. "You're not even spending the night?"

Dad shook his head. "They'd like me on the job tomorrow."

I glanced from one to the other, unable to squeak out a response.

Mom slung an arm around my shoulder. "Look at it this way. The sooner we leave, the sooner we come back. And since we already have a rental," she nodded toward the car in the driveway, "you don't have to drive us to the airport. Let's go inside."

"Wait. I have to put away the groceries."

"Which reminds me, we made another deposit into your account for food or whatever else comes up," she said.

"But I still have money left over from the car."

Dad held the door open for me. "We trust you to manage it wisely. I'll get the bags out of the car."

"Okay." Who were these people? Why such generosity now when before I had to pay back every penny or stay grounded? Why weren't they worrying and fussing over me? Why weren't they interrogating me on my friends and whether I'd seen any weirdoes lurking in the bushes? They'd done a complete one-eighty. Not that I minded. It was just very, very strange.

My dad lightened the Taurus' load, then my mom began putting the food away.

"I can do that," I told her.

She waved me away. "I want to see if you're still eating healthy."

Good. They hadn't been taken over by the pod people after all. No way would I mention the hamburgers.

My mom quickly went through the bags, eyeing the contents with approval. I folded each one as she emptied it. "You bought a ton of stuff. Feeding an army?"

Only Zack, one meal a day, which made up for the meal I had at his house. "I don't want to go shopping again anytime soon, so I got enough to last a while."

"That's my girl." Mom smiled, her eyes twinkling as she closed the fridge door.

They brought out a couple more suitcases from the attic and filled them up, then collected last-minute items. I glanced at the time on my cell, knowing Zack would be home soon. When he discovered I wasn't there, he'd come looking for me.

If my mom and dad were shape-shifters, a werewolf's presence would stress them out. If they were merely human, an unknown guy coming to the house while they were supposed to be away might put them on alert. They might even cancel their trip.

I darted upstairs to text Zack, telling him about

my parents and not to come over. Dashing back down-stairs, I followed them outside and sat on the front porch as they loaded up. Dad tossed a bag in the trunk before scanning the vicinity. My mom mimicked the move. It was strange the way they kept tabs on every-thing around them. It reminded me of how Zack always looked around to make sure danger wasn't lurking.

I approached them at the curb. "Is something wrong?"

"Why would you ask that?" She smiled in that way that told me I was her everything.

Suddenly, it all seemed right again. "I don't know. Just checking."

"Don't worry. We'll have a productive trip and be back soon," my dad assured me.

They finished loading and closed the trunk while I hovered. We did a three-way hug and they drove away. I waved until I couldn't see their car anymore.

Alone again.

Finding my phone, I texted Zack and gave him the all clear. He replied right away telling me to stay put, make sure the doors were locked and he'd be there in a few minutes. But I was fine. It was still light outside. Daniel wouldn't make an appearance knowing I had protection. Would he?

While I waited for Zack, I checked my email, then scribbled out a check for the bill Timothy had emailed for Zack's time.

True to his word, Zack drove up moments later and honked. I ran outside and he flicked a thumb to-ward the passenger side. "Get in," he said. "We're going to my house for dinner."

"And we can't walk one block?" I raised one brow.

"While we're there, I can pick up more of my things. Easier to drive my stuff back than carry it."

I hopped in. "Fine, but on the way back, I get to drive. Tomorrow too."

"Sure, it's your car. What's the deal with your parents?"

"Just stopping by between jobs. Dad thinks it'll take two weeks, then they'll be back. I don't know whether to be relieved or concerned. It's so unlike them not to drag me along."

"From what you say, they've never had any real time alone together. Maybe they realize it's not such a bad thing."

"You're probably right," I said.

At Zack's house, the smell of garlic and basil and other spices greeted me. I wondered what surprises waited for me in that casserole I'd peeked at earlier. "What's for dinner?"

"Smells like baked ziti. You're in for a treat. God, I love my Aunt Cara." He grinned.

Zack was right. It was delicious. After we ate and I helped him clean up, we did our homework. When we'd finished, we visited his mom. A few minutes later, he left me alone with her while he gathered more of his things.

"How are you and Zack getting along?" she asked.

"Fine. But—" I held her hand between mine, about to tell her that we didn't want to start something we weren't going to finish. But I couldn't do it. "We're taking things slow."

"You're such a nice girl. I'm glad he found you." She smiled sweetly and I ached for Zack, because this beautiful, wonderful woman would be leaving him soon. I barely knew her and my heart felt heavy as I contemplated her fate. Zack's fate too. He had to feel a hundred times worse than me and would miss her a thousand times more.

He came in, kissed her on the cheek and tucked the blanket around her. "Goodnight, Mom."

When I got into the driver's side of the Mustang, I saw a duffle bag and a box filled with tattered books and yellowed papers. "What's that stuff?"

He threw a quick glance into the back seat. "The books my dad left for me. You need to read them. They'll explain things a lot better than I could."

Good. It would occupy my mind. Then maybe I wouldn't notice I was alone in a house with a gorgeous guy who'd already demonstrated his attraction for me, in the yummiest possible way. Was there anything in the world more tempting than that? I didn't think so.

Back home, I curled up on the sofa with a blanket wrapped around me to ward off the frigid temperature of the living room. I'd turned down the air conditioner earlier, so Zack wouldn't sweat on the furniture. I didn't want any more of his scent permeating the house in case my parents returned unexpectedly, as they were prone to do.

But it might be a good idea to turn it back up before I went to bed or my room might be too cold for me to sleep. The last thing I needed was to be up all night, with nothing to think about but the scantily dressed boy on my sofa.

Zack sat in the recliner rereading one of his dad's books. I'd snagged an old, crinkled letter that his dad had written to him years ago. I unfolded the yellowing papers and turned toward the light of the lamp.

Lucio Gavino De Luca told how he'd grown up human, his lack of propriety and complete disregard for others, how he'd been turned into a werewolf and eventually worked for the king as a scout. But the indulgence and decadence had grown old. The abundance of willing women became meaningless and he wanted more from life.

He fell in love with Favianne and had planned to turn her so they could always be together, but then she'd become ill. He resigned himself to having her only a few more years when he learned she was pregnant.

I finished the letter, then read the ending once more.

This, Zack, and the other books your mother gave you, is all you have left of me. Use the knowledge wisely. More importantly, stay free. Value your right to create your own path and not be a part of a pack. Don't make the same choices I made. Don't join the king and don't become a scout. Run, if you must. And above all else, never trust a werewolf. No matter how nice they seem, how convincing they are or what they promise you—it's a lie. Never trust another werewolf.

Know that I am there with you in spirit and remember I loved you more than I could say.

Lucio Gavino De Luca

"Wow. I'm sorry." Tears pricked my eyes. I didn't know what else to say and couldn't decide whether Zack's father should be vilified or praised. Perhaps a little of both. "Your mom must've read this and thought it was pretty weird."

Zack abandoned the book in his hand and moved over to sit with me on the sofa. "She thought he was quite creative for making up such wild stories for me."

"He had a tragic life, trapped for centuries on a path he shouldn't have chosen." I snuggled closer in the blanket, thinking if I should adjust the thermostat now. Before I froze to death. "No wonder you've decided to run."

"Which I think is why he told the story the way he did. He wanted me to know the ugly truth, so I wouldn't make the same choices. My mom describes him very differently. The way she tells it, he was an honorable man who loved life and was always happy to spend every waking moment home with us. She was madly in love with him. Still is." He smiled, a faraway look in his eyes.

"I remember worshipping him," Zack continued, "and being so excited when he'd come home after a long business trip, although at the time I had no idea he was a werewolf or a scout. He spent a lot of time with me when he was home. He'd carry me on his shoulders everywhere we went. Sometimes, we'd work on the car together or we'd go fishing."

"Sounds like maybe he was a good guy, or trying to be."

Zack stared at the old letter still in my hands. "Or not. He was a scout, doing the king's dirty work. Even a bad person can love his wife and son. People can get good at hiding their true selves. And my mom... Love can be blind, so her version isn't all that reliable. Besides, he told me not to trust werewolves. He didn't exclude himself, because he knew werewolves aren't good."

I dropped the papers in my lap and turned to face Zack at the other end of the sofa. "You'll never convince me you're not good, Zack."

"If I was, then why did I bully Daniel the first time I caught him harassing you? He didn't physically provoke me, but he ended up shoved up against the locker anyway."

"You're not bad," I repeated.

"I've done bad things." He shook his head. "I was a total ass to you when we first met and you didn't deserve it."

"We've *all* made mistakes or made wrong decisions, whether human or werewolf. That doesn't make you evil. *Real* evil people don't feel bad about what they've done and they don't try to change." I didn't want Zack living with guilt when he already had so much to deal with, but I didn't want to get on a soapbox either.

My hand had slowly curled around his, but since he hadn't flinched and removed his hand, I left it there. "How did your dad die?"

With his other hand, he played with my pinky ring. "I'm not sure. My mom won't talk about it. All I knew was that one day he never came home." His gaze dropped to my mouth.

Butterflies danced in my belly and I refocused. "I can't imagine what that must be like, to lose a parent that way."

"Hopefully, you'll never know."

"I wish things were different for you, that your dad was still around and you didn't have to run alone."

He stopped twirling my ring and covered my hand with his. "I still miss him."

"I'm so sorry, Zack," I said softly.

My blanket had fallen to my waist and I shivered. His free hand skimmed my shoulder and traveled down my arm to my elbow, the warmth of his skin sending another shiver through my body.

Breaking contact, he took the papers from me and set them on the coffee table. Then he nudged the blanket aside and captured my hips, pulling me down so I lay flat. He hovered over me as if suspended in midair. My gaze locked onto his. I held my breath, waiting as he gradually eased his weight over me. Our lips a breath away, he closed his eyes and slowly inhaled, then opened them again and met my gaze.

Was Zack waiting for me to meet him half way? He'd already rejected me and told me he couldn't get involved. Knowing that, if I encouraged him, wouldn't I deserve the heartache that would surely come?

But I couldn't look away.

"Autumn," he said, so quietly I assumed it was my imagination. "You're not helping."

"You want help?"

"Yes," he pleaded.

To me, that was as good as his blessing to do as I wanted. As *he* wanted. I rose to meet him and nibbled his bottom lip. He moaned, which was all the encouragement I needed. My hands snaked under his loose T-shirt, my thumbs exploring the center line that separated his stomach muscles and led to his chest. He chucked off his shirt and returned to me.

I let my fingernails skate lightly over his shoulder blades and down his spine. He swooped and our tongues entwined, igniting a fire in my belly. I ached, wanting so much more, but then he eased off me just enough to separate our mouths.

"That's not what I meant," he said in a hoarse voice. "You're supposed to have better control than me. You're a *girl*."

It wasn't just that he'd ruined our moment. Again. He'd compounded his crime by saying something stupid. Regardless what came out of his mouth, it still equaled another rejection.

I squeezed my eyes shut and shoved him away. "Didn't you learn *anything* from last night?"

His brows furrowed.

"Did I try to stop you up in my room when we were half naked? No, I didn't. Here's a clue for you: Girls like it too." I gave his shoulder a jab, then rose from the couch and stomped toward the stairs to the thermostat. Even though I was too hot now.

"I'm sorry." He ran a hand through his hair. "Let's go for a run and work off some of our, uh, energy."

† † †

"This time, I won't forget. When you bark twice, I'll turn around," I assured Zack as we distanced ourselves from my house and went deeper into the forest.

"I won't need to bark. I'll talk to you telepathically," he reminded me.

"You can do that in your wolf form?"

"Sure. Everything's almost the same. When we're wolves, we're still just as aware and intelligent. But some things are different. In my human form, I don't want to kill a rabbit and eat it raw and I *do* care about showering and stuff. As a wolf, none of that matters. I chomp down on a fresh kill and I'm in heaven."

"Too much information, Zack," I chided, mentally pushing away the image of the bloody animal.

"Don't worry. I try to resist. I've gotten too paranoid someone will go hunting for whatever they think is killing the wildlife. I don't want to get shot at."

"Let's go." I bolted. I didn't know Zack's normal routine, but I intentionally expended double the energy I usually did. Ideally, once I got home, I'd be too tired to lust after Zack or do anything about it if I did lust.

After a hard run, Zack dressed and we strolled down a path toward the empty field that led to my house. Unsure who may pop up in the woods, I spoke silently. *"If I'm a shape-shifter, why don't I morph?"*

Zack froze, his jaw muscle going tight as he held up his index finger against his lips and squinted. The breeze picked up and I smelled him.

Get up in a tree, as high as you can. Now! he shouted into my head. My heart banged around in my chest, and I shot upward. In a flash, I was there, viewing Zack from above. He slowed his movements, plucking a leaf from a tree and rubbing the smooth, waxy surface. "Daniel. Nice of you to come by for a visit."

"Where is she?"

"Who?" Zack asked.

"Don't mess with me. I can smell her."

"You're not smelling *Autumn*. You're smelling *her scent*. It's actually *me* you smell." Zack flashed him a cocky grin.

Daniel's hands balled into fists. "No, it's too strong. She's close by."

"You think I'd bring a human on a run and let her see me morph? Whoever turned you should've clued you in on the rules by now. Look around if you want though. Keep in mind that I'm staying at her house these days and she's *incredibly* hot." Zack grinned. "Can you think of *any* reason why her scent would be all over me?"

Daniel stiffened, took a step closer and hissed, "I warned you that I wasn't finished with Autumn."

"She's *mine* now. Stay away from her."

I knew Zack was only trying to get Daniel to give up on me, but Zack's words *she's mine now* sent a thrill through my bones anyway.

Daniel growled.

"Careful." Zack angled his body to better dodge an attack. "I've been a werewolf my entire life. Which means I've had eighteen more years than you to build up strength."

"I'll take my chances." Daniel backed up ever so slightly, like he was about to spring.

CHAPTER TWENTY-THREE

"I'M DISAPPOINTED IN you, Daniel."

From the cover of the tree, I scanned the vicinity for the body belonging to the vaguely familiar voice. The next moment, he appeared beside Daniel—the man we'd seen at the dealership dressed in black. But today, he wore faded jeans and a T-shirt. Zack had said he was a scout and had probably been the one to bite Daniel. By his presence now, I guessed Zack was right.

"There's a time and place for everything but *I* say when and where." The scout held perfectly still just before his hand struck out. The force of the blow lifted Daniel off the ground, sending him crashing into a tree trunk. "I could end you as easily as I made you. Do not force me to remind you again." He motioned for Daniel to come, then turned on his heel and strode away.

Daniel rose and followed, his eyes shooting daggers at Zack over his shoulder. When I was sure they were long gone, I dropped to the ground.

It's getting crowded around here, Zack told me silently. *We need to find a new place to run,* Zack said as we headed back to my house.

So you've been morphing since you were born? I asked, pretty sure I'd heard Zack tell me a different story.

No, just the last couple years. He moved a branch out of the way for me.

I hurried past him, avoiding the end of the branch. *That's not the impression you gave Daniel.*

I told him the truth. He can take it however he wants. I learned that from you. Zack flashed me a grin. *But I'd probably still be stronger, because I've got two years on him.*

You think that makes a difference? I sidestepped to avoid an overgrown tree root.

He shrugged. *I would think so.*

We arrived at the field and took off running to my house. Once home, I wasn't sure I had the energy for anything but a quick shower and maybe a few pages of reading. Zack retrieved his blanket and pillow from the closet while I disappeared upstairs.

Energized after my shower, I changed into a tiny pair of flannel shorts and a spaghetti strap tank, then headed downstairs for water. The scents of soap and shampoo wafted from the bathroom and tickled my nose. Zack was lying on the couch, his hair wet and disheveled. Yum.

Propping his top half up on his elbows, he eyed me as I hit the landing.

"Everything okay?" I asked, wondering what the chances were of making out with him again.

"Yeah, sure. Just winding down." Zack looked around the room, anywhere but at me. "I was about to call it a night."

"Is the couch okay? Need anything?" I passed through the living room toward the kitchen doorway.

"I'm fine, thanks." Avoiding my gaze, he reached to the floor and picked up a book.

I was about to step into the kitchen when I caught him staring at my legs, so I paused.

His eye twitched. "Do me a favor and put on some real pajamas, okay?"

Biting my lip, I pretended to mull it over, then scrunched up my nose. "I have to cover up and you get to run around with that six-pack exposed?"

"I get hot at night."

I couldn't have agreed more, which made me want to throw myself at him. Jolting back to reality, I trudged to the kitchen and poured a glass of water. Not wanting to appear desperate, I did my best to keep my eyes off him.

Who was I kidding? He looked too good not to get my fill. I wanted to drink him up. Glass in hand, I stood in the doorway between the kitchen and living room and observed him while I sipped the cool liquid. He studied me, leaning against a pillow with his hands behind his head. From where I stood, I could hear his breathing change, his heart speed up.

My veins hummed just looking at Zack. Instinct told me that if I pressed, he wouldn't resist. But I didn't want him that way. I wanted him to want me without reservations. Most of all, I didn't want to be rejected again.

"Well, sweet dreams." Gulping the rest of the water, I set the cup on the counter and sprinted up the stairs.

Zack dropped me off at his house the next day after school and went to work. Once I finished my homework, I asked Cara and Favianne if they needed help with anything. They didn't. Bored, I rifled through Zack's backpack in search of notes that would tell me his assignments. I found them and did all his homework, fairly sure he'd get an A on everything. I checked in with Cara again and she asked me to set the table. As I placed the last plate, I heard Zack arrive in the Mustang.

"Honey, I'm home," he called out as he came through the door.

I chuckled. "Supper's about ready, dear."

When dinner was over, we spent some time with his mom, then gathered our things and went to my house.

"Why don't I morph?" I asked, leaning against a wall in the living room. Zack had the couch. I could've taken my dad's recliner, but even that was too close. Too comfortable. The temptation to flirt with Zack was too much.

"Everyone's different. I started noticing changes when I was sixteen. This was right after my mom quit working, because she kept getting sick. It was stressful having a job, doing the grocery shopping and everything else while worrying about my mom. From what I've learned so far, stress can bring on the first morph. It was another two weeks before I turned into a wolf though."

I recalled the first day I'd noticed changes. I'd just learned we'd be moving again and then I'd gotten grounded. The next day, I had the run-in with

Zack, then Gina got pissed off at me and later Daniel douched it up at my expense.

"You must've completely freaked the first time you morphed," I said.

"It was strange," Zack agreed. "But I had so much energy and this wild urge to... I don't know. One time I took off running and in my mind I was a wolf. I *needed* to be a wolf. And an instant later, I really was. It felt natural. Instinct, I guess."

I didn't feel any of those things, except the extra energy and the running part. "I haven't had the urge to morph."

"You probably won't. Shape-shifters are different. Relax. It'll come."

I shook my head. The sooner I learned to change into a bear or some other dangerous animal, the sooner I could protect myself. "I'd like to try *now*."

"Go for it." Zack pointed to his temple. "It's all in here."

"What if I can't change back? I'm afraid I might get stuck."

He chuckled. "Not gonna happen. If you can change once, you can change again. Once you morph, you'll see."

"Okay, here goes nothing." Focusing everything I had into being a wolf, my body heated up and a tingle that felt like it might turn into a headache traveled up the base of my neck.

"You're trying too hard," he said after a moment. "Think soothing thoughts and picture a specific animal. Visualize it. *Be* it. You have to *know* you can do it."

I imagined myself as a wolf. *I am a wolf... a wolf... a wolf.* I opened my eyes and held out my arms. They were blurry, almost translucent. It felt... like I was *meant* to morph. Peaceful.

"Yes," Zack whispered. "That's it."

My arms steadied and became normal again.

"Sorry. I guess I distracted you. Try again. This time I'll be quiet. Go on," Zack coaxed.

I focused again, the exact same way. The vibrations started, only this time, more controlled. Then, my body became lighter, almost weightless. Suddenly, I stood on all fours and the world appeared a lot different. Black and white, mostly. Ugh. I wanted to run now, but couldn't in the living room. I felt trapped and claustrophobic.

I thought about being human again, and the next moment, I was.

I felt the chill across my naked flesh and screamed. Zack gaped as I hunched over to cover myself. "The least you could do is look away," I hissed.

He turned around.

"You could've warned me." Snatching my clothes, I disappeared behind the recliner and threw on my shirt. My pants weren't on yet, but Zack couldn't see beyond the furniture. "You can look now."

"Kind of like when I was barking for you to turn around and ended up having to dress in the bushes. Twice." Zack raised a brow.

"Okay, Zack. Now we're even," I said, zipping up my jeans and sitting next to him on the couch. I was so irritated that I knew nothing could possibly happen between us now. Which made the close proximity to him totally safe.

"I wasn't trying to get even for the times I morphed and you forgot to turn around. I wouldn't do that on purpose." His eyes were riveted to mine. "Besides, there are less sneaky ways of getting you naked."

Why was I thinking the couch would be safe? This yo-yo business was getting painful. Standing up, I struggled to concentrate as I leaned against the recliner. "So it's always like that? You shift back buck naked? Kind of inconvenient, isn't it?"

"I never worried about it, because I've always been alone when I morphed." He shrugged. "If you wore one hundred percent cotton or linen—something from nature, or close—it would shift with you. When you're human again, you're fully dressed."

"Seriously?" That was great news. "I see a shopping spree in my future."

My first morph. I'd done it. I inched forward to sit on the arm of the recliner that was nearest to Zack. "What else should I know about us?"

"There's not much more." He leaned back and ran a hand through his hair. "Except that werewolves aren't very nice. According to one of my books that documented various crimes throughout history, all the really violent periods, werewolves were responsible. Like the Spanish Inquisition and Hitler, Charles Manson—they were all werewolves. The very worst of mankind weren't really men at all. They were monsters."

"But there are good ones, too." Zack was proof of that. "Like you."

"Sometimes I'm not good." He looked at me, his eyes intense. Hungry.

I swallowed hard, staring at him.

He let his head fall back against the couch and closed his eyes. When he focused on me again, his eyes were clear.

"Of course you're good. You always try to do right by me."

"Which isn't easy," Zack said. "You're like fast food."

I narrowed my eyes at him and crossed my arms. "How's that?"

"You know it's not a good idea, but you keep coming back for more anyway."

I wanted to get mad at Zack, be offended. But if he was compelled to spend time with me and even wanted to kiss me, how could that be a bad thing?

"I see why Daniel won't go away."

Now he'd gone and ruined my good mood by bringing *him* up.

Zack groaned. "Totally off the subject, but I just remembered I still have homework to do."

"I did it while you were at work."

Zack beamed. "You did my homework for me?"

Nodding, I returned his smile.

"Wow," he said. "Thanks."

Zack was openly staring and the longer he did, the more I wanted to kiss him. I pretended there were bars between us that were impossible to squeeze through. I would not invite him in, because if I did, surely we'd make out and I'd get my heart crushed all over again.

He rose from the couch, but when I sidestepped off the arm of the recliner to avoid him, he paused and seemed to shake it off. "Let's go for a run," he said. "I'm thinking of a spot more private, but we need a car. Mind if I drive?"

"Sure." I dashed upstairs to change, wondering where he'd pick. And wishing I wasn't so excited to be going into the woods with him.

† † †

We drove with the top down, so I gathered my hair in a ponytail and enjoyed the night air infused with the scent of pine.

"We can't allow the scouts to catch us together as werewolf and shifter," Zack said, eyes trained on the road.

"Right," I said, admiring his exquisite profile. "They'll want to enslave me."

"It's not just that. Shape-shifters and werewolves do *not* socialize with each other. At all. You guys are slaves and not worthy of us."

"Really?" I asked, an edge to my voice. Maybe that was the real reason he didn't want to be with me.

He spared me a glance. "Hey, I didn't make the rules. If I felt that way, I wouldn't be here."

I believed him. "Right. Sorry."

"Forget it."

We'd driven around winding roads and now cruised through a deserted area, one side a cliff and the other a mountain. Zack slowed and glided the car into a lookout spot, then grinned at me. "I can't wait to see what else you can do. Let's go."

CHAPTER TWENTY-FOUR

WE REACHED A dense part of the forest and could no longer see the car, the sky barely visible through the thick clumps of branches and leaves. I could smell moss growing on the ground and boulders where massive trees provided protection from the sun.

Zack stood, his arms folded. "What do you most want to be?"

I thought about it a moment, then closed my eyes and the vibrating began. Except this time, it was more like a shimmer, then the floating sensation enveloped me. A moment later, I roared.

Zack chuckled. "A tiger, of course. I should've known. Cream, not white or striped. You had to be different, didn't you?" His eyes traveled down my form and landed on my shoes at my feet. "You thought ahead. That's too bad, because your wardrobe malfunction earlier was rather illuminating. I'll have to sneak into your room and steal all your natural fiber clothes, so they don't morph with you."

I snarled at him and bared my fangs.

He laughed and morphed, then bolted off into the trees.

When we'd run enough to soothe the animal in us, we returned to the spot where we'd left Zack's clothes and my sneakers. I easily shifted to human.

Turn around, he told me silently.

I would've rather watched. So far, I'd seen his stomach and chest. Was the rest of him as flawless? But I grudgingly obeyed, listening to the fabric rustling as he got dressed. After finding my shoes, I put them on.

"I want to try something else," I said.

Better to practice another time," he said. "Morphing takes more energy than you think. You'll sleep like a rock tonight, but it'll get easier as you get stronger. You can turn around now."

As I twisted around, I got a glimpse of the muscle at his hips that cut in at his waist. Then it all disappeared, hidden by his shirt. Back to business. "I'll get stronger?"

"I did." He finished with his socks and located a shoe. "We should arm wrestle and see what you're made of. We can use it to gauge any future increase."

"I *am* curious, but we can do that tomorrow." I still had so many questions. But he was right when he said morphing took energy. I felt all used up, mentally and physically. "We should get home."

Zack led the way to the Mustang. Once inside, I leaned back and closed my eyes. What seemed like several seconds later, the car stopped and I popped up. How long had I been sleeping? I hated getting that tired. Embarrassing things happened, like drooling with my mouth open. Hopefully, he'd been concentrating on the road.

"Where are we?" I asked.

"Your house." He chuckled softly. "Where else?"

I wiped at my mouth, thankful it was dry, then got out and stumbled up the steps and into the house. "I'll shower in the morning when I'm more awake," I said as I made my way upstairs.

"Don't forget your book." He pointed to the box of his father's things.

I abandoned the steps to sift through the books, unsure which one I should pick. "What's this?" It was thin, like a pamphlet, but hardbound. The faded, threadbare cover wore the words *The Truth About Shape-shifters* in old, block style letters across the front. I flipped it open. On the inside cover, it read, *Brought to you by SWAAST.*

"What's SWAAST?" I asked.

"Shape-shifter Werewolf Alliance Against Slavery and Tyranny. They're a group of shape-shifters and werewolves who help others who've escaped captivity or defied the king. They try to spread the truth through things like this. But the king wiped out most of them. I doubt they exist anymore."

Interesting. I'd been close to retiring to my room, but my fascination with SWAAST reenergized me. "You don't think they're around anymore?" I asked.

"They're a threat. King Mortimer would do everything in his power to destroy them."

My eyes left the book to stare at Zack. "It's a whole different world with its own problems and politics, isn't it?" I examined the cover again, reading the title, and frowned. "Your dad was a scout."

"That's right."

"Then why would he have this book?" Zack opened his mouth to answer, but I didn't give him a chance. "If it's that dangerous being part of SWAAST, we can assume it's also dangerous to know them or even have these things in your possession."

"I never thought about the danger aspect of it. I just figured he left it for me so I'd know about shape-shifters, not because he actually supported SWAAST."

"But isn't it safe to assume that if he was against them, he would've gotten rid of this book and never let you see it? If he supported the king at all, he wouldn't have left it for you to learn."

He paused a moment with a bewildered look. "Yeah, it seems logical he wouldn't risk me getting caught with this book unless it was really important to him."

"And it would only be important to him if he was a believer." I hesitated a moment to let him absorb that. "Which proves my theory that good werewolves do exist."

A gamut of emotions flickered over Zack's face. "I guess so."

"What did he look like? Your dad." Now that I knew Lucio Gavino De Luca was worthy of the love Zack so obviously felt for him, I became more curious than ever. "You have pictures, right?"

"My mom had some photos, but they disappeared one day about ten years ago. Maybe my dad knew he wouldn't make it back and didn't want evidence he'd been there. If a werewolf ever saw the pictures and recognized him, I'd automatically be marked and a scout assigned to keep an eye on me until I came of age."

"So he was trying to shield you. They found you anyway." I glanced at the book again then Zack, tilting my head thoughtfully. "You don't remember what he looked like? Not even a little?"

"I was five the last time I saw him." His gaze returned to the box of his dad's books sitting by the couch.

I didn't think Zack would be up for idle conversation. Or for me grilling him more on our kind and I was exhausted anyway. I waited a beat, not wanting to barge in on his private moment. "I'm glad he wasn't a bad guy." I rose from the couch, my SWAAST book in hand. "Well, goodnight."

He gave me a half smile.

I made my way up the stairs with the book. Part way up, I glanced back. Zack rifled through the box like he was searching for something specific. He stopped and stared at a book intently while taking it with him to the couch.

† † †

"Autumn. Wake up."

My eyelids fought me, but I eventually triumphed and squinted at the intruder. "What?" I croaked.

"We're going to be late for school if you don't get up." He vanished from the doorway and I struggled to clear the cobwebs. I'd started the book, gotten my second wind and stayed up way too late reading it.

I sprung from my bed, pinned up my hair since I didn't have time to wash it, then jumped in the shower. When I was ready, Zack was waiting by the door.

"Don't you have an alarm clock?" he asked.

"My dad always woke me up."

He rolled his eyes. "Great. I've replaced your dad."

"If the shoe fits." I snorted. "*You* are the one who insists on being just friends."

We arrived at the driver's side of my car and I raised my brows. He shook his head and rounded the hood to the passenger side.

On the way to school, I thought about the book I'd started last night. "So apparently, your people and mine don't hook up because supposedly, mating makes both of them weaker."

Zack cocked his head. "Yeah, I remember reading that. Didn't pay much attention to it at the time, since I didn't know any shape shifters."

"So if we made out, you could lose to Daniel in a fight, because I made you weaker?" I spared him a quick glance.

Zack shrugged. "I guess. But by *mating* they probably mean... you know. Not just making out."

"But you're not positive, right? It could be physical contact and kissing. Why didn't you tell me *before* we fooled around?" I made a turn, wondering what else Zack had neglected to tell me.

"If that's all it took, we'd already feel weaker. And anyway, things like that don't occur to guys when they're kissing a hot girl. Besides, I read it like two years ago and forgot about it, 'cause I had no reason to think it would ever be an issue."

That was understandable. "It's odd—mating making us weaker." I stopped for a red light and studied Zack. "Could be just a calculated rumor to prevent forbidden love."

"Agreed. But since you and I defy the norm, who are we to say what's possible and what isn't? It could be some chemical reaction that sucks away our powers."

Maybe. Maybe not. "What if it's not true? According to the book, there are no documented cases except from the king's court. He doesn't like us and uses us as slaves. That's not very objective." I drove the Mustang past the gate and into the school parking lot.

"Yeah, but what if it *is* true? I don't think any shifter or werewolf would be crazy enough to risk it. Oh, and from what I remember, socializing at all is illegal. You'll read about that soon in one of those books."

That was news to me. "So we've already broken the law?" I cruised by rows of cars until I found a spot wide enough to hopefully prevent any car doors opening and dinging my Mustang.

"Yeah. Like I don't already have enough problems with the scouts. If we get caught breaking the law, the scouts taking me to the king will be the least of my problems."

I stared at him, shocked. "Zack, you could be killed."

He opened the car door, then stopped to eye me. "Then you'd better not let anyone find out you're not human."

As he hopped out of the car, I realized what he was risking. His life. For me.

CHAPTER TWENTY-FIVE

MY MIND FIXATED on what Zack had just said and I all but screeched to a stop. So he and I being together as boyfriend and girlfriend wasn't a matter of choice anymore? I couldn't hope Zack would fall violently in love with me and take me on the run with him, because even if he did, we couldn't do anything about it or we'd lose our strength and be easy targets. The future, the world and everything in it suddenly seemed so pointless and dismal.

I needed to move but my limbs felt too heavy. Zack nudged me as we walked away from the Mustang. Sluggishly, I followed, hitting the clicker to lock up.

"Hey," he said. "It's not like we could've been together anyway."

That didn't help. At all.

I whirled around to face Zack, yanking his arm and forcing him to halt mid-step. "I don't know why you're so cold about this, Zack. I *know* you like me. Why do you have to hide it?"

He stared at me so long, doubt for my theory crept up on me like a bedbug. Was it smoldering passion I saw in his eyes, because he wanted me so badly? Or annoyance because my assumption was horribly wrong?

"Never mind. It doesn't matter." I bolted ahead of him in a huff, a part of me wanting to lose him. But, to his credit, he kept up while still maintaining his distance.

In my cloud of temper, I hadn't noticed Daniel step in front of me. I bounced into his chest, my forehead clipping his chin.

Daniel's big hands clamped onto my elbows. "Come back to me," he said so quietly, I doubted Zack could hear. "I can't be without you. Please, Autumn. Give us another chance."

Sure, he was begging now, but in a moment, when he didn't get his way, he'd turn nasty again. "No means no, Daniel."

Zack's familiar scent surrounded me and his arm circled my waist. His hand slid over my hip, palm flattening over my stomach possessively as he pressed my back to his chest. Delicious. I naturally melted against his chest, my insides alive with little butterflies.

I looked into Daniel's eyes, but he'd zeroed in on Zack behind me. All softness and pleading had vanished, replaced by fire. I gazed into his soul and saw destruction and mayhem. It hadn't hit me until that moment that exposing Zack to Daniel put Zack's life in jeopardy. Because of *me*. If I went back to Daniel, Zack would be safe.

"She's with me," Zack rumbled, his warm breath caressing my cheek.

"You sure, Autumn?" Daniel growled. "I wouldn't do that if I were you."

"We're both *very* sure," Zack answered for me.

"She's not yours to keep. You'll see. And you'll regret this." Daniel released me and strolled off.

Zack spun me and cupped his hands around my face. I couldn't tell if he was angry at me or disturbed by Daniel.

"From now on, you don't walk ahead of me, no matter how pissed off you are. Got it?"

Angry. Definitely angry.

He left me at my first class and stormed away, making me feel guilty for racing off without him. As expected, he waited for me after every one of my classes. At lunchtime, we walked into the cafeteria and I spotted Daniel right away. Zack tensed.

Trevor appeared in front of us. "You think you can tear yourself away from your girlfriend for a minute? I need to talk to you."

Girlfriend. I liked the sound of that. Too much.

"If you want to hang out with Maya," Zack nodded toward our table where she sat, "I'll be right here."

I scoped out a spot with John and Maya where I could see Daniel. My friends took a break from their animated conversation to say hello. I returned their greeting, but it was half hearted. I didn't feel much like talking, not with the new knowledge about Zack and the future of our relationship. Or *lack* of future relationship.

A few minutes later, Zack returned and sat next to me.

He called me your girlfriend and you didn't correct him, I said silently.

He took a bite of a hamburger that smelled heavenly. *Yeah? So?*

But I'm not your girlfriend.

Right.

I'd hoped for a more encouraging answer, but wasn't surprised. *So why let him think we're together?*

He glanced at me as he chewed, one brow elevated. *I'm spending every night at your house, shadowing you at school, double dating with you and defending you against Daniel. What do you think the chances are of anyone believing we're not together? If we deny it, we look like liars.*

I'd wanted him to say, "Wishful thinking, Autumn. I know we can't be together forever, but can't we live in the moment?" I wasn't going to get an answer like that from him.

"Bathroom?" Maya nodded toward the cafeteria exit.

I nodded numbly and got up, not even glancing at Zack.

In the bathroom, she waited until the door closed before questioning me. "What's up with you two? You guys haven't spoken one word all through lunch."

Actually, we had, but she couldn't know that. I didn't sense Zack outside, but would've bet anything he was close by, still looking out for me but not near enough to listen in. I knew Maya meant well, but I had nothing encouraging to offer and didn't want to be interrogated. I stalled, going to the sink to wash my hands. "Nothing's going on. That's the problem."

"Wow." She stared at my reflection. "You superlike him."

I dried off my hands and shook my head. "I do *not* superlike him."

She spied my reflection in the mirror. "I know what happened. You slept with Zack, then realized you were madly in love with him. But he doesn't return your feelings, because he's in love with his neighbor's twin sister who just returned from the Amazon after everyone thought she was dead."

I laughed. "Maya, you've been watching too many soap operas."

She smiled and I realized she'd gone on her weird tangent to distract me. I turned and grasped her shoulders firmly. "I *do* like Zack. Very much. But, no, we're not hooking up. He stays on the couch and I sleep in my room. I promise."

"You've kissed him though, right? I don't see what the problem is." She searched my face to find the answer.

"Yeah, we've kissed but—" I was about to tell Maya the truth, that Zack and I weren't involved nor did we have plans to remedy that. But Zack's reasoning came back to me—she wouldn't believe me in a million years. "He wants to take it slow."

"Has he brought up exclusivity yet?"

I sighed. "No, and he won't either. His mom is the only thing keeping him here and she's not going to live forever. This'll never be a deep and meaningful relationship, Maya."

That sounded so depressing when I said it out loud.

† † †

Zack waited right outside my last class, walking with me toward the exit with his arm wrapped around my shoulder.

At the curb, I heard Ashley. "Autumn."

She appeared at my side as Trevor arrived and talked to Zack, who held my hand firmly—the perfect way for us to have separate conversations and still know where the other was. He gently squeezed every now and then. I couldn't take it personally. Getting my hopes up would lead to more disappointment.

"I was wondering if you wanted to come by my house Friday night. Just some close friends and a jam session. If you play anything, bring it. It'll be fun." She frowned. "Uhm. No one else is having a party that night, right?"

I chuckled. "Not that I know of."

"He can come too." Her eyes darted to my boyfriend. "And Trevor and Maya."

"I'll ask them and let you know. Thanks for the invite." I threw her a smile. "It sounds fun."

She wandered off, but Zack and Trevor were still talking. Cars. Trevor had been saving up and was almost ready to buy.

"What's your schedule like this week? I rarely see you around anymore except at dinner." Trevor gave him a knowing look.

"Right. And you're not always with Maya these days," Zack said sarcastically.

"Hey, Autumn," John said.

"Hi." Beyond John, I spotted Daniel staring at me like a stalker. It gave me the creeps.

John followed my gaze. "What's up with that guy? I didn't like him before and he wasn't nearly this disturbing."

The last thing I wanted was to involve John, so I lightened my tone. "Who knows?"

"How're your parents? Still traipsing around the Grand Canyon?" John asked.

"Oh. I didn't tell you. They came home and left again to Montana for a job. I got an email from them last night saying they'd arrived and all was well. They'll probably be home in a couple weeks or so." I giggled at John's surprised face. "I know. Crazy, huh? I guess they realized how unproductive it was to worry so much."

"You ready to go?" Zack asked.

"See you tomorrow, John." I waved to him as Zack dragged me away.

My day had been too deflating to enjoy my Mustang, so I tossed my keys to Zack and went to the passenger side. "So what were you reading last night?"

"Werewolf history." He opened the door and adjusted the seat to accommodate his longer legs, then started the car.

I waited to hear more, but he didn't volunteer anything else. Instead, his eyes fixed on the road ahead, hands stiff on the steering wheel. He definitely was not in a good mood. I wondered what the rest of the evening had in store for us, but had an idea it wouldn't involve having fun.

"Why read it again? What were you looking for?" I asked.

"I thought about what you said and wondered if there might be something about my dad in the history books. Or any mention of SWAAST. Maybe when my mom's gone, rather than run on my own, it might be safer to search for any who are left."

"Hanging out with those SWAAST guys would be even more dangerous. They're probably the most hunted people ever." My voice rose. "Being with them is *not* safer."

He glowered at me. "I won't live my life afraid to do the right thing. What kind of a life is that?"

"Yeah, you're a good guy who wants to do good. I respect you for that. But being stupid isn't smart."

Zack gave a quick laugh. "That's profound, Autumn."

"You know what I mean. You're young and no match for werewolves who are hundreds of years old. You said with age comes strength. You'd be better off joining the king and honing your fighting skills until you get stronger. So long as you're with them, they won't hunt you for being a traitor. You're no good to anyone if you're dead."

He glanced at me and nodded. "Okay. I promise to consider that before I do anything."

I didn't want to think about him leaving or getting hurt—or worse. If we didn't talk about something else soon, I'd explode. "You want to go to Ashley's little party Friday night? She invited us to a jam session."

"I heard her ask. I figured you'd tell her no," Zack said.

"Why's that? I like Ashley. And her parties are nice. If I'm able to go, I usually do."

"I assumed..."

Realizing what Zack hadn't finished saying, I flinched. "You assumed that I was too much of a snob to hang out with a junior. I thought we were past that." When he didn't deny it, my eyes burned and my throat swelled. After all our time together, I was still the stuck up girl he originally thought me to be.

"To hell with you, Zack," I mumbled toward my window.

CHAPTER TWENTY-SIX

WHILE ZACK WORKED at the auto shop, I stayed at his house, but hid in his room, so I wouldn't have to face his family. If they asked me what was wrong, I'd surely spill it. Zack wouldn't like that. Once I'd finished all my homework, I considered doing his too. I reached for his backpack, but kicked it across the room instead. If he didn't do it himself, he'd miss out on everything that his studies had to offer. I snorted at the thought and retrieved his backpack. I wrapped up his homework just as he arrived and Cara announced dinner was ready.

As everyone ate, I smiled at all the right times and made polite conversation. I noticed Cara and Favianne's occasional glance my way, but I didn't say anything. My goal was to get through it as painlessly as possible. When I got home, I planned to abandon Zack in favor of my room. I needed to separate from him emotionally. He would run alone tonight.

"Something's up with the car," he said as soon as we got on the road toward my house. "It sounds different."

"What do you think's wrong with it?"

He turned his head, like he was listening for something. "Not sure. I have tomorrow off, so we can take it in the shop and have it checked out." He guided the car into my driveway and killed the engine.

Once inside, I immediately hit the stairs. "Goodnight, Zack."

He stood at the bottom of the steps. "You don't want to go running?"

I turned and faced him, careful to mask the violent turmoil raging within me. "Not with you. No point in bonding, remember?"

Once in my room, I closed the door and locked it. Jumping on my bed, I covered my face with my hands.

"Autumn." He rapped on the door and when I didn't answer, the doorknob rattled. "Damn it, open the door." Seconds passed and he kicked at it. "Open the door or I'll break it down, I swear."

I believed him. I couldn't have my parents coming home, seeing the broken door and worrying that I'd been attacked or something. I wiped my eyes and got up. Before unlocking it, I took a moment to erase any emotion from my face.

Opening the door a few inches, I poked my head out. "What?"

"I can't leave you alone." He glared at me. "You know that."

"Then don't go running. Simple."

"That won't work. It's easy for you to resist, but not me." He sighed. "Can we talk about this?"

I flung the door open and turned away, knowing he

282

would follow. On my bed again, I leaned back against the wall, my knees up.

"Sorry about the Ashley thing." He cautiously sat at the foot of my bed. "I wasn't thinking. I know you're not like that anymore."

"Anymore? I was *never* like that, Zack!"

"That came out wrong," he said quickly. "I meant that I don't think that way anymore. About you." He ran a hand through his hair and growled. "I'm sorry."

That was better. But he wasn't there yet. I stared at him, my brows raised.

"Autumn..." He looked at me helplessly.

I had no intention of bailing him out. "Are you finished?"

"And I'm sorry for being so—"

"Cold?" I finished for him. "Impersonal? Unfriendly? Distant? Hurtful?"

He held up his hand. "I get the picture. Yes. All of those things." He studied the fabric of my purple comforter. "It's just that I've had a lot to process lately and some decisions to make." His voice lowered. "You're not stuck up. Actually, I think a lot of you. If I didn't, I wouldn't be here."

I couldn't make more of his words than they were. We had a mutual respect. Nothing else.

"I'm sorry I hurt you," he said softly.

I swallowed and glanced away, so he wouldn't see the tears in my eyes.

"Will you go running with me?"

"Sure," I forced out. "Give me a few minutes and I'll be down."

If he saw me cry, he'd probably feel sorry for me. We'd probably end up kissing and I couldn't open myself up like that again, expose my emotions, so he could stomp all over them. Still, he hadn't moved and I wondered what he was thinking. Hopefully, he'd take my reaction to mean that complete forgiveness wasn't his yet. Which it wasn't.

The mattress quaked as Zack got up. When he was gone, I leaned my head back and breathed.

I hated Zack.

I hated him for being the most gorgeous guy I'd ever seen. For being nice to even the nerds. For helping me and protecting me, for inviting me into his home and sharing his mother with me. I hated him for shielding me from the evil that was Daniel. I hated the way he joked and teased me and chuckled when he thought I did something cute. I hated him for thinking I was beautiful.

I hated him for being *exactly* who I wanted him to be.

Mostly, I hated myself for being desperately in love with him.

I couldn't go downstairs yet.

Closing my eyes, I imagined being a giant bird, almost weightless as I soared soundlessly through the sky. When I felt the tremor of my body beginning to shift, I relaxed my muscles and tossed the image away. But my moment in the make-believe wind calmed me enough to go downstairs. I took them one step at a time, wondering how I would do this with Zack day after day if he could never be mine. And knowing one day, he'd be gone.

As I reached the last step, we both instinctively zeroed in on the front door just before the bell rang.

He peeked through the gap between the curtains. *It's Gina,* he told me silently. Zack opened the door and she entered hesitantly.

Why did you let her inside? I asked.

I'm curious to know what would make her so desperate that she'd show her face at your house, he answered, one corner of his mouth curving up.

"What are you doing here?" I wanted to throw her right back out.

"I couldn't find Daniel and thought he might be here." She glanced at Zack. "But I see now that was never a possibility."

"Is he missing again?" Zack asked, coming up beside me and casually slipping his arm around my waist.

Gina made a strange sound between a laugh and a sob. "He keeps going MIA these days, especially at night." Her gaze fixed on the wood flooring. "He doesn't answer his phone and his parents can't reach him either." She returned her attention to me. "I think he's cheating on me."

A normal response would've been to say, "I told you so" or make a sarcastic remark and urge her to dump him. But if she followed that advice, Daniel might get freaky and stalk her the way he'd been stalking me. At least I had superpowers and Zack to protect me. Gina was probably safer *with* Daniel.

"He hasn't been here, Gina," Zack said. "I'd know if he was. I've been here a *lot* the last few days."

That wasn't subtle at all. Zack must've wanted to make sure Daniel knew we were still together. My gut told me Daniel was already in the loop.

"You're probably thinking if he was unfaithful to you, why would he be any different with me?" Her eyes welled up with tears. "And if he *is* with another girl, I deserve it."

"I doubt he's cheating on you," I said. She would never know the absolute truth, but I could give her part of it. "We've seen him at night when we've gone out and he was alone. Maybe that's all he wants. Solitude."

"Hope you're right. He's been different lately. It's hard to figure him out." She smiled and shuffled her feet awkwardly. "Well, thanks. Goodnight."

I opened the door and closed it after her, turning to Zack.

He clucked his tongue. "I want to hate her for what she did to you, but I feel bad for her. Daniel's evil. And she just doesn't see it."

I felt sorry for her, too. Hopefully she'd learn from the mess she'd made.

During the drive to the woods, Zack was quiet. Too quiet. I wanted to keep him talking, so I didn't have to think about how unavailable he was. Or how I was being stalked by a crazed newly-made werewolf or that if I wasn't careful, I could become a slave.

"That you know of, have there been any other werewolves around here besides Daniel and the two scouts?" I asked.

"I've noticed others over the last couple years, since I matured. But you mean lately?"

I nodded.

"When we first moved in with Aunt Cara, I ran across a couple wolves in the woods. As soon as they saw me, they took off running. I have no idea who they were and haven't seen them since. I thought I sensed wolf a few times on errands for my mom. Once at the bank and another time at the grocery store. There were always too many people around, so I couldn't locate where the energy was coming from."

"If you sense an energy, it could easily be coming from a shape-shifter too, right?"

"I guess so," Zack answered. "But I'm thinking that since they're weaker, sensing their energy isn't as easy. Like with you. Are you thinking of your parents?"

"Maybe." I averted my gaze.

"If you find out they're human, you won't be able to tell them what's going on. If they're shifters, they're in danger too. You should be prepared either way."

Zack parked and we bailed from my car, in a hurry to feel the wind. As soon as we were in the tree covering, we ran. When we stopped, I realized Zack had turned into a wolf.

Shift, he told me as he raced past trees. *Try something new.*

As I kept up with Zack, I pictured a lion. My body vibrated a moment, my step faltered, and then I was on all fours. I sprinted to catch up with him.

Zack slowed until I was running beside him. *Nice.*

I guess you like cats. You're the total opposite of me.

What a tool. Why did he take every opportunity to remind me how different we were and that it wasn't going to happen between us? Just when I felt like I might forgive him, he'd do it again. I veered off to get away before I swiped at him. Zack followed.

As we sprinted through the forest, I quickly bored of being a lion. Cheetahs were supposed to be fast, weren't they? I slowed to a stop, intending to morph. My body quivered and nausea rose up. My eyes blurred as I watched Zack become a boy again.

"Go to your human form first. Do it now!"

I fell to the ground, trees swirling around me as I shifted back to human. Thankfully, I'd worn all natural fibers.

He loomed over me, grasping my hand. "Are you okay?"

"I think so. The nausea is passing." I used the back of my hand to wipe the perspiration from my forehead.

"Human is your other half. It stabilizes you. Always go back before shifting into anything else."

"Got it." Something pulled at me. Something different. Something I needed to see. My eyes drifted to his chest, down his abdomen. "You look nice."

Zack's hands shot below his hips to cover his junk, but it was too late. I'd seen it all.

I sat up and grinned. "Now we're even."

"Where are my clothes?" He morphed back into a wolf and disappeared into the trees.

I turned into a cheetah, quickly catching up to him.

I saw more of you than you saw of me, Zack bragged silently.

You keep telling yourself that. I laughed which ended up sounding like a cross between a meow and a hiss.

After a few minutes of racing through the forest, Zack suggested we head home. He didn't want to risk running into Daniel, just in case he decided to switch forests, too. And there were at least two other were-wolves around to be wary of.

"You're improving." The engine purred to life and Zack put it in drive. "And you morphed twice. Not as tired tonight?"

"I'm good," I said, enjoying the open window and the breeze on my face.

He glanced over at me. "Um, Autumn..."

Usually confidence oozed from Zack, but now he seemed a little uncertain. Would he apologize? Perhaps say he'd changed his mind, because he can't stop thinking about kissing me again? That he wants to be with me despite the danger. Forever.

"Yes?" I asked.

"Did you do my homework or do I still need to do it tonight?"

I'd worked myself up into impossible fantasies and the only thing on his mind was homework? I sighed and turned toward the window, the air drying the would-be tears from my eyes. "I did it earlier. How did you ever manage without me, Zack?"

He snorted. "The extra time I spend with you now, answering your questions and helping you morph? I would've done my homework."

"Right," I muttered, staring at the passing trees.

At home, Zack tossed the keys on the dining room table and located the blanket and pillow. "It's late. We should get to bed, but first I'd like to test your strength." He returned to the dining room table and propped an arm up on his elbow, his hand ready to grip mine.

"It's kind of pointless, don't you think? As a shape-shifter, I'm not going to be as strong as you." I held my arm up opposite his on the table.

"It'll still be challenging. Plus, if we practice, you'll build strength and maybe next time, you won't lose as quickly. We'll have something to compare it with, so we can tell how fast you're changing."

"On three?" I asked and he nodded. "One, two, three."

Slowly, my arm descended in the wrong direction. I fought it as hard as I could and Zack's arm slowed. He put more power behind his push and I strained against him. Another thrust and the back of my hand lay flat against the table. I lost. Not exactly a big surprise.

He stared at me. "You're unusually strong."

"Not *that* strong. You beat me, remember?"

"But not as easily as I expected." He studied me another moment. "You're going to get stronger. I may not always be able to take you down."

"What? Aren't shape-shifters weaker than werewolves?

"Yeah. I don't get why you're different though." He tapped a finger on the table, studying a knot in the wood grain of the table. "We'll have to wait and see how tough you get."

"When will I max out?"

"Never. We just keep getting more powerful as we get older. But at first, there's a surge. From the moment I first noticed my body changing, my strength rapidly increased for a couple months before I leveled out. But that's *me*. I don't know what it will be like for you, since we're different species."

With his constant reminders, how could I forget? "So how else are you and I different?" I asked masochistically.

Zack toyed with the keys on the table. "Werewolves tend to be grumpier and shape-shifters tend to be more easygoing." He glanced at me. "Although, apparently, that isn't always the case."

I pouted. "I'm *not* grumpy."

"Whatever." He snorted, twirling the keys around on the table.

I put my hand over Zack's to stop the weird key frenzy.

Rising from the kitchen chair, he paced between my dad's recliner and the dining area. "So what else did you want to know?"

"Hm." I glanced at the box of his dad's stuff. "Any idea why the king is so opposed to shape-shifters?"

"That's in the book I'm reading now—the legend of Hannah and Eli." Zack returned to lean a hip on the dining room table. "Even before them, you guys were slaves. When Hannah and Eli betrayed the king, more laws were made and penalties became harsher."

"Who are Hannah and Eli?" Maybe it wasn't important, but I couldn't know what might help me and what wouldn't. "They must've royally pissed off the king."

"Oh, yeah. Hannah was a born werewolf betrothed to the king in the fourteenth century. Eli was a shape-shifter slave and the king's top blacksmith. They fell in love and escaped. It's believed though that they're dead. They became so weak as mates, they ended up dying of old age as mere humans."

The more I learned, the more impossible a relationship with Zack became. We had zero chance. Utterly depressing. "But no one knows for sure? For all we know, Hannah and Eli survived."

"With the entire werewolf kingdom hunting them? Can you imagine the king's rage when he discovered a *slave* stole his future wife?" Zack shook his head. "Besides, it's too easy to detect a werewolf or shape-shifter. I can't see them still alive after all this time."

"Wait. To detect a *shape-shifter*?" I squinted, trying to think with that. It didn't mesh with what had been happening to me. "If that's the case, why don't the scouts or Daniel already know about me?"

Zack stopped pacing and gazed at the floor. "Maybe because you're still maturing and your scent is light. That'll change."

This was not good news. "How long do I have?"

"Weeks maybe? I'm guessing your scent will increase with your abilities."

I didn't have much time before I became a fugitive. If I stayed with my mom and dad, assuming they were humans, how much danger would they be in as a result? Werewolves had rules about not hurting humans, but rules were sometimes broken. And anything could happen with scouts around like the one who turned Daniel.

Hanging out with Zack wasn't an option either, since socializing with a shifter would hurt his chance of survival. I'd have to run. Alone. The frustration burned through my throat like fire.

CHAPTER TWENTY-SEVEN

I GLARED AT Zack. "And you didn't think that having only a few weeks to be safe was a detail I needed to know?"

His eyes widened. "It didn't occur to me. We've had a lot going on."

Although I wanted to be mad at him, I couldn't be. Suddenly, my energy level dipped and fatigue settled in my muscles. "I'm going to take a shower and go to bed." I rose from the kitchen chair without looking at him and practically sleepwalked to the stairs.

"Goodnight," he said.

I was too emotionally paralyzed to reply.

† † †

When I awoke some time later, light from the moon peeked through the slit between the curtain panels. My first thought was of Zack. I wanted to tiptoe to the couch, sneak under his blanket and snuggle up with him. He'd be warm and sleepy and, very likely, would give me what I needed. But it probably wasn't worth the agony I'd feel when he walked away saying, "I warned you I was leaving."

In a few weeks, he would be on the run and so would I. Not to mention the other ramifications of my situation—I'd have to leave my parents, my friends, my home. What would I do all alone with no one to turn to? Even if by some miracle Zack wanted company on the road, I couldn't continue with him if he didn't love me.

But I couldn't stay away from him either.

To say I was screwed would've been like calling my situation *unusual* or saying Zack was *cute*. Both were gross understatements.

Huddled in my blanket, my eyes stayed fixed on the ceiling. I knew I should get up, maybe make breakfast. As I lay in bed, it grew lighter outside, the walls of the room visible without super-vision.

A shape formed in the doorway to my room. I turned my head to see Zack.

"Are you okay?" he asked.

"I guess so," I answered quietly. Hadn't I closed the bedroom door before I'd crawled into bed last night? I knew Zack hadn't opened it just now. He must have done it during the night. "Were you in my room earlier?"

"Why do you ask?"

Why was it such a difficult question to answer? Either he was or he wasn't. "My door is open."

"I checked on you a while ago to make sure you were okay." He averted his gaze.

"Why? Did you hear something? Was someone trying to get in?" I couldn't imagine not waking up if an intruder had tried to break in.

I rolled over and propped myself up on my elbow.

"No. Last night, you seemed upset, so I was checking on you." Zack took a step over the threshold, his fingertips wiggling against his thigh.

Just when I thought he didn't care, he did something nice to make me think I wasn't just any girl. The longer I watched him, the more his fingers twitched and his eyes roamed the room.

I wanted to pursue it further, but intuition told me it was a bad idea. We'd be kissing shortly or he'd withdraw further, just like before. I couldn't allow myself to think that his compassion didn't extend *equally* to all people. He had no special feelings for me. And if I remembered that without fail, my disillusionment wouldn't flatten me later.

"Thanks for checking on me." I flopped down against my pillow and stared at the ceiling. Zack disappeared as quietly as he'd appeared.

Knowing I needed to stop wallowing in misery, I bolted from the bed and headed downstairs. Still in my PJs, I fixed eggs. When we'd finished eating, without a word through our entire meal, I escaped upstairs into my sanctuary. It was getting uncomfortable with Zack. He must have sensed it too.

In my bathroom, I got out all my tools. If I was going to be down in the dumps, no point in feeling unattractive, too. I ironed my hair until it was straight as a pin before hitting the ends with the curling iron. After brushing it out, I flipped it over to make it a little bit messy. I threw on jeans and the same tank top Zack had previously told me not to wear due to it being unsafe. At the last minute, I switched bras, putting on a pushup. After donning a pair of sandals, I surveyed my reflection in the mirror. Not bad. Back to the bathroom, I started my makeup.

"Autumn." Zack tapped on the hallway doorjamb leading into my bedroom.

"I'm in here," I called out.

"Are you about ready?" he asked from right outside the bathroom, peering in.

I checked my cell. "You want to leave *now*?"

He nodded.

"We still have a half hour before we need to go. Either we wait here or we wait at the school. What's the diff?"

"I'm bored." He scratched at something on the wall. "At my house, there are always things to do. All my stuff is there."

"If you're going to be staying here longer, maybe we should use our extra time to get more of your things."

"Good idea." He passed through the doorway, getting a closer look as I applied mascara. "Why are you bothering with that stuff anyway?"

Did he mean that it didn't do any good on me? I feared getting permanent marks between my brows from frowning at Zack so often.

His palm flashed up as a shield. "I mean, you're just as pretty without it."

Calmer, I eyed my hand, realizing I'd been holding my mascara brush like a weapon.

A moment later, he was gone, but my spirits were lifted. At least I was likable enough that he still found me attractive. That was *something*.

Zack did the driving to school. I'd have plenty of time alone with my car soon enough. Besides, I enjoyed watching him be master at the wheel. He was as confident with that as everything else.

But it was less painful when I wasn't looking at him. I sighed and shifted until I was gazing out the side window. "You never answered me about Ashley's party. It's tonight."

"I think we should go."

My eyes snapped to his. "Really?"

"Yeah. I'm not sure how smart it is to have us cooped up in your house so much."

I knew why *I* thought it wasn't a good idea—Zack was too much of a temptation for me. But I was curious why *he* thought so. "Why?"

He fidgeted, his gaze elsewhere. At a stop sign, he focused on me. "Didn't I already tell you how pretty you are?" He smiled, the dimple in his left cheek peeking out.

For the first time in what seemed an eternity, I felt good. I warmed all over.

Despite our extra stop at his house, we were still a little early for school. Once he parked the Mustang, I got out of the car. Zack was already a few feet ahead of me.

"Daniel's waiting for you."

I caught up to him. "Maybe he's standing there for some other reason."

"No. He's waiting for you."

"How do you know?"

Zack stopped and faced me. "I'm a guy, Autumn. I know how the minds of guys work. Plus, we know Daniel." He held me by my shoulders. "Promise me you won't make any deals with him."

Since I'd almost agreed the last time Daniel approached me, I couldn't blame Zack. But his urgency alarmed me. "Okay."

He released my shoulders and resumed walking, giving me a lopsided smile. "People aren't talking about us enough. We're going to have to do something about that."

In that moment, I forgot all about different species, shape-shifter slaves and even Daniel. It was just Zack and me. We looked at each other with goofy grins until we touched the curb.

"Autumn," Daniel said. "Can I have a word with you?" It was a question, but the way he spoke, it sounded more like a command.

I put a hand on my hip. "Is that an order?"

"Yeah, is it?" Zack took a step toward Daniel.

Daniel's eyes darkened, his shoulders straightening. The corners of his mouth lifted, but the energy around us crackled with tension. "Of course not. May I please have a minute of your time, Autumn?"

Zack stepped back, but stayed close. I stood two feet from Daniel, my brows raised.

"I've made my position clear and you've had several chances to make this right." He shifted toward me.

I backed up. "Do you have a point? Because those are the same tired things you've already said."

His eyes narrowed a moment. "This is your last chance."

"Going, going, gone. You can leave me alone now."

His eyes darkened. "When I kill Zack, you'll get to watch him die. But I'll keep you alive." His voice lowered. "For a while anyway."

"Way to make a girl love you, Daniel." My stomach knotted. "How about I call the police and file a report? Anything happens to us and you'll be the first person they come for."

"Do I look like I'm afraid of the police?" Daniel laughed. "All that matters is that in the end, we'll be together."

His complete disregard for his own life made him even more dangerous. "You think you could murder Zack or me and suddenly I'll want to be your soul mate? If you really believe that, you're even crazier than I thought."

At that, I made my way to Zack as casually as I could on trembling knees. All I wanted was to get lost in him. I wanted him to hold me, kiss me and make me forget how dirty Daniel made me feel. I struggled to keep him in my line of vision as the shapes around me spun. I'd stood my ground, but I may have made the biggest mistake of my life by putting Zack in danger.

He met me halfway, snaked an arm around my waist and pressed me against him. With his other hand, he brushed some strands of hair off my forehead. He dropped a kiss on my cheek and pulled away. I gazed into his eyes. Zack... so beautiful and yet impossible to have. My chest ached.

His mouth lowered and I lifted my chin as if Zack's kisses were the most natural thing in the world. His hand moved to my nape, holding me in place, then his mouth covered mine and our tongues danced. I felt pangs of desire for him in places I could never tell my parents. My hand slid up his muscular bicep to wind around his neck and I got lost, forgetting Daniel or anyone else was there.

Slowly he released me, his eyes locked on mine. *It was the only thing I could think of that would distract you. You didn't look so good,* he said soundlessly.

He'll try to kill you, I said.

He won't succeed. Are you okay?

"I guess so," I said quietly. "If the kiss was to distract me, what was the *second* kiss for?"

"That time *I* was distracted." He grinned. "We better go or we'll be late."

I was so engrossed in the memory of the kisses, I didn't notice whether Daniel was still lurking or how many people saw the show. Daniel had kissed me at school before, but it had never been like that. I felt my cheeks flush.

Zack opened one side of the double doors for me to pass. *Sorry again, but we accomplished a lot with that kiss.*

Yeah? How's that? It was all I could manage to say. My mind was like apple sauce, incapable of holding much shape.

For one thing, everyone's staring. Zack chuckled as he dropped me off at class.

CHAPTER TWENTY-EIGHT

LATER AT HOME, I hid in my room. Sitting cross-legged with my computer balanced on my thighs, I logged into my email. I could've taken my laptop downstairs and sat on the couch with Zack, each on our own computer. But that would've been unhealthy for me. I didn't want to be tempted into bringing up the last kiss again. Further, talking to him at all was a bad idea, unless absolutely necessary.

We would go to Ashley's party later, have fun, come home, go for a run, then go to bed. Our *own* beds. That's it. I would not stay up late at night unable to sleep for thinking of his full, perfect lips. I would not remember his musky scent, nor would I sneak downstairs to watch him sleep, hoping he would wake up and, in a sleepy haze, forget all his reasons to stay away.

Sitting alone and thinking about the kiss wasn't healthy either. We needed to set boundaries, so we knew what to expect. If Zack were allowed to touch me anytime he wanted, it was really going to mess with my head.

When he appeared in the doorway, I didn't have to see him to know he was there. My gaze stayed on my computer screen.

"What time do you want to leave for Ashley's party?" he asked.

"Nine?" A moment later, I peeked up at him from under my brows.

"Sounds good." He wiped a smudge off the door frame and made a show of inspecting it for flaws. "I think it's better to go running after, not before. Less chance of running into anyone else the later it gets."

"Okay." I pretended to be fully engrossed in whatever was on my computer screen.

"We forgot to take your car in," Zack said. "I called Timothy and he said I can use the garage over the weekend. I have a key."

"That was nice of him." I forced my mouth to curve up.

Zack's gaze wandered over to the window, then to my little antique French desk I never used. He scratched his chin and turned to go.

"Zack?"

He spun around. "Yeah?"

I mustered my courage, erased all emotion from my face and met his gaze. "I don't want you to kiss me again."

He just stared, blinking once. Evidently, he wasn't expecting me to say that.

"I *like* kissing," I explained. "And you already know I like you. I haven't exactly kept it a secret." He took a step forward and my heart pounded. I held up my hand to stop him, because I couldn't go there again, only to have him pull away. "But it's all or nothing. If you don't want to form any ties, because you're leaving, then *don't.*" My blood roared in my ears and I forced myself to breathe, so I could finish. "You can't kiss me and act like it means nothing. Because it means something to *me.*"

He nodded slowly. "Alright."

"I'll come downstairs when it's time to go. I have some things to do first."

He nodded again, but didn't move.

The strain in the room was stifling, so I smiled in hopes of easing it. "I appreciate everything you've done for me. I don't know what I would've done without you."

He stood poised and ready bolt. At the same time, he appeared permanently stuck to the floor. Would he take his cue and be thankful I gave him a way out? Or would he stay and whisper in my ear what an idiot he's been and tell me he can't imagine being without me. If he walked away without a fight, then he didn't care enough anyway. In that case, I wasn't losing anything, right?

"Well, I'll be downstairs if you need anything." Zack's gaze held mine another second or two before he turned to go.

As he left my room, my earlier inner pep talk didn't comfort me at all. Regardless of philosophies, logic or anything else, the bottom line was that any hope I'd had that he'd come to his senses was lost. My eyes stung and my throat ached. I wanted to scream and run after Zack and tell him I loved him. Instead, I leaped off the bed, wiped my eyes and quietly closed the door.

Zack was a total gentleman, locking up the house and escorting me to the passenger side of my car, then putting the Mustang's top up, so my hair wouldn't get messy. But he practically went out of his way not to touch me, like when he made a wide circle as he opened the car door for me.

When we arrived at the party, he spent most of his time with Trevor, but he always positioned himself to include me in his peripheral vision. The distance between us should've made things easier on me, but it didn't. I wanted him just as much as before.

I surveyed the living room of Ashley's parents' house, people spilling out the front door. The other day, she'd said "just some close friends" but this was a lot more than that. Yet she handled new arrivals graciously, immediately introducing them to someone, so they'd feel at ease.

Ashley's parents were strict, inspecting the punch and other drinks to make sure no booze had been smuggled in. I thought it was pretty cool of them to allow parties at all. If anyone wanted alcohol, they could wait for Daniel to throw one.

A pale, plump gothic-dressed girl wailed away on a make-shift stage, strumming her acoustic guitar while a tall guy in skinny-pants plucked at his bass. The music was loud, but I had no problem picking up the other sounds throughout the house. Girls laughing in the hallway, glasses clinking in the kitchen.

Despite the sheer number of people, it was a good crowd. Why hadn't I come to more of her gatherings? Now that Gina and Daniel were out of my social circle, I looked forward to spending time with people I enjoyed. Real friends who'd still be there for me, even if I wasn't popular.

At least until I went on the lam.

Zack loitered at the other end of the room with Trevor and a couple other guys, his gaze always coming back to me.

Maya looped her arm through mine. "Love that dress. Looks like it's been glued to you. I bet as soon as Zack saw it on you, he immediately started scheming how to get it off," she giggled into my ear. "Where did you buy it?"

"It's Gina's." I admitted, then snickered.

"No!" Maya high-fived me. "Whatever you do, don't give it back."

"I wasn't planning to since she didn't return all my stuff." She could keep the shoes, because seeing them would remind me how she'd betrayed me with Daniel.

"It's like there's a blaze of passion around Zack, festering. You need to satisfy that poor guy soon."

I burst out laughing. "Maya."

"It's true. God, I wished Trevor looked at me like that."

"He does. You're just blind to it. And anyway, I think you're misinterpreting Zack's expression."

"Yeah," she mocked. "And I'm *sure* I misunderstood that smoldering kiss by the curb this morning too. Gee, whatever did that mean?"

It had been foolish of me to deny it in the first place. "Okay, I get it. You're right. He's *madly* in love with me." I snorted.

Her face lost all traces of amusement as she discreetly eyed him again. "Actually... I think he really is."

I wanted to plug my ears. I did not need her crazy ideas banging around in my brain, giving me false hope. "It doesn't matter. I have no plans of sleeping with him when I know he's leaving. He'll have to carry on unfulfilled."

"Good girl," Maya said, patting my arm. "Don't settle."

I *wanted* to settle though, since it was the only way I'd ever get Zack. Even as that thought formed in my head, I discarded it. If I didn't stand my ground, I'd never truly have him in the way that mattered.

But what if Zack liked me more than he let on? His actions certainly hinted at it.

Oh, who was I kidding? Zack was not crazy in love with me. The attention he showered over me was temporary while he educated me, like he wished had been done for him. Duty, that was it. With that thought, it was as if my heart was being repeatedly impaled by an ice pick.

"Uh-oh. I smell trouble." Maya's lips tightened.

I spotted Daniel at the front door scanning the room. I slunk back, hoping Maya might shield me from his line of vision. Ashley and her parents didn't deserve the kind of scene Daniel might make. My gaze shot to Zack who was already heading my way, Trevor by his side.

"Excuse us for a moment." Without missing a beat, Zack gently turned me around. With his fingertips at my waist, he steered me away. His musky scent curled up my nose and tingles spread over my chest.

I peered over my shoulder to see Daniel staring after us, his face twisted with loathing.

At the corner of the room, Zack pressed me against the wall, turning so he could keep Daniel in his peripheral vision. Gently, he skimmed my cheek with his knuckles and gazed into my eyes, his thigh brushing against mine.

"Let them think I had to have you to myself for a minute. Less conspicuous than having an outright war. Do you want to leave or just avoid him all night?" he asked.

I mentally kick-started my brain, which had stopped as soon as Zack touched me. "He won't give up. Why don't I find out what he wants?"

"Autumn, we've already been there. He wants *you*."

"Unlike you," Even as the words left my mouth, I regretted them. Especially when I saw a strange look flit across his face. But it was gone before I could analyze it.

You can't make a scene in front of all these people. Go away, Daniel, Zack said.

I jolted at his voice in my head. How was it possible to hear his thoughts as he sent them to Daniel?

Zack's hand rested at my hip, his thumb at the soft spot on my waist. A blaze began in my belly. Sadly, it was all pretend, unlike the fire he ignited inside me. If I got any more worked up, I'd give up everything for him.

"I know what you're thinking. Don't get any ideas about sneaking off and making any deals with Daniel," Zack said, keeping his voice low enough that Daniel couldn't possibly hear over the music. "Do you know how I'd feel if someone negotiated with a guy like him to save *my* life? I can't be responsible for that. And it won't make me leave or stop trying to protect you."

I nodded. "Okay."

He exhaled and rested his cheek against my temple. I heard his raspy breathing, despite the noise in the room. I repositioned my leg, so I wouldn't feel his against mine. I could think more clearly without being *that* close.

"You spoke to Daniel telepathically. Did he answer you?"

"No." He withdrew to look at me. "Why?"

"I heard what you said. You told him he couldn't make a scene and to go away."

"Interesting. Wonder how you could've heard that when I didn't send it to you. Let's try it again." He visually located Daniel who'd moved to the other side of the room. *You can't win this one. You may as well leave.*

Hand over Autumn. Now. Or I'll mess up some of your pretty little friends. Daniel smiled smugly.

I don't respond to threats. But I'm sure William does.

Daniel's face flushed, his fists clenching, which made me wonder what William had done to punish Daniel the last time he'd disobeyed.

William's not around. It'll be my word against yours.

"Did you get that?" Zack asked softly near my ear.

Goose bumps skittered across my bare skin where his breath had whispered. "Yeah," I said.

"Fascinating." He gave me a crooked grin. "It's like three-way calling."

I gave a nervous laugh.

Maybe when I'm done here, I'll stop by your house. Your mom's dying anyway, isn't she? Daniel's lips curved up. *I'll tell William you were so upset when Autumn dumped you that you went on a rampage. Such a pity I couldn't stop you.*

A blaze ignited behind Zack's eyes. When I searched for Daniel again, he was gone.

CHAPTER TWENTY-NINE

ADRENALINE ROCKETED THROUGH my veins
and my heart raced. I took a deep, calming breath and
sensed Daniel's energy. He hadn't left the party and
gone after Zack's family. Yet.

Should we call the police? I asked.

*They can't help us. If he's that crazy, he'll tear the
cops apart.*

Zack inhaled, but I could feel his muscles tense
and alert as he draped an arm over my shoulder, then
guided me back to Trevor and Maya. When he released
me, she grabbed my hand.

"When did Daniel get so creepy?" Maya gave a mock
shiver.

Glancing over my shoulder, I saw Zack and Daniel
across the room glaring at each other. Were they talking silently? If so, I couldn't hear anything.

"I think he's always been like that," I said. "He's
just not trying to hide it anymore."

The boys separated and Daniel left the room. Zack
reached into his pocket for his cell, dialed and held
it to his ear. I couldn't hear him over the roar of the

music and I wished I could read lips.

He shoved the phone back in his pocket and squeezed through the crowd toward me. *I don't know what he'll do next, but staying here puts everyone else at risk. We need to go.*

But by leaving, *we* would be the ones in danger. *What are we going to do?*

Do you trust me?

I nodded and he took my hand.

We said our goodbyes to Ashley, Trevor, Maya and a few of the other guests, then headed for the car. Outside, my eyes raked up and down Ashley's street for any sign of Daniel. I didn't sense him or any other werewolf. "What if he's on his way to your house?"

"He's not. Let's just go," Zack said, opening the passenger side for me.

I stopped at my car and faced him. Even as the fear built in me, I knew how important it was to keep my cool and my voice level, for Zack's sake as much as my own. He had much more to lose than I did. "Daniel threatened to kill your family. How are we going to keep them safe?"

"I told him I was going to call Charles and tell him about our conversation. Which I did. If Daniel does anything, Charles will be all over William, then Daniel will be dead meat."

"Good thinking." Still, Daniel was more unstable than ever. He wasn't used to a girl rejecting him and couldn't seem to accept it. Especially now that it looked like I preferred Zack to him. "How do we know he's not going to follow us home?"

"No point in worrying about that, since he already knows where you live." Zack scanned the vicinity briefly, then motioned me into the car.

"True. But he could be waiting for us when we get there." I climbed inside, strapped on my seat belt and leaned against the headrest. Dealing with Daniel had sucked the life right out of me.

"There's nothing we can do about that." He shot me a glance. "Unless we sleep in a motel tonight."

I tried not to conjure up images of us in a motel room together. But the pictures snuck in anyway and warmed my cheeks.

"He'll find a way to get to us, no matter where we go," Zack said, starting the car. He sounded way too calm.

"So that's it?" Panic crept into my voice. "We just sit around and wait for him to ambush us?"

"I doubt it'll be tonight, because he knows we're expecting him. He'll want the advantage of surprise." He pulled away from the curb. "We'll have to deal with it when it happens. In the meantime, let's stay alert and not dwell on it."

My fists unfolded and I released a breath, knowing I needed to chill. Worrying about it wasn't going to change the outcome. "So when I walked away, did you guys talk?"

Zack's lips tightened. "Yeah."

"I couldn't hear either of you."

He signaled to turn. "I wonder why."

As we passed houses and street lights, I reconstructed the last few days in my head. "The first time we saw Charles, I heard him ask you about me. I thought it was just me, losing my mind."

Thinking back to the exchange at the dealership, I remembered that Zack had been holding my wrist and moved in front of me. At the party, he'd been wrapped around me.

I gasped. "Zack. Each time that happened, you were touching me. When you let go and I was standing with Maya, I couldn't hear anymore."

"Fascinating. It might come in handy up the road." He white-knuckled the steering wheel.

I shook my head, my hopes plummeting. "Except the scouts will already know about any new abilities we discover."

"Right." He blew out a noisy breath. "Daniel's so new, he might not. *He's* the problem right now."

"What did you guys talk about?"

"Nothing important." Zack lifted a hand off the steering wheel and waved it off. "Just how much he'll enjoy killing me."

"No, Zack. Not because of me. You should stay away." The pitch of my voice had risen and I made a conscious effort to keep from sounding hysterical. "If he gets William to help him, we're dead meat."

"As far as William knows, you're human. He has to obey werewolf law and he knows Charles is keeping an eye on things. I doubt killing me is worth the risk. And I'm *Daniel's* vendetta, not William's. We'll stay in tonight."

"Can you do that?" My eyes cut to his. "I thought it was too hard not to morph."

Zack drove the car into the driveway of my house, jumped out and got to my side before I'd even opened the door. "Difficult, yes, but not impossible."

"We should go out. You *need* to."

"No. I won't put you at risk. We'll figure out another way."

I wondered what that other way could be. I wouldn't let Zack suffer to keep me safe. I couldn't. I unlocked the front door while Zack kept guard. Inside, we checked for Daniel's scent, but he definitely hadn't been in the house.

Usually by now, we were already back from the woods. A run was overdue and I itched to get out. It must've been harder for Zack.

Dropping the keys on the kitchen table, he paced.

"Is there anything I can do to help?" I asked, taking off my sweater.

"You'll have to watch over me, make sure I don't shift."

"But... so what if you do?" I dashed around making sure there were no places the curtains didn't cover, then did the same upstairs. When I returned, a black wolf awaited me, restlessly trotting through the living room.

Go to sleep. I'll be fine. When I hesitated, he added, *If you're worried about me taking off, it's not like I can open a door with my paws.*

I giggled. "True, but you might suddenly feel desperate to run. If you turned human, you could open the door. I'll stay."

Suit yourself. He took off and sprinted down the hallway.

I prayed he didn't damage anything. To save my cuticles from my worrying teeth, I switched on the TV. It had been forever since I'd relaxed and did something mindless. Normal. While keeping an ear out for Zack, I flipped through the channels until I came across a comedy.

About a half hour into the movie, Zack plopped onto the other end of the sofa, back in his human form and dressed. "What's on?"

"Who cares? It's got Vince Vaughn and Owen Wilson." I shot him a smile, but he didn't return it. "Was that not enough? Do you still need to go out?"

He shook his head. "I'm fine, for now."

Why was he staring at me? "Then what's wrong?"

"You're in my bed and I'm tired. Although that's not what I was thinking." He grabbed a decorative pillow and leaned against the end of the sofa. "I'm not comfortable with you so far away. It would take Daniel two seconds to break through your window and snag you. I wouldn't be able to get there in time. Now that he's upped his threats, we can't afford to sleep at opposite ends of the house anymore."

"I could sleep in my dad's chair." I eyed the recliner uncertainly.

"You take your bed. I'll sleep on the floor in your room."

I shook my head. "No way. That chair will be more comfortable for me than the floor. It's hardly fair to let you be uncomfortable when you're only here for my safety."

"Okay. It's late. Let's get ready for bed."

Get ready for bed. That sounded good. I turned and went upstairs to clean up. Out of the shower, I blow dried my hair then contemplated which PJs to wear, settling on a set that covered nearly every inch of me. I wanted to avoid tempting him, which would then torture me.

Delaying my reunion with Zack a few more minutes, I rifled through my closet in search of what I would wear tomorrow, running my hand along the skirt section, then the jeans and tops. Stopping at the dresses, I picked up the hem of a gown covered in paper. Where the protective wrap ended, gold and cream fabric peeked out. I fingered the delicate lace.

"Hey."

I jumped, my eyes darting to Zack who stood in the doorway, bare-chested and hair wet. My stomach did a little flip.

"It got too quiet and I got worried that..."

With great effort, I smiled and tried to keep my eyes on his when I really wanted to ogle his six-pack. "I'm fine."

"What's that?" he nodded toward the hem of the dress in my hand.

"Daniel planned on taking me to prom, so I got this. Now, the thought of going anywhere with him makes me want to vomit." I glanced down at the gown again. "Waste of a perfectly good dress."

"Why not go anyway?"

Was that his way of asking me to go with him? Since we were pretend boyfriend-girlfriend, why not pretend go to the prom together? I waited for him to ask.

"People go stag all the time," he said with a shrug of his shoulder.

"Hell, no." I gave him a dirty look. "I'll be down in a minute."

He backed away and disappeared, his footfalls getting fainter the farther he got. "Come down soon. Having you so far away makes me nervous," he shouted from below.

If only he meant that comment the way I would've meant it.

When I joined Zack downstairs moments later, he'd already become one with the couch, his blanket tucked around him. I turned off the lights and curled up in the big chair, reclining it all the way back. The plush cushions enveloped me and I should've instantly relaxed. Instead, I lay there wired. Snuggling deeper into my comforter, I hoped I'd be able to take my mind off Zack. Eventually. It had been easier up in my room where he was farther away.

I didn't get Zack at all. He had to like me. Otherwise, why did he take every opportunity to kiss me? Could it really be that simple, like he'd said so many times—I was hot and he was still a guy? No connection other than having the right equipment?

Feeling the energy radiating from Zack, I knew he wasn't asleep. What I was about to do was scary and risky. Bad things could happen by putting myself out there and opening myself up. But I just had to. "Zack. If two people like each other, why is being together such a crime? I don't mean mating and risking our chances of winning a battle. I'm talking about enjoying the moment with someone you care about."

"With that reasoning, I could hook up with Maya or Ashley, because they're attractive and I like them too." He exhaled loudly. "Earlier today, you asked me not to kiss you again, because *it meant something to you*. Did you change your mind?"

He'd just lumped me in with every other girl, basically saying I wasn't special to him, even a tiny bit. It felt like a massive weight pushed into my chest, the pressure crushing my heart and lungs. I wondered if I might stop breathing. How long could I live without oxygen?

"I'm sorry, Autumn. You know I care about you or I wouldn't be here. But what you're asking for isn't something I can give you. You have to let this go."

I forced my lungs to take in air. Inhale... exhale... inhale... exhale.

"I never meant to hurt you," he said.

But he *had* hurt me.

Maybe it was a good thing. Maybe I could finally get him out of my head. The truth shall set you free, isn't that what they say? Yet, I didn't feel free and the truth didn't make the rejection go down any easier. But at least now, once and for all with absolute certainty, I knew where we stood.

"Don't sweat it," I said. "You did me a favor. Now I can move on."

He'd warned me all along. How could I be mad at him? It would've been helpful if he'd exercised more control, but who was I to talk? I held as much blame for our make-out sessions as he did.

It had been exactly two weeks ago today since I'd first seen him and most of that time, we'd been at odds. I couldn't be in love with him. Someday, I'd fall in love for real, with someone who could love me back.

Zack's breathing stayed uneven, telling me he was still awake. Mentally, I wanted to cut my ties to him, but even in the wee hours of the night, he was still all I could think about.

† † †

Saturday morning, we slept in and awkwardly went about our morning business, me pretending I didn't care. He'd said good morning to me, but those were his only words until I invited him to breakfast. I'd put coffee on, then whipped up omelets and made toast.

Zack looked like hell. He was pale, his hair exploded in every direction and he moved slower than usual.

"You didn't sleep well?" I saw him eyeing the salt and passed it to him.

"I've had better nights." He sprinkled the shaker over his eggs.

"If feeling sorry for me disturbed your sleep, it shouldn't have," I said, forcing a smile. I couldn't tell what he was thinking, since his face was void of expression. "You warned me that first day car shopping. I should've listened. In any case, I'm fine," I choked out when I really wanted to yell at him and play the blame game. But that would make us both miserable.

The responsibility was on me anyway.

"So, what are your plans today?" I asked in an effort to change the subject.

"We have to take your car in." He spread jelly on his toast and took a bite. "The last thing we want is for it to break down when we need it most."

I took another bite of my eggs. "Can we take it in later? I wanted to do laundry and some cleaning. We also need to get groceries and maybe spend some time with your mom while she's up for it."

"Sounds like a plan." He scooped up another bite of the omelet. "This is great, by the way. So far you've only scrambled them and they were good, but this is amazing."

"Thanks. It's time-consuming though. School mornings I'm too rushed to do it right."

"Then I should wake you up earlier." He grinned.

"Ha ha." I chuckled, relieved at the lighter atmosphere.

"I think doing the car thing later in the day is good," Zack said between chews. "The shop will be closed. I won't have to wait to use any of the equipment and we won't be in anyone's way."

We finished breakfast, then divided up the chores and went our separate ways. After lunch, I finished the last of the mountain of our laundry while he went through the fridge sniffing things and tossing out anything bad. I made my shopping list, consulting him now and then.

Ready to hit the supermarket, I realized all the curtains were still closed. I peered through a slit in the panels while I waited for Zack to stow his clean clothes. A suspiciously familiar black Audi approached.

"He drove by earlier this morning when I took a break from cleaning the kitchen," Zack said from behind me. "Nothing to worry about. It's a scare tactic." He found the keys and opened the front door like he didn't have a care in the world.

I abandoned the window to face Zack. "You don't find it annoying? Maybe a little bit unsettling?"

"Why stress over it? I can handle Daniel." He ushered me out and locked the door.

I glanced around, scrutinizing every inch of the neighborhood, but didn't see Daniel or his car anywhere. When would he attack—today or tomorrow? Could Zack really handle him or would Daniel play dirty and somehow catch Zack off guard?

Maybe Zack wasn't scared. But I sure was.

CHAPTER THIRTY

WE FINISHED AT the market and arrived at Zack's house before dinner.

"Mmm. Lasagna. I love you, Aunt Cara." He leaned over and kissed her on the cheek.

Meat lasagna. How could such a temptation be denied? I briefly considered throwing the whole vegetarian thing out the window. No point in fighting it. But I'd had enough craziness in my life without losing control over some stupid piece of food. I would resist, just as I had all week.

Cara wiped her hands on her apron and smiled at him. "You better not love me just for my cooking. I left a corner of it without meat," she told me. "We don't want you going hungry."

"Thank you. That was nice of you."

"Well, it's the least I can do, since you feed Zack every morning. Your mom's waiting for you, Zack. She's more tired than usual today. You should see her while she's still up for it." Zack opened his mouth and she cut him off. "Go. Both of you. I don't need any help just yet."

"You sure?" I asked Cara as Zack disappeared into the hallway. Staying busy would make me less antsy about waiting helplessly for Daniel to pounce. It was coming. I could feel it. "I don't have anything to do."

Trevor burst through the front door and spotted me right away. "Hey."

"Autumn." Maya sprinted to me and filled me in on everything we'd missed after leaving Ashley's party the night before. Ashley's mom had stepped in vomit, almost slipping on the bathroom floor. When they were breaking up the party and sending everyone home, her parents found partiers making out in their bed. Cigarette butts were strewn across the lawn, a bed of flowers trampled beyond saving and a trash can tipped over with garbage littering the driveway. Now Ashley was limited to a certain number of guests—if she'd ever be allowed to have parties again.

"That's terrible." I said, distributing a stack of plates around the table. "It seemed like everything was under control when we left."

Maya narrowed her eyes. "Somebody spiked the punch and I don't mean with booze. I think it was Daniel. He probably figured her parents wouldn't be able to tell the punch was drugged."

"Such a jerk," I said. It made sense in a twisted way. If he wasn't able to ruin my evening by harassing me, he'd upset me by messing with my friends.

"I couldn't agree more," Maya said. "We're going to that carnival tonight. You and Zack should come. It'll be fun."

I was so not in the mood. "Don't you and Trevor ever want to be alone? You know, a real date, without us tagging along?"

"We get plenty of time alone. It's fun having you two go out with us, especially when you're getting along."

"I'll ask Zack, but he's worried about my car. He wants to go to the garage and check it out."

Maya rolled her eyes. "On a Saturday night? Oh, please. You're coming with us."

I decided to let Zack handle her. I barely had any brain cells left after worrying about Daniel's imminent attack, much less anything else.

† † †

After dinner, Zack helped his mom to bed, while I started on the kitchen. He joined me a few minutes later, washing the pots and pans while I rinsed and dried them.

"What are Trevor's chores? Or do you do everything?"

"I clean the kitchen."

"Oh, that explains why you were so anxious to dump it on me earlier."

He laughed. I'd missed the easy camaraderie. Soon, Daniel would interfere and who knew what the outcome would be?

He'll come for us tonight, I think, Zack said silently. *The more prepared we are, the better our chances. Always stay close to me, okay?*

I'd had even less time to relax than I thought.

"You guys are coming to the carnival, right?" Trevor asked.

Zack glanced at his cousin, shook his head and continued scrubbing. "Nah. Thanks, but I'm too tired. Slept crappy last night."

Trevor wrapped an arm around Maya. "What do you think? You and I can go to a movie tonight instead."

"Only if I get to choose which one," she said, a gleam in her eye.

"Sure," Trevor agreed.

Maya looked smug. She went for chick flicks. I giggled to myself, knowing he'd regret agreeing so readily. The happy couple went to Trevor's room to check on movie times and we finished in the kitchen. Setting the sponge on the side of the sink, Zack wiped his hands on a dish towel and turned to me.

"What now?" I asked out loud.

Visit with my mom, then we meet up with Daniel.

If he isn't out front to see us leave, how will he know where we went? I asked. *Or did you already arrange it with him?*

We didn't talk about it at all. But how do you know he's not around to watch where we go, just because we don't see him? He headed down the hallway toward his mom.

I followed, a rush of trepidation making me sluggish.

Crap. That sucked. *Maybe it won't be tonight. He might wait a few days,* I said hopefully.

Daniel's used to getting his own way and wasn't gifted with patience. The only leverage he has left is surprise. He'll attack and he won't wait a second longer than he has to.

Zack was probably right. Just great. I hated being so dependent on Zack and wished I'd taken a self-defense class. Or two.

He tapped on Favianne's door and opened it gradually. When his mom signaled for us to come in, he urged me ahead of him. As soon as she saw me, she patted the side of the bed. I scooted up onto the mattress and she took my hand.

Trevor poked his head in. "Goodnight, Aunt Favianne."

She smiled sleepily. "Goodnight."

"Can I borrow you?" Trevor asked Zack.

Zack glanced uncertainly at his mother and she waved him away. "Don't stop your life for me. If I fall asleep, I'll see you tomorrow."

He hesitated a moment, then slipped out of the room.

"When do your parents get back?" she asked.

"A week or two, I think."

She smiled. "Then Zack will sleep here again?"

"Yes."

She scrutinized my face. "When I go, his family will take care of him. But it would be nice to know he has a girl to love him and watch over him."

I couldn't be there for Zack. He'd never allow it. My eyes watered, but I didn't wipe them. "I'll do my best."

"I'm sure you will. Don't let him push you away. He can be very independent and stubborn." She leaned her head back against the pillow and closed her eyes. "He loves you, you know."

I blinked, unsure how to respond. What could I say? That her mother's intuition was off? That Zack and I would never be together and what she thought she saw was a lie? "We've been hanging out a week. Love might be too strong of a word."

"He's been slow to open up since he lost his father, but I see that he cares for you. Love can mean many things. Caring for someone, wanting to be near her for who she is. That's the best kind of love."

Should I deny it? Tell her that he and I were thrown together, because of Zack's habit of helping damsels in distress?

Her deep steady breathing told me she'd fallen asleep and didn't require a reply. As gently as I could, I eased off the bed and left. In the hallway, I heard Zack and Trevor. I followed their voices, poking my head through the doorway of Trevor's bedroom.

"They're okay cars, but for that price, you can find one with fewer miles on it." Zack looked doubtfully at the laptop monitor. "Be patient. Don't be in such a rush that you buy a problem. Besides, you have my Jeep when you need it." He glanced at me. *Is she asleep?* When I nodded, his face fell. I'd make sure he spent time with her tomorrow.

If we were still alive.

He waved to Trevor and as we re-entered the hallway, he called out goodnight to his aunt. Handing me my purse, he ushered me out the door and to my car. Once he'd seen me safely inside—not without first scanning the area thoroughly—he started the Mustang and backed out of the spot.

"Should we go straight to the auto shop?" I asked, lowering the window to feel the wind.

"Yeah. Listen," he cast me a quick glance, "if Daniel shows up, you have to remember not to do anything that'll tell him you're a shifter, no matter what."

"He'll fight dirty, Zack. You know he will. If he's about to hurt you, I can't sit there and do nothing." I took in a deep breath and stared ahead. "You can't ask that of me. You can't expect me to stand by and..." I couldn't finish it.

"Autumn, if they find out about you, it's over."

I wasn't going to let Zack get hurt if I could help, but I let the subject drop. "Why are you so sure he'll go to the shop?"

"He's not going to follow us into a crowded place with witnesses. The garage is in an industrial area and deserted most of the weekend. There's no better place to launch an attack. I think he knew that and did something to your car, so we'd have to go there."

"We should've taken my other car or your Jeep." Anything was better than falling in line with Daniel's plan.

"He'd just do something to those cars too, if he hasn't already."

"Oh, my God, Zack." I wasn't sure how much more I could take. There seemed to be no way to avoid a confrontation with Daniel. "Why are we even leaving the house?"

"He's determined to get what he wants. You think some walls and windows would stop him?"

I gripped the edge of my seat. "How about weapons?"

"There are plenty at the garage."

"That Daniel can access also," I added.

Zack shot me a smile. "But I know how to use the good ones."

My eyes snapped to his. "You had all this figured out and you didn't feel the need to tell me?"

"You would've gone crazy worrying."

I didn't reply. Zack's protectiveness was getting annoying. But I *was* grateful I hadn't had all that time to chew on it.

"Thought of all the ways this could go," Zack said, switching lanes. "My house is the safest place for you, but Daniel would just wait it out. This is the way it needs to go down."

Shades of red and orange painted the sky as shadows elongated. It would be dark in a matter of just minutes. "But why didn't you insist we do this earlier? He'd be less likely to attack in broad daylight. Staying alive is a little more important than laundry and chores, don't you think?"

"If he's going to come, I'd rather be the one to orchestrate it, so we know when and where to expect him. This way, we can be prepared. Plus, it's easier to hide a body in the dark."

I shot him a glare. "What?"

"Just kidding. Sort of. Hey, we have to be prepared for anything."

My stomach felt queasy and I pressed a hand to it. "It's a bit of a stretch that Daniel would sabotage the car with all that in mind." I hoped Zack was wrong.

"Maybe. I smelled Daniel's scent on the hood when I checked to see where the noise was coming from." He waited until we were several blocks from the shop before speaking again. "He's been around the car again today, but I'm not sure when."

"You smelled him?" My belly roiled.

"Yeah. All over the seats." He turned to me. "He's just messing with us."

"Why didn't I smell it?"

"While you were doing laundry earlier, I slipped outside and checked out the car. When I smelled him, I cleaned the seats."

"Really, Zack? What else are you hiding?" Anger was good. It took my mind off my churning stomach.

He nodded toward my hand pressed against my abdomen. "Look at you. If we switched places, would you want to tell me?"

"That doesn't make it right," I mumbled. We were almost at the shop and staying focused on any topic would be difficult. I'd argue with him later.

"I was thinking about this three-way calling business." Zack began slowing the Mustang way before the stop light. "If Daniel's touching either one of us and we talk telepathically, he'll hear us and know about you. We should be able to direct our thoughts. You know, he shouldn't be able to hear us if we block him."

"How do we block him?" I asked. We were moving again, but barely. Zack was stalling, probably since we were close to the shop and he had more to say.

"I'm guessing it's the same way you morph. You visualize it happening. See it the way you want it to be."

Apparently, he utilized his spare time trying to find a way to beat Daniel, while I used mine trying to get Zack to want me. His time had been much better spent. I slumped in my seat, feeling useless.

He eased up off the accelerator a little more. "On the other hand, it might not work and he might over-hear everything we say to each other and he'll know you're not human."

"So we don't do it unless there's no other way," I said, recognizing the auto shop sign up ahead.

"Right. When we get there, we'll open the garage, drive the car inside, then close and lock it."

"Sounds simple enough," I said.

Waiting in the turning lane, he glanced at me. "The timing will be tricky though. The garage door isn't au-tomatic. We'll both have to leave the car to open it and come back together. I can't leave you alone."

With the Mustang's top down, I felt vulnerable. "We should put the top up."

"No, that would make your car higher and give Daniel something bigger to hide behind if he snuck in somehow. We need to see everything around us."

The nausea became more intense and I swallowed to keep from gagging. As Zack pulled into the desert-ed lot, he squeezed my hand. "It'll be fine. You'll see."

I looked into his green eyes and, for that moment, I believed him.

"C'mon." He opened the driver's side door and got out, eyes scanning the lot. Not a soul in sight.

In unison, we moved to the lock on the immense garage door. I kept my back to the wide door while Zack slipped a key into the padlock and pulled the chain through the thick brackets. Still hanging onto the chain, he pressed his back to the door and bent at the knee. Grabbing the handle, Zack rose, bringing the door up with him. He motioned to the car. On high alert, we got in at the same time.

Slowly, the car eased into the empty garage. To my right was ample room where five cars could park side by side.

As soon as Zack killed the engine, I smelled him.

Daniel.

I sucked in air to shout out a warning to Zack who was rounding the hood, but Daniel was already at my side, stuffing a rag over my mouth. Instead of air, I sucked in something vile. He yanked me out of the passenger's seat and snaked an arm around my neck.

Zack froze two feet away. *Autumn, he drugged you.*

I'd figured that out by the stink up my nose and the fog in my brain. But I wasn't completely unconscious. Apparently, drugs didn't affect me like they would a human.

Act like you're out. Zack told me silently.

I pretended to go limp, resting the back of my head against Daniel's chest. Knowing he couldn't see my eyes with my back to him, I kept them open.

"Don't do anything stupid, Zack. One move and I'll snap her neck."

If Daniel had heard our three-way calling, he would've

skipped the threats and fast-forwarded to the snapping. I inwardly breathed a huge sigh of relief that Zack was able to block Daniel from our silent conversation.

"Okay." Zack took a step back and held out his hands. "You're the boss."

"That's right, I am." I felt a tremor in Daniel's chest as though he were laughing. "You should've walked away when you had the chance, moron."

"So what now, Daniel? You think you can get away with her dead weight holding you back? You'd never make it."

"You're going to step aside and let me walk away, because you don't want her to get hurt."

"Hm." Zack nodded thoughtfully. "Why would you think that?"

Daniel chuckled. "Because you like her. Duh."

"Yeah, well, she *is* hot. But she's just a girl. A *human* at that. You want to kill her, go ahead. You're not leaving here alive though. Not after you've insulted me and tried to take what's mine."

With his free hand, Daniel picked a knife from his back pocket. He held its razor sharp edge to my neck below his arm. If he pressed any harder, he'd draw blood. "You sure about that, dude?"

"You went through all this trouble for her and now you're okay with killing her?" Zack laughed. "You're an idiot, Daniel. I can tell you though, she's worth the wait," Zack said, a slow smile spreading over his face.

Daniel's arms stiffened, then he released me and I allowed my body to crumple the way I imagined an unconscious person would fall.

CHAPTER THIRTY-ONE

I WENT DOWN, twisting my body and turning my head, so I'd be able to keep tabs on them. My shoulder hit the concrete with a light thud, a few wisps of hair settling over my eyes. Unless he looked closely, Daniel wouldn't notice me watching them.

Daniel lunged, swiping the knife at Zack's torso.

Zack laughed, dodging the blade. "You can do better than that." *Stay down, Autumn, so this isn't all for nothing.*

I gritted my teeth, but obeyed as Daniel sprang again. Zack ducked, grabbed a wrench and on his way up, clocked Daniel on the side of his face. Daniel stumbled into a table laden with tools. He gripped a tire iron and swung. When it crashed into Zack's side, he staggered and fell, his back slamming to the ground. Daniel jumped on him, sending them both rolling. Daniel landed on top with his back to me, Zack struggling beneath him. Daniel wielded the iron again, but Zack swung the wrench, hitting Daniel's inside elbow. Daniel lost his hold on the iron and it skittered across the cement.

Fists flew, but from where I lay, I couldn't tell who was winning.

The wrench clattered to the floor, which left Zack without a weapon. I couldn't take it anymore and moved to get up.

Don't distract me by doing something stupid, Autumn. I got it.

With Zack still trapped underneath Daniel, I wasn't so sure about that. But I held still and hoped.

Zack's legs and arms shot out at Daniel. A fist hit its mark, tossing Daniel off. Zack leapt to his feet and flipped a switch behind him, then grabbed the nozzle of a hose. When Daniel went in for another attack, Zack squeezed the handle and blasted air into Daniel's eyes. He screamed and covered his face. Zack captured Daniel's arms and shoved him back, immobilizing him against the side of a sturdy table. "Touching you this much is like my worst nightmare. You're not my type."

"I'll kill you!" Daniel screamed, eyes squeezed shut.

"News flash for you, loser. That's exactly what you'll have to do. Because if you want Autumn, you'll have to go through me to get to her. I'll die before I'd let you get near her again."

Daniel opened his eyes, then closed them again. "I can't see."

"Stop being such a wuss." Zack easily blocked Daniel's blow, then another.

Even without vision, Daniel put up a good fight, his fists thrashing wildly and relentlessly. Zack dodged them, but I knew any second, Daniel would be able to see again and Zack would be right back where he'd started. Killing him would be the most effective, but I didn't want to think about that and certainly wouldn't want to witness it.

Autumn, look away. You don't want to see this.

Apparently, Zack was one step ahead of me, as usual. The next moment, Zack jammed the nozzle into Daniel's eyes while he released the air. Daniel wailed as blood trickled down his cheeks. The tossing in my stomach returned and the possibility of throwing up was too real.

"Stop screaming like a girl, Daniel." Zack stepped away to search the table, finding a roll of duct tape. "It could take an hour or two before you can see again, although I'm not sure if you'll live that long. That depends on you."

"Zack, let him go." William, Daniel's maker, stepped into the garage in a flurry of rage, but he went directly to his fledgling, seizing him by his shirt and throwing him to the ground. "You halfwit. I told you not to involve the human." He leaned over and slapped Daniel, hard, followed by a series of punches to his face.

"She's doesn't know anything." Daniel curled up in a ball in an attempt to shield himself from the onslaught. "She didn't see me when I chloroformed her."

"But she's *here*, isn't she? She'll know it was you, pinhead. What if she goes to the police?" With one hand, William picked Daniel up by his shirt and set him to his feet. He backhanded Daniel with so much force, a bone cracked. "You just don't listen." A strange energy emitted from William, almost a vibration. I guessed his patience with Daniel was used up. "You better pray you dosed her properly and she wakes up."

"She will. I only gave her a little bit." Daniel rubbed his eyes with quivering hands.

William released Daniel and he reeled backward, bouncing into the edge of the table. "You and your foolish vendetta. You will be punished for defying me."

"I have to see Autumn. Where is she?" Daniel extended his arms and groped sightlessly.

William didn't answer, backing away and sneering, like he enjoyed seeing Daniel suffer. Zack stuck out his leg and Daniel stumbled over it, his hands shooting out to break his fall.

"You'll never have a chance to get close to her again," Zack said. "She's mine. You got it?"

Daniel growled and leaped up blindly, but Zack easily avoided him.

William stepped in front of Zack, clamped a hand around his neck and raised his arm until Zack's feet dangled. "You might be even stupider than Daniel. I could waste you in a second and you dare cross me by antagonizing my recruit?"

Zack clutched at the hand clamping his throat.

"One more stunt like that and I'll kill you myself," William hissed.

The energy in the room seemed to change somehow, like the air became thicker. A pair of cowboy boots appeared in front of me.

"That won't be necessary," Charles said. "Put him down."

340

William glared at the latest arrival, but complied. Zack rubbed his throat.

Great. Now we had three werewolves to contend with. If Charles became hostile, Zack and I would never make it. I closed my eyes as Charles approached me.

"Turning someone out of spite. That's petty, even for you, William," Charles said.

"I'm picking up a rogue wolf nearby," William growled. "You were the only scout in the area, but you weren't available. I needed help."

Charles gave him a low, gravelly laugh. "Or you turned him, because you thought you'd use Daniel to hijack my recruit. I already warned you to stay away from Zack."

"You must think I have nothing better to do." William laughed, but there was no humor in it.

"Don't you?" As Charles bent closer to me, his earthy scent became stronger. "She's a pretty little thing. Zack, if you decide to turn her, make sure you get approval beforehand. I'm sure you went through the proper channels to change Daniel. Right, William?"

"Of course," William answered in a voice slightly less steady than a moment ago.

"And I'm sure if I called your supervisor, he'd assure me of that. Or would Kyle tell me that you haven't applied for a permit since Colorado about two years ago? If he asked me why I was inquiring, I'd tell him I was checking on something, but would get back to him within twenty-four hours." Charles sighed, sounding immensely pleased. "If I disappeared for any reason, I imagine he'd check into the matter."

I didn't understand why a permit held such significance. But if it got William and Daniel out of the way, it was fine by me.

"You will leave this city, this state and not return for a minimum of six months," Charles ordered. "If you do, I'll have that talk with Kyle. Come to think of it, there are a few other things I've been meaning to discuss with him." The fabric of his clothes rustled as he moved away from me. "You and your pup will leave tonight as soon as his eyes are healed. Daniel's proven to be quite resourceful. If he can procure chloroform, I'm sure he can handle the situation without raising suspicions from the mortals. See it through, William. And if you ever bother one of my recruits again, I will make sure that the entire werewolf community knows all your dirty little secrets, especially King Mortimer."

I heard William growl and drag Daniel away, then silence. One second... two seconds... three seconds.

"He's disgusting, even for a scout." Charles made a low sound in his throat. "You'll have to make something up to tell the girl, so she doesn't involve the officials. They'd want to find out what she was given, which would involve blood tests and the pup will be their most promising suspect. We can't have the mortals investigating one of our own."

"Yes, sir," Zack answered.

"Tell her she passed out. I'll hang around a while to make sure William and his pup don't come back or try anything else."

Zack lifted me up off the concrete. I heard the car door open as he gently laid me in the passenger seat.

"Put the top up, so she isn't noticed."

"Yes, sir." Zack went to the driver's side and did as he was told. I stayed in the car seat, my head leaning against the window, while he straightened the shop and cleaned up spilled blood.

"If you need anything, call me. If you see William or Daniel again, I want to know right away."

† † †

Zack and I didn't speak a word on the way home as I pretended to be asleep. He cruised into the driveway of my house, parked and swiveled in his seat. *If I carry you in, your neighbors might see and it would draw attention to us. It's probably okay if our werewolf buddies see you awake now. Act weak. If we see Charles, he'll assume you woke up during the drive.*

Racing around the car, he opened the door for me. Gingerly, as though I was still disoriented, I got out.

Charles appeared out of nowhere, meeting us at the path to the front door. "Hello. I had no idea we were neighbors. Everything alright?"

He seemed so nice. Not at all like my first impression at the dealership. Standing less than an inch shorter than Zack, he wore his long, brown hair loose. It framed brown eyes and lightly tanned skin.

"Uhm, yeah. She fainted, but she's okay now." Zack draped an arm around my shoulders. *You think we're safe now?* he asked Charles telepathically.

Yes. They won't bother you again.

You're sure? Zack asked.

Positive. If I turn out to be wrong though, call me. I'll be close by. He switched to talking aloud. "I'm glad you're alright," he told me, then turned to my escort again and tipped his hat. "You two have a nice evening."

Zack looked a little dazed. I probably did too.

CHAPTER THIRTY-TWO

WE WENT STRAIGHT for the sofa without turning on a light, Zack on one end and me on the other.

"I can't believe you did that to his eyes. That was so disgusting." A giggle slipped out, even though it wasn't actually funny.

"I didn't gouge them out or anything. Just messed them up." Zack half snorted, half laughed. "I wanted to kill him."

"Why didn't you?" Not that I'd wanted him to, but I was curious.

"I was hoping I wouldn't have to. I figured since I know that shop inside and out, I had an edge on him. Planned on tying him up with duct tape so tight that even morphing into werewolf, he couldn't get away. Stuff him in the trunk, drop you off, then call Charles. If things got ugly, I would've killed him to keep you safe, but it's not something I was looking forward to. And there'd still be a werewolf inquisition and I'd have to prove it was self-defense."

I shuddered at the thought of Zack being jailed or worse for protecting me. "I'm glad it didn't come to that."

"Once William showed up, I knew Charles would follow," Zack said. "I'd given Charles the heads up earlier and suggested he keep an eye on William, which guaranteed that if William showed, I'd have help."

"You had everything all figured out and you didn't think maybe you should clue me in?"

Zack left the couch, then switched on a light and stood in front of me. "I didn't want you to worry. At the same time, I didn't want you getting your hopes up by thinking we were in the clear."

"You think it's over?" I asked.

"With Daniel, for now, yes." He settled into the recliner. "But so long as I'm a werewolf under the king's rule and you're a potential slave, it will never be over for us."

"You put such a positive spin on things." I sighed and relaxed my shoulders.

"Sorry, I don't mean to upset you, but you need to understand the situation."

"Trust me, I'm fully aware of the situation." Part of me wished I wasn't. "But Charles was surprisingly nice. Maybe he's not so bad."

"He's a werewolf and a scout, Autumn. You're forgetting how creepy you thought he was. Besides, he wants the same thing William wants. The *king's* best interest, not mine."

"Your father was both those. Don't forget *that*. Most important, *you're* a werewolf. We're not even supposed to get along and yet we do."

"Don't be so optimistic that you're not prepared for the worst." He pulled the lever and the footrest came out.

"Well, that's something you don't have to concern yourself with, because I *am* prepared for the worst," I said softly, taking a deep breath. "Now that Daniel's gone, you don't need to protect me. I've got my car now, so that frees up your afternoons and weekends."

Zack didn't comment. Good. I didn't want him to say something nice and give me false hope. I needed to cut him from my life as quickly and painlessly as possible. The sooner he left, the sooner the healing could begin. But I'd still see him at school and it would be excruciating. Monday seemed like a million years away though.

"Imagine how glad your mom will be when you go home tonight and tell her Daniel is no longer harassing me," I said, my chest tightening at the thought of Zack not staying the night.

"Until I'm sure he's gone, you're not out of the woods. I'll stay tonight. But tomorrow, you probably won't need me anymore."

Oh, but he was so wrong.

"In the morning, we'll get your car fixed and you can drop me off."

I'd forgotten about the car. "You don't need to bother with that. I can take it in on Monday after school."

Zack growled, low and deep. "Autumn, we'll fix it tomorrow. I'm not taking any chances."

"Fine." I waved my hand in surrender and rose from the couch. "Goodnight."

"Autumn," he groaned.

A part of me hoped that at last, knowing that tomorrow we'd barely see each other, he'd finally realize what a mistake he was making by turning me away. "Yes?"

His mouth thinned to a straight line. "I need to morph tonight."

"Right." I turned away, my eyes misting. Stupid Autumn. "Sorry. Shouldn't we stay in?"

"Yes."

"Okay." And like the night before, I closed the house up tight.

† † †

Sleep hadn't come easy. In the morning, the sun filled the room and bright light shined through my eyelids. I turned over, hoping for a few more minutes of sleep. I didn't want to face the hole in my heart and what my life had become. I wasn't looking forward to anything in my future.

When I opened my eyes, I saw my bedroom door standing wide open, which meant Zack had checked on me during the night. I wondered if he was still downstairs. Would he be anxious to get away from me? Or would he be as happy to continue as friends?

He appeared in the doorway, his arms spread to embrace the doorframe as if it would fall any second. "Hey," he said.

I tried to smile, but couldn't make my mouth do that particular function. Hopefully, he'd think my odd facial expression was because I wasn't fully awake yet. "You were in my room again."

"Yeah, so? You've had a rough week. I was just checking on you."

I squinted, thinking his week had been twice as stressful. "Well, I didn't have to stick a nozzle in Daniel's sockets to destroy his eyeballs. I think you win."

"Yeah, I guess I do." He didn't smile, watching me another moment, then he disappeared.

I didn't want him to leave without saying goodbye and didn't know how much more time I had with him. So I jumped out of bed and threw on some clothes. After racing down the stairs, I searched the house for Zack. He had the fridge open and glanced over when I entered the kitchen.

"Up for an omelet?" I asked.

He grinned. "Always."

I licked my lips, suddenly aware I hadn't even checked myself out in a mirror. "I'll be back in a couple minutes."

When I was pretty sure my face and hair were no longer scary, I headed downstairs and something caught my eye. Zack's duffle bag, box of books and other things waited by the front door. This was it. The end. I could swear there was an imaginary blanket over my face, suffocating me.

"After breakfast, we can go straight to the shop, then I'll go home. You know, rather than breaking up our day."

"Right." I mustered up a smile from God knows where and headed to the fridge where I could hide in the omelet process. Ten minutes later, I called Zack for breakfast and set a plate in front of him.

He nodded, taking a bite of food and chewing. "Mm. This is good. I'm going to miss your weekend omelets."

But would he miss *me*?

I rose to put the cheese and other items away, then grabbed a sponge to wipe the counters and wash the pans. By the time the kitchen was clean again, Zack's food had vanished.

"You know..." He placed his plate in the dishwasher. "It's silly to drag you to the shop with me. There will be nothing for you to do there anyway." Seeing egg bits in the sink, he turned on the water and swished it around. "I'll go by myself, then bring your car back as soon as I'm done."

"Okay. Call me when you're on your way back and I'll have lunch waiting. It's the least I can do."

"Nah." He shrugged. "No offense, but the vegetarian thing isn't working for me."

I knew he didn't mean it as a subliminal message, that *this* vegetarian wasn't working for him. Zack was too open and straightforward to hide behind cruel remarks under the guise of help or friendship. But his reminder hurt just the same. He had to go.

I tossed him the keys and forced a smiled. "Thanks so much for doing this."

"No problem. I don't think I'll be gone more than an hour. If it ends up being complicated, I'll let you know."

I nodded and closed the door.

† † †

The first part of that hour after Zack left couldn't have been better spent. What could be more awesome than worrying if your neighbors hear your gut wrenching cries of anguish and fearing that they'll call the police for fear you were being attacked? Soaking your pillow and going through two boxes of tissues was reason to be grateful for being alive.

I reveled in that first glimpse of my face in the mirror—splotchy skin around swollen and bloodshot eyes.

The last part of that hour was spent on repairs. I became the surgeon, painstakingly reconstructing my face after a gruesome accident and the artist, carefully layering the canvas.

Zack texted me when he was on his way to my house, saying he'd already stopped at home to drop off his belongings. Since all our business had been concluded, I hovered in the doorway and smiled as he handed me my keys.

"I'll walk home. It's a nice day." His eyes darted away as he mashed his lips together. "As far as everyone else is concerned, Daniel's still around, which is the reason we've given my family for me spending the night here. We have no idea how he's going to handle his banishment and we're probably not going to find out until Monday. So..."

"You have to sleep here tonight?" My stomach clenched at the thought of being subjected to Zack when he didn't want me. At the same time, my heart soared at spending more time with him.

"No. My mom and Cara just need to *think* I'm sleeping here."

"Oh." I wasn't sure what that meant, but it would be a bad idea to invite him in, even though I desperately wanted to. If he asked, the answer would be yes.

"I have a way around that," he said.

Asking him to explain and engaging in further conversation would only stretch out my agony, so I kept my mouth shut. When I offered only a smile, I thought I saw a hint of sadness in his eyes. In a flash, it was gone and he smiled. "See you at school tomorrow."

"Yeah. Thanks for everything." My chest felt heavy as he walked away. "'Bye."

CHAPTER THIRTY-THREE

I PAUSED, MY back against the closed door. There had to be a way to get through this heartache. Other people survived broken hearts. I could too.

Breathe in. Breathe out. Breathe in. Breathe out. Steadier, I grabbed my laptop. I needed an escape, something to take my mind off Zack and how he'd left me.

Scrolling through the movie thumbnails, I considered downloading a horror flick, but feared having nightmares again. That went double for anything with vampires or werewolves. That kind of thing was too real now. And I didn't want anything depressing or stressful either, so that eliminated the dramas. The action flicks would remind me of Zack and how he saved me. The love stories would also remind me of him for obvious reasons.

I finished scanning the new releases and discovered there wasn't anything that wouldn't make me think of Zack. In the end, I picked a couple of my old favorites, the ones where I knew exactly what to expect—a sappy, happy ending.

I made some popcorn, soaked it in salt and hot butter, then flopped onto the sofa and started the first movie.

† † †

When I awoke hours later, I was still on the couch. I felt stiff from tossing and turning all night. What time was it? I fumbled for my cell and saw it was after four. All that time trying to escape thoughts of Zack and here I was again. What would I do to keep my mind off him now? I dashed up the stairs to my room, threw on some sweats and flew out the door. If I ran now, I could be back before the sun came up and maybe I could stay home tonight when I'd be more likely to run into Zack.

I'd missed my runs. It was nice to know I could live without them, but I was grateful to be free again. Morphing into a cheetah, I ran as fast as my long, furry legs could carry me.

When I returned home, I was just as emotional, but physically, I was less sluggish from my Zack hangover.

I killed the rest of the extra time getting ready. Since hitting new lows on the depression scale, it was more important than ever to do everything possible to feel better about myself. I wore a sundress and sandals, then took the time to curl my hair.

Sailing into the school lot, I realized by the lack of cars it was still too early. If I stayed, I'd see Zack arrive and perhaps *accidentally* run into him. On the other hand, not seeing Zack was the quickest way to get over him. Plus, I'd feel less pathetic.

Despite knowing I must avoid him to get over him, I scanned the lot one more time for the red Jeep. Disgusted with myself, I got out of the Mustang and saw the red Jeep drive into the lot. I leaned into my car pretending to dig into my backpack.

"Autumn!" Maya shouted. She stuck her head out of Zack's Jeep window and waved to me.

I waited for them to park. As far away as she was, I could still hear what she said to Trevor.

"I'm going to talk to Autumn. I'll see you in a couple minutes."

He nodded and said something to Zack, but I didn't listen in.

"Hey." She sprinted to me, a little out of breath. "Did you hear about Daniel?"

I shook my head innocently. "No."

"You're not going to believe this. Apparently, he ran away over the weekend with his new love. He's gone."

"Ran away? Why couldn't he stay here with this mystery girl?" A strange story, but not final enough to warrant a permanent disappearance. I waited for the rest of it.

Maya's eyes widened. She looked like she was bursting with fascinating news. "Not a *girl*."

"What?" My mouth gaped. "An older woman?"

"He met a *dude*. Supposedly, it's the same guy he'd met when Jeff said he'd been dragged away by a wolf. Can you believe it?"

Actually, I could, except for the *love* part. I knew the male lover bit wasn't Daniel's idea. He most definitely liked girls. William must have thought it an amusing penalty for disobeying and humiliating him.

It was perfect.

"You know what homophobes his parents are," Maya went on. "They're so pompous about their money and knowing all the right people. Their reputation is more important than their own son. As soon as Daniel came out, they disowned him."

"Wow. That sucks for Daniel," I said. It was a brilliant plan since being disowned cut all ties, which would make life as a werewolf easier.

Maya giggled. "I guess we don't have to worry about him stalking you anymore."

Zack passed by, giving me a nod. I smiled, hoping it appeared genuine. It was the best I could manage.

"C'mon." Maya motioned for me to go with her and the boys.

"I'll see you at lunch. I have something I need to do." Like hide my head in the sand, so I couldn't do something pathetic like throw myself at Zack.

I made a beeline to the bathroom. As soon as the door swung shut, it opened again. Gina waltzed in, eyeing me coldly.

"You think you've won, don't you?"

"Uh, I didn't know there was a contest," I said. "And it's not like Daniel left you for *me*."

She gave a forced laugh.

"And besides," I rifled through my purse for my lipstick. "Zack and I aren't together anymore." I glanced at her briefly to see her eyes shooting daggers at me.

"You're such a liar. You'll do and say anything to hurt me and get what you want." Apparently, she was almost as delusional as Daniel.

I applied the lip color, then rubbed my lips together as Gina's face flushed and her eyes hardened. If she'd approached me without the attitude, I would've smiled and went about my business. "You might get my leftovers if you act quickly." Dropping my makeup in my purse, I pushed past her.

It was masochistic of me to paint a bull's-eye on Zack, when there was a chance he might go for it. If he hooked up with her though, I'd lose respect for him and getting over him might be easier. If it went the other way, witnessing him reject her was worth the risk and would make my day slightly less dreary. It was a win-win situation.

At lunch, I waved at Zack's table from where I sat with John and Janine. Maya had tried to talk me into hanging with her and the boys, but Zack had come to my rescue, telling her it was healthy to socialize with other people now and then. Apparently, no one noticed Zack and I weren't together. Or maybe he'd already told them something. I was dying to know.

Where did you sleep last night? I asked Zack from across the room.

He smiled. *At home. Where else?*

But I thought you were supposed to be at my house, I said, focusing on my lunch.

Everyone had to think *I was with you. I left and later snuck back into my room through the window.*

Clever. I took a bite of my grilled cheese sandwich, grateful that with silent communication, I didn't have to worry about talking with my mouth full. *What did you tell Maya about us? I'm wondering why she's not interrogating me.*

I told her you missed your other friends. She was so wrapped up in the whole Daniel thing, she moved on.

Why not tell her the truth? I asked. *That we're not together.*

I wasn't sure if you'd want to deal with that yet. Good old Zack—always thinking of me. I wished he'd stop that. He made it so difficult to hate him.

Well, thanks. I returned to my meal, but saw Gina approach him in my peripheral vision. Maya didn't even notice, too engrossed in Trevor.

I told myself not to listen in on Gina and Zack. But, unable to resist, I peeked at them from under my lashes and tuned out everyone else in the lunchroom.

"Hi, Zack."

"Hey, Gina." He gave her a friendly smile.

"I wondered if you wanted to go for coffee after school. We haven't been working on our science project and it's due soon."

"Can't today. I have a shift at the auto shop."

"What about Friday night? We could hit a movie after."

Zack turned away, frowning. "Well, I got to thinking. We should stick to working on it here after school. Except for our mandatory school project, I don't want to associate with someone who betrayed her best friend by sleeping with her boyfriend."

Gina's mouth dropped open and her face turned bright red.

Zack took a bite of his burger and ignored her.

Ouch.

Through my guilt, I couldn't help gloating. But damn him. Now he was even more appealing than before—if that was even possible. I'd never get over him.

Ever.

† † †

Later that afternoon, I zipped upstairs to my room to change into some ratty, old sweats and a faded T-shirt from eighth grade. To take my mind off Zack, I buried my brain in homework. But I finished too quickly and was alone again with my thoughts.

The dead silence made me miss my parents horribly. I'd emailed them on Saturday and needed to send another one soon. But I didn't feel like it. The depression hung over me like a heavy mist, strangling me.

Why didn't Zack like *me* enough to run away with? Or at least be with me for what little time we had. What was wrong with me? Fighting for my life with Daniel was almost easier, because at least then, I stood a chance. A tangible evil could be fought. How someone feels about you couldn't be changed.

But his feelings didn't fit with his actions. He'd gone above and beyond, even told Daniel he'd have to kill him to get to me.

Minutes passed as I stared at the television I hadn't yet turned on.

Why would Zack do so much for me if he didn't feel anymore for me than he did for Maya or Ashley? How was it possible?

Wait.

Air whooshed out of my chest as the clouds in my mind parted and the sun shone.

Why hadn't I seen it before?

I snatched my keys from the dining room table, left the house and locked the door behind me. I sprinted down the block and knocked on Zack's door.

Trevor answered, looking surprised to see me. "Oh. What are you doing here?"

"I've been around almost every day for the last week and you act like it's strange for me to be here?" I raised my brows.

Trevor blinked. "He's been so crabby, I thought you two broke up."

That was impossible since we were never together in the first place. But Trevor didn't know that. "We wouldn't be the first couple in history to have a disagreement. But I have some ideas how to fix it."

Trevor grinned. "Good. He's more fun when you guys are getting along."

"Is he here?" I peeked past Trevor's shoulder.

"Yeah. He's in his room." Trevor swung the door open for me.

I headed to Zack's room, but he met me in the hallway.

"Autumn, what are you doing here?" He spotted Trevor and waved him away.

"I need to discuss something with you. Alone."

"What? Why?" He leaned against a wall, fidgeting.

"I want to talk to you about *us*," I whispered.

He inhaled deeply. "I don't want to go through it again."

I blinked. "You mean you won't even give me five minutes? Really?"

He shook his head, avoiding my gaze. Crap. What would I do now?

"Zack," his mother wheezed from the doorway of her room. Apparently, we'd been too quiet for Trevor to hear from the living room, but Favianne was just off the hallway where we were standing. "What's going on?" she asked.

Maybe her overhearing us wasn't so bad. Zack's mom liked me and wanted me with him. She'd help me if I played my cards right. "Zack's trying to dump me. I'm trying to work things out with him, but he won't even talk to me."

Stop this, Autumn. Let it go, he screamed into my head.

What are you going to do if I don't? Dump me?

He glared, resembling an overheated steam engine.

"Is that true, Zack? Autumn wants to work things out and you're refusing to talk?" Favianne closed her eyes and leaned against the doorway.

I became aware of her heart thudding, her lungs

crackling. It must've been difficult getting out of bed, which made me feel guilty for making a scene.

"What did she do that was so bad you can't give her a few minutes?"

"Yeah, Zack. What did I do that was so bad?"

Zack clenched his fists. "Mom, you should be in bed. Let me help." He reached for her.

She swatted his hands away and breathed in again. "Zack, I raised you better than this. I can't tell you who to date. But I *am* asking that you go someplace where you can talk privately and give her fifteen minutes. And both of you," she glanced from him to me, "need to *explain* yourselves better. Be patient and respectful. Promise me you'll give her a chance, Zack."

"Okay, I promise. Let's get you back to bed." He picked her up and carried her back into her room, while I waited in the hallway.

I will never forgive you for this, Autumn.

CHAPTER THIRTY-FOUR

ZACK STORMED PAST me and out the front door. I had to sprint to keep up with his long strides. *You think, for once, you can leave my mother out of your mischief?*

"It's not my fault you were being mean where your mom could hear. And by the way, our fifteen minutes doesn't start until we're inside my house." I followed him down the street, a smug smile stretched over my face.

I unlocked my front door and he pushed past me. Rude.

He had the nerve to check the time on his cell. "Clock's ticking. Let's get this over with, huh?"

"Time out, Zack. You promised you'd be patient and respectful." I folded my arms over my chest.

He covered his face with his hands and took measured breaths. He stood taller and rolled his shoulders. "Okay. I get the point. Talk."

I sat on the couch, bringing my knee up, and swiveled to face him. "When Daniel and I got together, it was easy because he was a safe bet."

"Daniel? *Safe?*" He gave a sarcastic laugh.

"He was popular, which gave me security. And I

knew he liked me. Since I wasn't crazy in love with him, the risk was minimal. Safe." I glanced at my knees and noticed my old, faded T-shirt and ratty sweats. It didn't do much to bolster my confidence, but I'd come too far to stop now. "But I don't want safe anymore. Not if it means losing a piece of myself. If I want something, I'm going to stand up and fight for it. And so should you."

He sighed, his eyes drifting lazily around the room.

I forged ahead, determined to break down his resistance. "I got to thinking. I couldn't figure out how you could do everything you've done and not want me enough to be with me. You went all-out with the Mustang. You could've let me go on and on searching endlessly, but you jumped in, found me the perfect car and made the deal for me."

Zack rolled his eyes. "It's called a job. You were paying me."

"Quiet. I'm not done yet." I waved an index finger at him. "You protected me over and over again from Daniel, had me for dinner at your house, double dated with me when you didn't have to, watched over me in the woods when you were a wolf, helped me figure out who and what I was, told me everything you knew about our kind." I took a moment to breathe, softening my voice. "You kissed me, touched me. You did all these things like you really cared about me."

"Autumn—"

"Shhh. I'm not done and my fifteen minutes aren't up. I get an extra minute, by the way, because you keep interrupting. Add another minute because you're being impatient." I raised one brow.

He growled.

"As I was saying, all these things were going through my head while I tried to figure out how anyone could do all that and not care deeply about the person. I kept buying into your explanations, but they never completely sat right with me. Then it hit me." I smiled. "The answer is so simple. I can't believe I didn't figure it out before." I paused a moment to let it sink in. "The answer is... it's *not* possible. That's the answer."

"What?" He looked baffled.

"It's *not* possible. You can't do all that and not want me."

He blew out his breath. "That's what this is all about? A guy would have to be dead not to be attracted to you. That's all there is to it."

"And I understand that. But you're trying to convince me that you only like me as a friend. That I don't mean any more to you than Ashley or Maya. But I know your feelings run deeper than that. I know this like I know your kiss, the color of your eyes and hair. Denying it doesn't change what I know. It'd be nice, though, if you admitted it."

He folded his arms over his chest. "Keep talking. Three minutes left."

"You think it's easier if you leave and pretend you never felt anything and I'll get over it. You think you're protecting me, protecting yourself and you're saving us both a lot of pain. But it's not easier. Sometimes easier isn't easier."

"Don't go into philosophy." He smirked. "No one would understand you."

"You know what I mean. It's like when you don't want to do your homework. You think it's easier not to do it. But later, when you get grounded for getting an F, it's so much harder and you wish you'd taken the time when you had the chance."

"How does that have anything to do with us?" He moaned and sat at the other end of the couch.

"I'm getting there." I got up to pace. "You think you're doing me this huge favor by pushing me away. You think it's honorable, but it's actually stupid. According to you, the plan is to walk away in the end, go our separate ways. And you *know* that's going to hurt. Your rejections have hurt me more than anything else you could ever do." I stopped in front of Zack as he absorbed that, his face softening. "And it hurts you too. I know it does. So what if we're together, then we have to split up because one of us has to run? Okay. We knew it could happen. Separating is a risk in any relationship. But for the next few weeks, we can live every possible moment like it's all we've got."

"It's too dangerous, Autumn. It's not safe for you to be around me. What if the scouts realize what you are?" He stood up and we were toe to toe. "Don't you see? Everything I've done, I've done for *you*."

That was probably as close to an admission as I was going to get. It was good enough for me. I laid a palm on his cheek. "You would have left me believing that you didn't care enough. It's unthinkable." I sniffed

366

as a tear escaped, remembering one of his lectures. "You have to do what's right, even if you're afraid of the consequences. Otherwise, life isn't worth living."

He hung his head and sighed. "You're impossible."

What did that mean? After all my effort, would he still blow me off? How much of the last three minutes did I have left?

"You have no idea how exhausting it's been." He looked into my eyes. "I tried to hate you when we met and I was doing pretty good until you wore that damned purple dress."

I grinned. Zack was finally mine. And he knew it. I leaned in and snaked my arms around his neck.

"Autumn." He held my shoulders, like he was about to push me away. "This doesn't change anything. I'll still be leaving in a few weeks and you won't be able to come with me."

"Then we don't have much time together. We'd better make it count."

"This is crazy." He snagged my waist and pulled me closer. "It's stupid to risk your life that way."

"Haven't you listened to anything I said?"

"Shhh." He laid an index finger across my lips. "I heard you, but I need to make sure you've considered everything."

"I want to be with you." I turned his hand toward me, then dropped a kiss in his palm.

He rested his forehead against mine, then squeezed me tighter and buried his face in my hair. "You just couldn't give up on me, could you?" he whispered.

"No." I savored being this close to him. "Believe me, I tried."

He drew back slowly. "We can't afford to get weaker. I can't risk your life by putting myself in a position where I'm incapable of protecting you."

Zack, thinking of me first, as he always had. "We've kissed before and it didn't affect our powers," I reminded him. "We can do all of that we want."

He smiled, a dimple appearing, eyes lighting up. "I can live with unlimited kissing."

So could I. When I rose up on the tip of my toes to get started, he held me back.

"One question," he said.

"Zack, I know I forced you to talk to me, but no more talking now, okay?"

"I'll be quick." He laughed deeply, his firm abdomen moving against mine. That made me want him more. "Do you still want to wear that dress you have wrapped up in your closet?"

"You mean..." My eyes narrowed.

"Would you go to prom with me? As my girlfriend. Officially."

Now *that* was worth the interruption. I beamed. "Yeah. Now, don't open your mouth again, unless it's to kiss me."

Holding his grip on me, he backed up and we tumbled to the couch, me on top.

"Easy," he warned. "I've already used up my resistance against you." Entwining my legs with his, he turned us and maneuvered our bodies so I lay sandwiched between him and the back of the couch. "There. Now you can't get away."

Like I wanted to. I was about to tell him to zip it when his warm, soft lips covered mine. Yeah, that was what I'd been waiting for. Only this time, I wasn't worried he'd leave me. I melted against him as his hands grasped my hips and he pulled me closer. Hot tendrils of sweet sensation spread through me as I snaked my hand under his shirt. I wanted him with a yearning like nothing I'd ever felt before. All of him.

I wished this perfect moment, this perfect kiss could last forever. But we needed to stay strong. I had to resist. I could do it. I *would* do it.

My head buzzed with questions and worries. Like what was Zack going to do about Charles? Could he really survive on his own without a pack? Were my parents shape-shifters or had I been adopted? I wasn't going to get any answers just yet, but right then, I didn't care. I locked away those mysteries in a corner of my mind for later. For now, Zack was finally *mine*. And I would find a way to keep him.

THE END

If you enjoyed this book, please recommend it to friends, reader's groups and discussion boards or tell others how much you enjoyed it by reviewing it on Amazon, GoodReads or your own site.
Thank you and happy reading!

ACKNOWLEDGMENTS

I CUT MY Young Adult teeth on My Wolf's Bane and, actually, wrote it before Something Witchy This Way Comes and A Bite's Tale. It's my favorite of all my titles—maybe because it was my first YA and a big step toward accomplishing my dream. Or maybe it's because I fell in love with Zack! :) Whatever the reason (or combination thereof), it's been an amazing journey with too many revisions to count and a never-ending supply of frustration in order to perfect this baby.

I'd like to thank my sister-in-law Allie who inspired me to write My Wolf's Bane; Susan Hatler who is the greatest critique partner ever; Katie McGarry for her encouragement and sweet words; my cousin Danette for her valuable insight; Suzanne Lazear for her fantastic feedback; Erica for her moral support; Niki for making me laugh; fellow authors Sarah Billington, Robin Haseltine, Carol Braswell, Becky Lees, Lynn Marshall, Lea Nolan, Felice Fox, and PR Mason for all their wonderful suggestions; proof readers Starla LeBarron and Samantha Gaudreault for making me look good; beta readers Samantha H, Mandy, Mary,

Calyn, Sausha, Jen B, Karie, Jyl B, Kat, Hayly, Athena, Celine, Norma, Lee, Courtney, Juli, Jen W and many others whose enthusiasm for my work keeps me believing in my writing.

And a heap of gratitude to my special peeps (you know what you do and it means everything to me) Megan D, Julie W, Ashley D, April P—you gals rock! And a huge hug goes out to Kat who keeps my head on straight during the crazy times.

A warm and fuzzy thank you to my mom who reads my very scary first drafts, Sara E who is ALWAYS there for me; a very special nod to Rose Nomura for her FABULOUS cover design!!! Lastly, my wonderful husband who exercises superhuman patience when I'm working frantically to meet a deadline and forget he exists. Baby, you're the best in all the land!

VERONICA BLADE

More Titles by Veronica Blade

A newbie witch enlists help from the scrumptious school bad-boy to make her life and death choice between two battling covens.

The witch queen must make the impossible choice between abandoning the throne and her people, or spending eternity with the man she loves.

Sofia lays her hard-won anonymity on the line by saving the most popular boy in school. Worse, she's been exposed to the vampire hunters who attacked him.

A Cinderella who spends her nights as a wolf. A prince with a taste for blood.

More Titles by Veronica Blade

Should a woman who's unable to forget her first love give "happily ever after" one more try?

When good-girl Maddie switches places with her famous bad-girl twin Jackie, she has some pretty high stilettos to fill.

When Hunter realizes he botched the annulment of his marriage to his longtime friend, he must decide if she and their marriage are worth fighting for.

A micro trilogy including Single-Handed, Singled Out (book two) & Single-minded (book three).

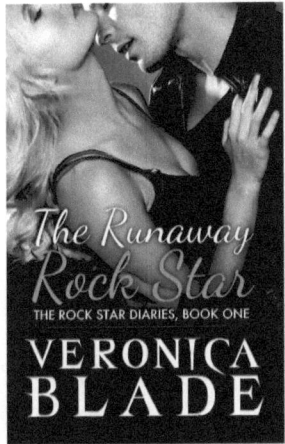
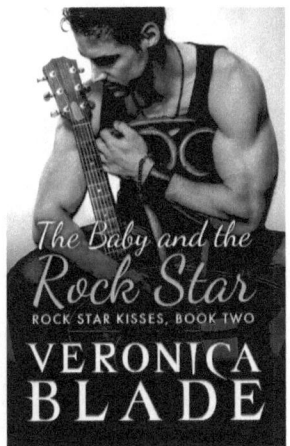

ABOUT VERONICA BLADE

VERONICA BLADE LIVES near Carson City, Nevada with her husband and furbabies but also spends a lot of time in southern California. She writes sweet romances to live vicariously through her characters. Except her heroes and heroines lead far more interesting lives—and they are always way hotter.

)

You can visit Veronica Blade on Facebook, check out her website at VeronicaBlade.com or follow her on Twitter @VeronicaBlade. You can even e-mail her at veronica@veronicablade.com. She loves hearing from readers!